wanderlove

wanderlove

KIRSTEN HUBBARD

DELACORTE PRESS

Text copyright © 2012 by Kirsten Hubbard
Jacket photograph copyright © by Laurence Mouton/PhotoAlto/Corbis
Interior illustrations copyright © 2012 by Kirsten Hubbard

Visit us on the Web! randomhouse.com/teens
Educators and librarians, for a variety of teaching tools,
visit us at randomhouse.com/teachers

Library of Congress Cataloging-in-Publication Data
Hubbard, Kirsten.
    Wanderlove / Kirsten Hubbard. — 1st ed.
        p. cm.
    Summary: Bria, an aspiring artist just graduated from high school, takes off for Central America's La Ruta Maya, rediscovering her talents and finding love.
    ISBN 978-0-385-73937-5 (hc) — ISBN 978-0-375-89751-1 (ebook) —
ISBN 978-0-385-90785-9 (glb)
    [1. Travel—Fiction. 2. Artists—Fiction. 3. Love—Fiction. 4. Central America—Fiction.] I. Title.
    PZ7.H8584Wan 2012   [Fic]—dc22   2011007435

The text of this book is set in 11.5-point Goudy.
Book design by Vikki Sheatsley

Printed in the United States of America
10 9 8 7 6 5 4 3 2
First Edition

to bryson, my travel partner for life

wanderlove

PART I

The Lake

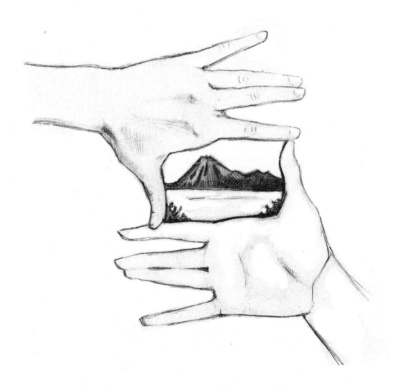

You mix a bunch of ingredients, and once in a great while, chemistry happens.

~Bill Watterson

I hope the leaving is joyful: and I hope never to return.   *~Frida Kahlo*

1

Day 1
Arrival

Travel companions
Overpriced organic fruit & nut bar from
    airport terminal
Ergonomic travel pillow
Phone with astronomical roaming charges
Sketchbook (knockoff Moleskine)
Assortment of pens and pencils

Left behind
Old version of myself

As soon as I see the blond girl bouncing down the aisle, I know she's heading for the empty seat beside me. It's just my luck. A woman in a floppy hat already fills the window seat. After three minutes of laboring at a sudoku puzzle, she starts to snore—even though our plane's still at the gate of LAX.

The girl tosses herself into the seat with a gusty sigh that practically rattles the double-plated windows. She's wearing a stretched-out sweater and drawstring pants, her dark blond hair in a sloppy pile on top of her head. Her fingers are covered with wooden rings.

I'm wearing quick-dry khaki capris, a crispy Windbreaker, and hiking shoes that make my feet feel like Clydesdale hooves. They're brand-new. Like my too-short haircut and my purple suitcase, along with everything in it.

I'm pretty sure the woman in the window seat is wearing a tent.

"So where you headed?" the girl asks, wedging her skinny knees against the seat in front of her. I shut my sketchbook and slip it between my legs.

"Guatemala," I reply, "same as you."

"Well, obviously. But where *in* Guatemala, exactly?"

"All over the place."

"Where first?"

I grasp for a name and come up with nothing. I never read the itinerary for my Global Vagabonds group tour. "I don't really travel with a set plan. It's too restricting."

She raises her eyebrows. "Is that right?"

Once I start, I can't stop. "I've found it's the best way to travel. Heading to whatever place intrigues me, you know? If I feel like sunbathing, I go to the beach. If I'm hungry for culture, I hike a Mayan ruin. I'm a photographer, really."

What I am is full of shit. My mom gave me the camera for

4

my birthday last month, with a warning not to tell my dad. Just like the stack of art books my dad slipped me last year, when I was preparing my portfolio for the art school I'm not attending. I think their secret presents make them feel like they're each gleefully undermining the other in their endless uncivil war. At least I get consolation prizes.

"You're a photographer?" The girl's blue eyes widen. "How old are you?"

"Eighteen."

"You must be *really* talented."

It's the *really* that gets me. She doesn't believe me. And why should she? It's not like I look particularly well traveled. Or talented. Whatever *that* looks like. My Windbreaker makes crunching noises as I shift away. I should have brought a better jacket, something funky and artsy. But even in the days I considered myself an artist, I never had the guts to dress the part.

Plus, the Windbreaker was on my Global Vagabonds Packing List:

1) *photocopy of passport*
2) *under-clothes money belt*
3) *crispy Windbreaker the color of gutter*
   water

And like always, I followed the rules.

Just when I'm about to implode with embarrassment, the woman in the window seat taps my shoulder. "I couldn't help overhearing," she says. "I'm traveling in a big group. I could never travel like you do. I think you're so *brave*."

I grin. "Thanks! It's no big deal . . . I just know how to take care of myself."

I think I sound pretty convincing.

It all began with a stupid question:

Are You a Global Vagabond?

The cashier at the sporting goods shop jammed the pamphlet into my bag, like a receipt or a coupon for a discount oil change, something easily discarded. But to me, it seemed like an omen, appearing the exact moment my resolve started to crumble.

Blame my wilting willpower on my best friends, Olivia Luster and Reese Kinjo. They've never agreed on anything—except backing out on our trip.

The trip had been my idea in the first place. We'd chosen Europe, the obvious choice for eighteen-year-old travel virgins fresh out of high school. But after just a couple weeks of emailed images of the Louvre and La Rambla, links to online travel guides and airfare deals, Olivia and Reese dropped by my house. They never hang out together, so instantly, I knew something was up.

"We've decided we can't travel with you this summer," Olivia said. "The timing's just not right—we're sorry."

I sat on my bedroom floor involuntarily, like someone had snipped my marionette strings.

"Look, Bria—we're not trying to be assholes," she continued while Reese's nonconfrontational eyes scanned my ceiling. "We're only thinking of you. You're just not in the right headspace for traveling. Remember what happened on your birthday last week?"

"Yeah, I remember," I said, annoyed. "You almost fell off the balcony flashing half of Tijuana in the hot body contest—"

"I'm talking about the fifty billion kamikazes you threw back before puking in the taxi on our way home. You're lucky we didn't get into worse trouble than that. What if it happened in Czechoslovenia?"

"There's no such place as Czechoslovenia."

Reese, who hadn't gone to Mexico and probably never will, squatted beside me. "We just don't think you're in the right headspace to take a trip, Bria," she said in that amateur philosopher's voice that makes my eyes spiral. "You and Toby have been broken up for, like, six weeks, and you've barely left the house. You didn't even go to prom. You're obviously still healing—running away isn't going to expedite the process."

"You guys don't get it," I protested. "I *need* this . . ."

They waited, but I couldn't continue.

"We're really sorry, babe," Olivia said. "We'll have an epic summer right here in town, all right? I'll find you a new boy before college—or several. Remember, no strings!"

Reese waited for Olivia to leave, then gave me one of her feeble, girlish hugs. "Maybe we'll travel next summer. After a year of college, we'll have so much more perspective for a trip like this, anyway." A piece of her black hair fell into my open mouth.

As soon as my bedroom door shut, I noticed the plate of raspberry bars on my nightstand. A typical Reese Kinjo gesture: reconciliation by fresh-baked goods. I've known her since second grade, Olivia since eighth. They're like the opposite poles of my personality. Mild-mannered, responsible

Reese is who I used to be, while in-your-face Olivia's who I *want* to be—with a few sharp edges dulled. We've never been a threesome. More like two twosomes, with me in common. I should have realized the three of us traveling together would have been uncomfortable, to say the least. And spending boatloads of money to serve as a pal's crying shoulder *is* a lot to ask. But why couldn't we have figured that out earlier?

I guess it's good they never learned my real motivation for heading abroad.

This particular trip may have been my idea, but traveling was Toby's. It was a fantasy we planned in pencil. All through early senior year, we passed notes in class layered with sketch upon sketch. I'd draw him; then he'd draw me. Him in a beret. Me with a baguette. The two of us clutching suitcases, floating on gondolas, beaming cartoonishly from painting frames. After we broke up, Toby didn't believe I would travel without him. He'd *told* me so. My own fault, for calling him to boast. I just couldn't teach my fingers to forget his number.

"You know you're not going anywhere, Bria," he'd said, as if our fantasy had never existed. "You're just not the traveling type."

I picked up one of Reese's bars. Slowly, so I could savor the feeling, I crushed it in my fist. Big drops of raspberry jelly oozed onto my thighs. It was a small thing, but it was enough. I stood, empowered by an unexpected surge of resolve.

Maybe Toby was right about my friends, but he wasn't right about me. The thought of travel had been the only thing sustaining me in the aftermath of a fantasy gone rotten. I had no art to comfort me and no hope for art school, and I was stuck in a too-small house with parents who aimed the word *divorce* like a rocket launcher set to maim. I wouldn't let Olivia and Reese take it away from me.

I would do the last thing anyone would expect me to do: I would go anyway.

Cue inspirational music.

My resolve lasted approximately an hour and a half.

In the sporting goods store, where I was surrounded by heaps of travel crap—sleeping bags and luggage tags, airplane carry-ons and astronaut ice cream—doubts whirred in my ear like a swarm of mosquitoes. I hadn't even bought my plane ticket yet, and there I was, squandering the money I'd earned pushing papers for my father on a clearance-rack suitcase.

I felt like a fraud.

And to make matters worse, when I thought of Europe, I could only picture cold greasy chips and streets gone haywire. Teetery double-decker buses and gargoyles dappled with bird crap. And me, navigating the crooked streets with my hands in my pockets—trying not to think of Toby and Chicago, where he'd move without me in September.

What was I going to do in Europe all alone, anyway? Look at buildings? Go to art museums and feel guilty for all those months I didn't draw or paint?

So forget Europe. But where was there to go *besides* Europe? Where *did* people go?

I had no idea. That's why the Global Vagabonds pamphlet seemed like such a prophecy. Travel made easy. All the thorns chipped off. Prepackaged, preplanned.

Perfect.

In my bedroom, I ran my finger down the table of contents. All the tours had gimmicky names: *Incredible India. Thailand Trek. Jungle Escape*—that was Peru and Ecuador. *Arctic Expedition.*

La Ruta Maya. What was that?

I flipped to the page and was greeted by the grins of four young, jubilant travelers posing with their arms linked. Behind them, a ruined Mayan temple loomed from a thickly forested backdrop.

La Ruta Maya. The Maya Route. Three weeks exploring Mayan ruins in Central America. I read the name of each ancient city out loud, stumbling over the exotic pairings of consonants: Tikal, Copan, Lamanai, Chichén Itzá, Palenque. I'd paid little attention to Central America on the maps in my father's office. Guatemala was vaguely synonymous with Mexico. I'd always thought Honduras was a Caribbean island, like Haiti. And I wasn't sure I'd even *heard* of Belize.

I decided not to read any further. I wanted to be a blank canvas, untainted by any preparatory information. That way, my mind would be fully open upon my arrival in Guatemala City.

"Bria?"

My mom stuck her head into my room. She gasped.

"Honey, you're not *suicidal*, are you?"

Meet my mom—who's only forty to my dad's fifty-two, goes clubbing twice a month with her dental hygienist friends, and has stretched out way too many of my tank tops with a gigantic chest I did not inherit. We do not "get" each other, to say the least. She likes to joke that she found me in a basket wedged among my father's rosebushes. *How else can we explain that art thing of yours?*

10

"Mom!" I exclaimed. "Are you kidding me? No!"

"But your hair . . ."

I reached up and touched it, like I'd done compulsively the whole drive home. I had paid twelve dollars for a cosmetology student to sever my long dark hair to my chin. "Your eyes look much larger now," the student had said, feigning expertise as she'd scrunched wax into my choppy bob.

"I was ready for something different," I told my mom.

Her surprise was understandable. I've been a creature of habit my whole life. My parents haven't known what to do with me in the six weeks since Toby and I broke up, other than try to coerce me into shopping trips (my mom, who loves deals) and hover awkwardly behind me (my dad, an accountant who is intimidated by teenagers) during my epic triathlons of television, breakfast cereal, and art blogs viewed on my laptop.

"I suppose it's all right," my mom said. "It would look better if you smoothed it out more. You can borrow my flatiron, if you promise to return it."

"Thanks a million."

"Dinner's ready. It'll be just you and me again, since I doubt I'll be able to pry that man out of his damned office."

As soon as my mom shut the door, I scrunched up my hair even more. I could already hear her yelling at my dad. I swear they're addicted to the adrenaline from their nightly hollering matches. They'll probably forget they ever had a daughter once I'm gone.

Okay, maybe that's harsh. But there's just so much my parents have overlooked. They never asked about the plastic tubs of art supplies I crammed under my bed after art school acceptances came out. They never questioned the nights I

11

lingered, dreading the cold seats of Toby's car. I know it sounds borderline psychotic, but sometimes I found myself wishing for the testimony of a bruise. If my parents could have seen my injuries, maybe they'd have understood. But I've never given them any reason not to trust my judgment.

So they believed me when I said that I *wanted* to stay in town after graduation, that attending a state school instead of art school was *preferable*, that Toby and I were doing *great*, I *swear*, *geez*, guys, everything's *fabulous*! until it was too obvious to lie anymore.

Enough about Toby. I pressed my palms over my ears, sat back in bed, and closed my eyes.

I could picture it already.

I would glide from ruin to ruin along La Ruta Maya, in a caravan of beautiful, happy people, and I'd be the mysterious one, gracious and profound. Butterflies would float down from the jungle canopy and alight on my bronzed skin. I would wear silver necklaces and ankle-length skirts that shifted in the breeze.

And above all else, I would do what Olivia suggested I do, the day after Toby broke up with me: I'd only hook up with guys I didn't care about. From now until forever. So when we parted ways, I could easily forget.

The blond girl scribbles in a journal for the remainder of the plane ride. When I finally muster the courage to open my sketchbook, she gives me a *look*, like she's accusing me of copying her.

My face heats up. *I have one trillion sketchbooks*, I want to tell her. *I could build you a sketchbook house.*

But I don't. Because then I'd be admitting I'm an artist. Or rather, that I *used to be* an artist, since I haven't drawn as much as a chipmunk in months. I have an urge to hide out in the airplane bathroom, but then I'd have to climb over the girl's legs. So I put my sketchbook away and stare past tent woman out the window, trying to ignore the ache in my chest. It's totally irrational—I mean, it's just *drawing*, Bria, come on now—but the longing skewers me just the same.

I expect instant culture shock when our plane touches down, but the Guatemala City airport looks like every other I've seen. Just with more Spanish. I lose sight of the blond girl as I attempt to navigate all sorts of foreign customs, like Customs. I reach the baggage claim just in time to see her dive into the arms of a pair of scraggly backpacker boys. One's freakishly tall and wears a stocking cap. The other has a ponytail.

I figure they're backpackers because of the backpacks.

No one's there to meet me. No signs proclaiming BIEN-VENIDA, BRIA! I want to sit down, but I can't find a seat. When I settle on the metal lip of the baggage conveyor belt, a security guard scurries over and orders me off in Spanish. So I stand there with my purple suitcase wedged between my legs, my hands in my pockets to safeguard my money belt. I try to ignore the huddle of middle-aged tourists across the room, along with the sinking feeling in my stomach.

At last, a woman excuses herself from the group and approaches me. She's got knobby knuckles and pearly, lacquered nails. She reminds me of a velociraptor.

"Are you Bria Sandoval?"

Dumbly, I nod.

"You're with us." She calls to the others: "I've found her!"

"I'm with you?"

"Yep. I'm Marcy, the guide with Global Vagabonds. I thought I recognized you from your photo, but you had such long hair. . . . Anyway. Glad we found you! You're the last one. Now we can jump on the shuttle to Antigua."

I give the group of tourists a hard stare, as if my eyes have the power to transform them. I see mustaches, baseball caps, doughy calves marbled with varicose veins. Where's my caravan of beautiful people from the Global Vagabonds propaganda? "But—but the people in your flyers were so much *younger*. . . ."

"Unless you want to camp out in this airport for three weeks, what you see is what you get. They're not so bad. You should have seen the last group—the highlight of their trip was the McDonald's in Chimaltenango. They couldn't get over the home-delivery service."

There's nothing left for me to say. I pop out the telescoping handle of my suitcase and follow Marcy to the Vagabonds, who frown at me with varying levels of irritation.

Great. They hate me already.

Just when I think my night can't get any worse, the blond girl and her boyfriends choose that precise moment to walk our way.

On the squeaky-clean airplane, she looked out of place. But now that we've landed, I realize she's perfect. All three of them are. Perfectly disheveled, perfectly irreverent. Real-life vagabonds with mismatched clothes and jewelry, scuffed leather sandals, and too much sun. The kind of traveler I didn't know I longed to be until right this very second, as Marcy and her husband, Dan, whose comb-over is flipped the wrong way, attempt to herd me outside.

14

The blond girl passes me without a word. But somehow, her silence is worse than any criticism. Suddenly, my Windbreaker feels even crispier. My haircut is too trendy. My new shoes feel like blocks of lead. I've only been in Guatemala half an hour, and already I've gotten everything wrong.

The freakishly tall guy in the stocking cap passes next, whistling. But I don't get a good look at him, because the guy with the black ponytail has stopped beside me.

"Tough luck," he says. He nods at my tour group, which is filing outside.

I shrug, duck my head, and follow my people into the night.

The Global Vagabonds logo of a crazed giraffe beams from the side of our shuttle van. Beside it, drivers lean against dilapidated cabs, watching us with distaste. I crawl into the backseat and scoot to the farthest corner. Too soon, I sense the mass of another person sitting beside me. And just because my life is like that, it's tent-garbed woman from the plane.

"Hi! I'm Glenna Heron, professional beadworker," she says, handing me a card with a tiny Ziploc bag of seed beads attached. "And you're a liar."

So much for reinvention.

2

Day 3, Morning
The Mayans

My Dad's Maps

Maybe it was Toby Kelsey who inspired this trip. But I have to blame my dad's maps for infecting me with the travel bug in the first place.

My dad has three maps in his home office—what my mom calls his hermit cave, since he pretty much lives there when he's not at work. One is a world map. The second is a map of ancient Greece and Italy. The third, hanging right above his desk, is a map of North America.

He seems to think his maps evoke the impression of a world traveler, landlocked by responsibility. But really, he's only taken one trip his entire life: a train journey across Canada, at age thirty-three, to fetch an engagement ring

*from his great aunt in Ottawa. It was the holidays, and he
could only afford a flight as far as Vancouver.*

*In the days when I spent entire afternoons drawing
beneath his desk, sometimes he would beckon me out to
share. With an ink-stained finger, he'd trace his itinerary
on the map of North America. "Saskatoon," he'd say,
pointing. "That's where an elk wandered on the tracks
while the conductor was out smoking cigarettes. A big
mangy buck. It took six men to scare him off."*

*Then he would slide his finger down the track marked
in blue ink. "Here there was a forest. I remember the trees
were all the same height, like a mowed lawn."*

*Once I asked him if he ever climbed off during the stops
and walked around.*

*"No need," he said. "My view from the car was
perfect."*

*As I got older and hung out in his office less and less, I
started to see the maps differently. The idea of my dad on
that train—sitting alone on a bench in coach, maybe with
a blanket over his knees, watching the landscape blur
by—might seem romantic to some people. Sappy people.
He was retrieving a ring for my mom, after all.*

*But hadn't he wanted to walk around under the
evergreens? Sift his hands through the pine needles? Touch
the ice-blue lakes?*

What's the point of travel if you never get off the train?
~ July 14, somewhere in Guatemala

I close my sketchbook. It always startles me when words
come out of my pen instead of pictures. I never did much
journaling before this trip, but it's never too late to start.

I glance up. I can hear the Mayan market before Dan shuts off the engine. It sounds like the low bellow of a far-off ocean, or a hive of bees. The hum of humanity. Kind of exciting, but after yesterday, I'd rather hide out in the van. Possibly for the remaining nineteen days of this trip.

We spent all day in Antigua, an ancient city that was adored by everyone but reminded me of a dishrag. Clouds slumped in the sky. Water the color of my Windbreaker pooled in the cracks of the cobblestone streets. The buildings were constructed in endless pastel-colored strips, without any gaps between the storefronts. Because most lacked signs, I never knew what one held until I peered inside.

Usually, backpackers.

I should have expected them, after the girl from the plane and her airport boyfriends. But they never stopped astonishing me.

The beautiful, beautiful backpacker girls, dressed in clothes that fit exactly wrong: baggy drawstring pants with muddy threads around the ankles, skirts with patches and stripes, droopy shirts displaying wing bones and the ribs on top of their chests. Careless hair and faces so tanned the whites of their eyes looked shocking.

And the backpacker boys. They wore tattered shorts beneath embroidered shirts open at the neck or plaid button-down work shirts, so perfect out of context. Shadowy chins and shaved heads, or hair gone feral. Hiking shoes, crusty Chuck Taylors, or leather sandals flaunting unabashedly manly toes.

My fingers ached to sketch them. Their straps and patterns. Their creases and tatters, beards and bra straps. The way they stood, posed, *leaned*. Sometimes with galaxy-sized backpacks and smaller daypacks, multiple Mayan totes slung over their shoulders. Everything they needed fastened to their bodies while they explored remarkable places.

Unlike me, they've learned the *right* way to travel. But where? How?

Who are these people?

Even though I attended a liberal Southern California high school, I've never seen anyone like the backpackers. Closest were the surf kids who slouched into class late with salt-crusted hair. But the surfers I know care only for waves. These backpackers strolled down Antigua's streets with Pulitzer prize–winning novels and Spanish textbooks under their arms. At cafés, I overheard them discussing foreign film and politics while sipping espressos—or, considering what we'd been served at breakfast, Nescafé served in espresso cups. They danced among the crowds of tiny Guatemalans, giving coins to children, buying fruit from carts and using pocket knives to peel it.

But when they passed my tour group, they didn't glance our way.

Not at Marcy, not at Dan, not at my personal barnacle, Glenna Heron, who loves beads a little *too* much, and definitely not at me. I've never been the most gorgeous girl, and certainly not the most captivating. But until yesterday, I'd never felt completely overlooked.

It was probably a good thing, though. Because even if the backpackers could forgive my quick-dry khaki capris (oh God, they were *pink* this time) and clompy horseshoes, I don't doubt they could see right inside my brain.

Which still resents my parents.

Which is still filled with thoughts of Toby Kelsey.

And, in all likelihood, is still shaped like a square.

Dan swivels in front of me, paging through a guidebook. "Let me tell you about Chichicastenango."

Marcy hushes us, even though no one's talking.

"The native market takes place twice a week. It's one of the largest outdoor bazaars in the Americas. The town's name means 'place of nettles'—"

"Why nettles?" I ask.

He glances at his guidebook, looking befuddled. "I don't see . . ."

"Never mind."

"Among the popular sights in Chichicastenango is the Church of Santo Tomás, built atop the remains of a Mayan ruin. The church reflects a spiritual marriage of Catholic and Mayan religions . . ."

I tune him out. He's like every history teacher I've ever had—reducing the colors of the past to a series of bullet points.

At long last, Marcy and Dan slide open the door to the van. I slip my straw bag over my shoulder, wedge my sketchbook into the back pocket of my shorts, and climb out. As soon as I round the corner, the market comes into view.

And—*wow*.

From the hill where we stand, it unfolds like a Mayan blanket: a chaos of market stalls stretching as far as I can see. People flow along the tilted streets, dressed in indigenous clothing of clashing prints and patterns. An old man in a cowboy hat staggers past, bent double, carrying a pile of quilts. Cooking smoke distorts the air. Stray dogs bark; babies squall. I smell incense, hot grease, the smoke of firecrackers.

It's claustrophobic. Overwhelming.

And I want nothing more in the entire universe than to

dive headfirst into the kaleidoscope of colors, to let them whirl around me until I become a fractal of light. *This* will be an experience worth writing home about. Worth my biggest canvas, if I was still painting. I pull my camera from my bag and take a picture, then a second, a third.

"Seems kind of crowded," Glenna remarks.

She looks traumatized. In fact, the entire Tourist Brigade looks traumatized, and they haven't even entered the market yet. To my left, Dan's violating a map with his index finger. *Poke, poke.* Marcy's talking about the dangers of pickpockets, stray cats, and leprosy. Forget being a fractal of light—I'm already part of a gaggle of ducklings. This is going to be worse than our tour of Antigua. How can I touch the ice-blue lakes if Marcy's dragging me along by the hand?

"I'm going off on my own!"

The other Vagabonds stare at me, as shocked by my declaration as I am. I didn't mean to yell, but there you go. Marcy peers at me with her reptilian eyes. "That's not safe, and you know it."

I turn to Dan. "What time did you say we're leaving? Three?"

Scandalized, he nods.

"I'll see you back at the bus at three, then."

And I'm off.

I feel like a fugitive as I dart through the aisles of the marketplace, clutching my bag against my chest, hopping, reeling, gritting my teeth to protect my brain from the noise. The market's filled with angles, which means I'm probably running in hexagons, but I don't slow until both my sides feel speared. Finally, I stop and glance around, panting.

I've done it. I'm beautifully lost.

In that exact moment, my eyes lock on a retreating back. It's undeniably familiar—the bouncy gait, the rough white shirt. The black ponytail.

I stand on my toes, attempting to peer over the crowd.

But it's too massive. The vendors surge around me, shouting, parading their wares, which include everything imaginable: splintery barrels of beans, live birds in handmade cages, lacy panties and bras, creepy animal masks, handcrafted Mayan souvenirs made of jade, yarn, mahogany. I spy disoriented tourists, Central American sightseers, and the everpresent twentysomething backpackers, though the Mayans outnumber the visitors ten or twenty to one.

I'm so drunk with the pandemonium I forget about the ponytail guy. My face begins to ache. I realize I'm grinning. How long has it been? I can't remember.

I hold out my camera at arm's length, aim it at myself, and snap a photo.

When I turn around, I see Dan's church. It rises above the marketplace like a hulking angel, perched on a set of ancient steps covered in flowers. Incense smoke billows from smoldering sticks. I intend to approach it, but every few steps I'm distracted.

Unfortunately, it's almost impossible to browse without buying. Anything I touch—or even glance at too long—is seized by the shopkeeper and shaken out, displayed.

"You like?"

Even when I say no, *lo siento*, the vendors override me with a price. Sensing my reluctance, they drop it by half, two-thirds. When I finally pull myself away, they keep calling to me, plaintively, shaving the prices until I feel so besieged and guilty I go back and make some silly purchase, and we both feel swindled.

Crap I Am Shamed Into Buying
Terra-cotta bird whistle
Orange apron
Sticky tamarind candy I can't get off my
    fingers
Wooden flute
Chicken-shaped pot holder with pinto bean
    for eye

At one point, I come across a row of butcher stalls, where raw chickens, hams, and unidentifiable hunks of meat dangle from hooks. The air dances with flies. A few vendors unenthusiastically wave newspapers at them. I pass what looks like a pile of pink masks and step closer. They're faces.

Deflated pig faces.

I snap a photo.

When I emerge from the meat market, I nearly bump into Dan. He's haggling with a shopkeeper who looks about ten years old. "No, I said *less grand*," I hear him bark, as if it's the volume of his words that prevents understanding.

I hurry around the corner, where I notice a tiny old man standing apart from the fray. His table is stacked with paintings.

I drift over and pick up the first one I see: a lake, surrounded by volcanoes. It looks amateur, like a child painted it. The volcanoes are flat blue cones. Hairline waves upset the surface of the water, probably scratched in with a toothpick.

A bright white boat hovers in the very center. Bad composition. Plus, the perspective is way off. I flip through the other paintings, but I keep coming back to the lake. Finally, I hold it up to the old man, who's missing all his teeth.

"Where is this? *Donde?*"

"Atitlán."

I run my finger along the frayed canvas. "*Cuánto cuesta?*"

Pathetically, it's one of the few Spanish phrases I remember. Even though my grandfather on my dad's side is from Spain, I thought being twice removed from my heritage released me from linguistic obligations. Already I've forgotten most of what I learned during my two required years of high school Spanish.

"Five dollar U.S.," the old man says.

All I have left is quetzales, the Guatemalan currency, which is something like six or eight to a dollar. I try to calculate the exchange rate as I reach for my straw bag.

It's gone.

I clap my hands to my face. "Oh, *shit*," I say, my voice muffled by my fingers. I turn to the old man. "My bag! It was right here. Did you see anyone take it?"

The old man shrugs. Does he not understand? I point at my shoulder, miming the strap of a bag. He shakes his head. Thank God my sketchbook's in my back pocket—I pat it just to check. What do I do now? Call the police? Damn these people! I was actually starting to like this country.

"It's gone."

I whirl around.

It's the ponytailed backpacker boy. He's wearing a white work shirt with the top few buttons undone and the sleeves rolled up, revealing an elaborate dragon tattoo on his super-tanned right forearm. His pants are cut off below the knee, and he's got forty or fifty string bracelets stacked partway up his left calf. His eyes are dark blue. He's not smiling, but the threat is there. In fact, he looks almost amused.

I try not to feel offended by his expression, because I need his help. "I set it down just thirty seconds ago. Whoever took it has got to be nearby. If we hurry, we can—"

I shut up as he grabs my shoulder. Is he trying to abduct me? He leads me around the corner, where the jumble of stalls opens into a courtyard teeming with people. "So who was it?"

My shoulders sag. "What . . . what about the police?"

"Was your passport in your bag?"

"Of course not—I have a money belt."

"What about your credit cards? Anything like that?"

"Money belt."

"Then what's in your bag that's so important?"

"My camera! And some snacks and things." I know better than to mention the terra-cotta bird whistle. "But it was a really nice camera. . . ."

He shakes his head. "The police won't be interested. They might file a report, if you beg. But come on. They've got more important things to deal with than a tourist who lost her *camera*."

I gape at him for a second. Then I turn and walk away.

"Hey, wait up." He falls into step beside me.

"That was mean," I say.

"You're right. I'm sorry."

"How do you know I'm not a photographer? Or an artist?"

"Are you an artist?"

"*No,*" I reply a little too loudly.

25

He looks taken aback.

"I mean no, I'm not an artist," I continue, tugging my shirt over the sketchbook in my pocket. "But you didn't know that. And just because I'm part of a stuffy tour group doesn't mean I'm really a *part* of them, okay? It was a mistake—I thought I was signing up for something else. And now I'm stuck with them for three weeks, seeing only what they want me to see, and there's nothing I can do. Today's the first time I've gotten a moment to myself."

"I see."

"You see," I repeat.

"Well, I believe you, so now I see it. Believing is seeing, right?"

Before I can correct him, he catches my arm. "Hey, do you smell that?"

"Huh?"

"Come with me."

He leads me to a booth where five barefoot women are making tortillas. First they reach their floured hands into a plastic tub filled with dough, pinch off a hunk, and roll it into a ball. Next they slap the ball from hand to hand, beating it flat. Then they toss it onto a griddle suspended over an open flame.

A tortilla dangles in front of my face. "Be careful," he says. "It's hot."

I hesitate, remembering what happened yesterday in Antigua. While the rest of my tour group browsed market stalls, I bought a chicken tamale from a street vendor. Before I could unwrap it from its banana leaf, Marcy velociraptored up behind me and snatched it from my hand.

"Rule number one," she said, mashing the tamale into

26

a blob of corn flour. "Unless you want to be hunched in the bathroom for three hours, exploding from both ends, don't buy anything from street vendors. Or from pushcarts. Or from roadside markets. You can't afford to be naïve—this isn't the first world, you know. Standards of cleanliness are much different here."

> **Global Vagabonds Rules for Third-World Travel**
> *Don't shake hands with the locals.*
> *Don't drink the water.*
> *Don't touch your face after touching the water.*
> *Don't eat street-cart tamales, or buy street-cart tamales, or approach street carts, or even make eye contact with street-cart vendors.*
> *If any water gets in your mouth while you shower, gargle with hand sanitizer.*

Feeling like a rebel, I accept the tortilla and take a bite. The hot dough melts on my tongue. "Wow! Tijuana's got nothing on these."

"You're from Tijuana?"

"What? No!" I laugh. "I'm from Southern California. But I've been there once . . . with friends. We had quesadillas."

Great—now he probably thinks I'm trying to be multicultural. Good thing I didn't bring up the kamikaze shots. At any rate, he doesn't seem eager to ditch me, and that says something. We head toward the outskirts of the market, where the streets are less crowded.

"So where are you from?" I ask.

"Hard to say."

"What do you mean?"

"I grew up all over." He crumples a tortilla into a ball and stuffs the whole thing into his mouth. After he swallows, he says, "Take a look down there."

He points to one of the steepest roads I've ever seen. At the very bottom, a village of tombstones designed to look like churches juts from a hill. The colors of Easter. Why do American cemeteries look so gloomy? It never occurred to me before. They should look like carnivals, celebrating life.

"Let me guess. You're staying in Panajachel tonight, right?"

When I turn back, he's perched atop a low stone wall with his hands on his hips, like Peter Pan. I can totally see him spreading his arms and soaring straight on till morning.

"It's usually the next stop for tour groups," he adds, "after here."

"Um," I reply. I don't want to admit I haven't read our itinerary. I'm starting to realize how idiotic my blank-canvas policy was. "Right."

"So what has your group got planned for you this evening?"

"I'm not a hostage," I insist, even though he's got it right. I'm pretty sure Glenna Heron said something about a Paraguayan restaurant. As if Guatemalan weren't exotic enough.

"So you can come across the lake for dinner?"

The sun emerges from behind a cloud. With my head tipped back, I have to squint to see his face. "The lake?" I repeat, thinking of the painting. I feel a flutter of excitement. "What's across the lake?"

"Three volcanoes and twelve other villages, for starters."

"I *know* that," I lie.

"We're staying at this guesthouse in Santa Lucía. It's called La Casa Azul. Your typical backpacker haunt. The only one in the village. But it's not so bad. Everyone cooks. You should come."

I wonder about the difference between a good backpacker haunt and a bad one. "How do I get there?" I ask, unsure whether I'm playing along, or whether I'm really considering going.

"*Por lancha*. By boat. Just head straight down Calle Santander—that's the main road—to the lake. The boat drivers will descend upon you as soon as you get there. Make sure to catch the six o'clock to get there in time for dinner."

"Should I, like . . . get your number or something?"

"I don't have a phone." He hops down from the wall and waves. "Bon voyage!"

I watch him stroll through the crowd. His hair's as dark as that of the locals, his skin almost as tanned. But even though he's not particularly tall—maybe average height—he towers above them.

All of a sudden, I think, How strange. We never exchanged names.

3

Day 3, Evening
The Most Beautiful Lake in the World

The Art School Girl

Anytime I've thought about art in the months after I gave it up, my mind has always wandered to the same incident: when our advanced-drawing teacher, Mr. Chiang, brought us to three Los Angeles art colleges in one day. I was a sophomore. Toby Kelsey didn't go to our school yet.

Back then, I ate art for every meal and slept with it under my pillow.

The classrooms and faces smeared together with time, except for one: a girl with tangled hair, barefoot, her paint-stained jeans scrunched over her knees. She burst out of a doorway at my end of a long, dark corridor. In

one hand, she gripped a paintbrush. I watched her soar
down the hall, limbs flying, bare feet slapping, and vanish
into a doorway at the other end.

Until the moment I saw her, I didn't know a person
could radiate so much joy it seemed tangible. I could feel it
shimmer through the hall. Ever since, I've wondered what
it felt like to be that happy.

The first time I see the lake, I think I understand.

July 14, near Lake Atitlán

As our shuttle maneuvers the steep, cratered roads of the Guatemala highlands, the drops plunge deeper and deeper, until I'm certain the only thing keeping us from plummeting over the edge is my own willpower. I'm concentrating so hard my cerebellum aches.

Then the lake appears through a crease in the mountains.

It's like a shock of blue light. A thrill punches my heart. I want to cry out, but stop myself just in time.

The lake vanishes as we round a bend. I glance at Glenna Heron, passed out in her usual seat beside me. After showing me every one of her Chichicastenango purchases, she fell asleep—quite a feat, considering the bloodcurdling roads we've been scaling. I try the next seat over, because I want someone, anyone, to share the moment with. A white-haired couple stare at matching Dean Koontz novels. In front of them, Marcy distracts Dan's driving with her animated screeching and flailing claws.

No one seems to have seen the lake. But how could they have missed it? It was the color of a gas flame, so blue it nearly stung my eyes.

I sit back in my seat, feeling like I've caught a glimpse of someone else's dream.

Forget being a blank canvas. This time, I want to know. I pull out my Global Vagabonds itinerary from where I stuck it in my sketchbook, and unfold it. I locate *Day 4: Chichicastenango* and drop my finger to the next heading.

Panajachel and Lake Atitlán, Guatemala

Scenic drive (approx. 2 hrs) from Chichicastenango to Panajachel, a Mayan village on the shores of Lake Atitlán—famously called "the most beautiful lake in the world" by *Brave New World* author Aldous Huxley.

"'The most beautiful lake in the world,'" I read out loud.

Suddenly, the minibus lurches to the side. A chicken bus—a retired American school bus painted in riotous hues—has careened into our lane to pass another. It swerves back just in time. For an instant, I look into the faces pressed against the oily bus windows.

My gut still churning, I glance again at Glenna. No signs of life.

We crawl through the narrow streets of a village called Sololá, a cluster of shabby buildings and courtyards surrounding a bustling park. Then we begin to descend. When the lake comes into view again, this time it remains. The stunning shade of blue isn't just the lake—it's the contrast of sky against heaps of white clouds, and the three volcanoes arching over the water like hooded gods.

My heart's so swollen with lake-love, I decide to wake Glenna.

"Are we there yet?" she asks, rubbing her eyes.

"Almost. But look—"

"Why'd you wake me up, then? I was having the most wonderful dream. Let's see, there was this man with a mustache, and he had a briefcase, and I think he was selling—"

"Glenna! Look out the window."

"Pretty," she says, without looking. "Anyway, I forget what the man was selling. But there was this field of butter beans . . ."

I open my sketchbook, tracing volcano shapes without ever actually touching my pencil to the page. From time to time, I glance back out the window, wondering which village is Santa Lucía. In the center of the haze of blue water, I think I see a boat.

In our shared hotel room, Glenna sits on her bed and watches me fix my makeup. I've showered and changed into a pale blue tank top and a flowy white skirt with silver piping along the hem. As I drape a silver necklace around my neck, I imagine Toby Kelsey sitting in Glenna's place. Watching me get dressed to attend a hostel party with a bunch of aimless ruffians.

Picturing his face helps me ignore the anxiety prickling inside my stomach. With the exception of Tijuana, it's been way, way too long since I've gone out.

Parties weren't Toby's thing, but he hated when I attended them without him. I quickly learned the fun factor of holding back Olivia's hair wasn't worth the ensuing interrogation: *Was Mark Schulman there? I saw him checking you out in physics. I hope it was worth it, because you realize we've got to send in our*

33

portfolios in just three weeks, right? In a way, it was nice having someone care so much, since my parents could be so damned useless in that department.

And then, after Toby and I broke up, breakfast cereal and serial television trumped putting on my party pants every time.

And now . . . it's like my social muscles have atrophied.

But I know I'll regret it if I don't go.

I established my alibi as soon as we arrived at our hotel. "Tonight, we'll be having dinner at a Paraguayan restaurant on Calle Santander," Marcy announced, clapping her hands. "After you drop your suitcases off in your rooms, meet us back in the lobby."

Once the rest of the group had filtered upstairs, I approached Marcy. "I think I'm going to skip dinner," I said. "I'm not feeling too well."

She smiled knowingly. "You ate something from a street cart, didn't you?"

Thank God I didn't tell her about my stolen camera.

Now I check the ancient clock radio beside my hotel bed. "I promise I'll be back tonight," I say, for my benefit as much as Glenna's. I'm not a hundred percent certain I can trust her, but telling her seems like the responsible thing to do. In case the boat is overtaken by lake pirates or something.

"Okay," she replies, adjusting her flowered hat.

"It's just for the evening. Please don't tell Marcy."

"I won't."

I touch my waist again to make sure my money belt is under my skirt. It's not the sexiest accessory—more like a top secret fanny pack, or one of those vintage belted maxi pads our grandmothers suffered through as teens—but I don't know how else to carry money since my bag was hijacked. I wave goodbye to Glenna, who looks almost wistful.

As I walk down Calle Santander, several apple-red motor taxis whiz past me, beeping gaily. I pass a man selling snow cones from a pushcart. *"Granizadas!"* he calls, pointing to a row of syrups in skinny bottles like crayons. Wildflowers grow in the gutters, and butterflies flicker in the alleyways. At the end of the volcano-dwarfed street, the lake draws me toward it like a whirlpool of blue.

But when I see the Mayanet Internet café, I can't help stopping by. Just for a minute.

To: "Olivia Luster"
<olivia.luster@gmail.com>
Subject: I met a guy!

I pause, fingers hovering over the keyboard. Bizarrely, I start to feel guilty. As if somewhere across the lake, the pony-tailed guy knows exactly what I'm doing.

Delete.

I jog the rest of the way to the lakeshore, where I'm the final passenger on the six o'clock boat. The driver cranks the motor, and as we roar into the fading light, the water changes from clear to pale blue to deep blue-black. It reminds me of all the times I sat on the beach back home, staying out until that last scrap of sun dropped below the horizon. The wind rushes against my face, tangling through my hair. I should be feeling weightless, wonderful.

But the farther the boat rumbles from shore, the more nervous I get. I'm not even at the hostel yet, and already my hands feel like Mickey Mouse gloves. I sit on them, ordering my knees not to jiggle. I wonder what it would take to turn the boat around.

A tsunami? A kraken?

Maybe I could jump out and swim to shore. I'd probably be stuck there, but that's all right. I could build myself a hut of sticks. Make sketchbook paper from chewed-up trees. Spend the rest of my days in solitude. *Whatever happened to Bria?* everyone would ask. I'd be like La Llorona, the weeping lake-lady from the Mexican ghost story. Haunting, beautiful—and deadly.

"Santa Lucía!" yells the boat driver.

I jump to my feet but am knocked back as he cranks the wheel. Grimy water laps over my sandals, soaking the hem of my skirt. Fabulous.

The boat bumps against the dock. Santa Lucía looks much smaller than Panajachel. Tin-roofed homes stagger up a sweep of hillside. About twenty yards up the road, which looks practically vertical, I see a hand-lettered blue sign: LA CASA AZUL. I reach for my camera. And then I remember.

"Click," I mutter sadly.

The dogs find me hiding in the doorway. There are two of them: massive, woolly black beasts that bark like disgruntled sea lions. I stand very still as they snuffle their insolent noses against my hands and skirt. Just inside the room, I hear laughter.

"Osa! León!" calls the bartender.

The dogs back off—but now I'm exposed. I cross my arms and survey the space: part pub, part restaurant, and part collective living room. Six picnic tables are arranged on a dirty plank floor. One wall is propped open like a garage door, letting the evening in. Beyond it, there's a patio deck furnished with potted plants and colorful hammocks. And everywhere, there are backpackers.

I see:

> *tanned skin*
> *tattoos—including, inexplicably, a winged*
> > *hot dog*
> *bare feet (hairy ones)*
> *dreadlocks*
> *knit caps, including one with fake*
> > *dreadlocks attached*
> *and lots and lots of linen*

But I don't see the ponytail boy from the market anywhere. Distraught, I head to the bar.

"They'll be done cooking in about twenty minutes," the bartender tells me in an (Irish? Scottish?) accent. He's short and lean, with freckled skin and pink knuckles ideal for rapping people's skulls. "It's five American dollars for the meal. Six if you want a Gallo as well."

"I don't know what that is," I admit.

"Haven't been in the country long, have you?" He opens the refrigerator behind him and withdraws a beer bottle bearing the red-and-yellow rooster logo I saw on signs all over Antigua. "*Cerveza.* Gallo is Guatemala's national beer."

"Why a rooster?"

"Down enough and you'll be crowing like one."

I manage a smile. "Just dinner," I say, rummaging in my money belt. The bartender grins. I realize I have my hand down the front of my skirt.

"You're not staying here, are you?" he asks.

Why, is it that obvious? I shake my head. I consider asking about the ponytailed guy, but I don't know his name, and I know how lame that will sound.

"Nice to meet you. I'm Henry Cavendish, like the Brit who discovered hydrogen—but that's our secret. Call me Hal!" He opens the Gallo for himself and slurps noisily. "I'm the owner. But you don't want to talk to me. I'm old and boring. You should run along and meet people. This crowd's pretty friendly, as long as you don't betray an interest in Top Forty radio."

"I'll try to keep it quiet," I say, stepping away from the bar.

I scan the room for someone sitting alone. Or an empty bench where I can sit by myself. I should have bought the Gallo, anyway. I hate beer, but at least I'd have a prop.

That's when I see her: the blond girl from the plane.

She's talking to a pair of skinny backpacker girls, and she looks even more backpackered out than before. Backtastic, even. Backtacular. She sits on a table, monkeylike, with her bony knees splayed out. Her drawstring pants pool around her thighs.

Of course she's here. I can't believe it never occurred to me. I focus all my mental energy on creating an escape hatch in the floor.

When nothing happens, I duck my head and inspect the bookshelf beside me. I grab a book—*The Canterbury Tales* in French, but at least it's illustrated—aim it toward the room, and peek over the top.

Now she's laughing, her head thrown back. Her feet are bare, nut-brown except for a V-shaped flip-flop tan line. She has even more wooden rings on her fingers, and her toes glitter with silver. As I watch, she winds a turquoise Mayan scarf, endlessly long, around the wheat-colored bundle of her hair.

I glance down at my white skirt, my surf shop sandals. They seemed passably bohemian back in my hotel room. But here they look almost pretentious. Though it's not as if anyone's looking my way. My invisibility is a good thing, I decide. It means I can escape unnoticed.

As surreptitiously as possible, I edge around the room, toward the night and the lake and the safe, boring numbness of my Global Vagabonds companions on the other side. Five dollars is a bargain for the lesson learned, I tell myself.

"Hey! Where you going?"

Smiling innocently, I turn back.

The backpackers who surrounded the blond girl have dispersed. She's staring at me with her head tipped to the side, the loose ends of her turquoise scarf draped over her shoulders like pigtail braids.

"Just . . ." I trail off.

"Come over here! I hate shouting."

She pats the table beside her. Like a good little square, I obey, crossing the room and perching on the table. Up close, I notice a scar on her bottom lip. Probably the ghost of a piercing.

"Funny finding you here!" she says. "But the travel circuit's small round these parts, I suppose. Where are all your buddies?"

I try not to scowl. "They're not my buddies. And they're back at our hotel in Panajachel."

"Your hotel's in Panajachel?"

I nod. "I just came here for dinner."

"But the last boat to Panajachel left here at six-twenty."

I sit very still.

"Wait," I say. "That was my boat—I *got* here at six-twenty. Nobody told me it was the last one."

"Did you ask?"

Mutely, I stare at her.

"Always, *always* ask! Don't take anything for granted when you're in another country. Especially when it comes to transportation." She twirls the ends of her scarf dismissively, as if she didn't just pull a Marcy and accuse me of being a travel moron. "Lucky for you, you're in civilization, instead of somewhere out in the jaguar-infested jungles. Everyone who's here is sleeping at the guesthouse. And I guess that means you too now. My name's Starling, by the way. Starling West."

"Starling? Really?"

"Yes, *really*. Wiseass. What's yours?"

"Bria Sandoval."

"Sandoval? Isn't that Hispanic? My brother's part Mexican. Do you speak Spanish?"

I shake my head. I'm sure she knows all sorts of Spanish herself. She's probably fluent in eleven languages. Including indigenous Mayan.

"So how'd you end up here, Bria Sandoval? Did you read about this place in a guidebook? Lonely Planet, perhaps? Rough Guides? Or are you a Rick Steves type of girl?"

"I was invited," I insist. "By the guy with a ponytail."

"A ponytail?"

"But he's not even here." The lump in my throat returns,

but this time it tastes like outrage. "Who does that, anyway? He knew I was staying in Panajachel."

"The guy with the ponytail."

"He was with you at the airport. He's got really tanned skin, with a dragon tattoo on his—"

"Oh, *Rowan!*" Even as Starling touches my arm reassuringly, she looks delighted. "I should have known. This is just like him. Reformed troublemaker, my *ass.*"

"Are you saying this is a joke?" I think I can feel my brain start to simmer. "Like, a prank? It isn't funny. It's insanely screwed up!"

"That boy can be *such* a misanthrope. I thought he was done with pranking tourists—it must have been Jack's influence. Five minutes with him, and Rowan's getting into trouble again. I wish we weren't meeting up in a week, but it's not my decision."

I have no idea what she's talking about, so I just gape at her.

"Relax, girlfriend, we'll get it all figured out. Here! Have my beer." She pokes her Gallo into my fingers. "So let's say Rowan misled you on purpose. What's the big deal? You've got a place to stay. We're good people, not savages. Even Rowan, for the most part." She grins.

And then it dawns on me: she's his *girlfriend.*

She has to be. My face turns hot. I mean, it's not like he made any sort of move on me. And to be honest, he's not even my type—he has a *ponytail*, for crying out loud. But I'm humiliated just the same.

"Hey, Rowan!" Starling yells at the top of her lungs.

I thunk the beer on the tabletop as the kitchen door swings open. Out steps the ponytailed guy from the market, that dark-haired demon, wearing a greasy apron over cargo pants. His chest and feet are bare. "Star, what the—" he begins. Then he sees me. "Holy shit, you made it!"

"How could you *do* this to me?"

Starling cracks up. "Whoa! Easy there, lioness."

Rowan holds his spatula in front of his face like a shield and cautiously approaches our table.

"You *knew* I couldn't have dinner here and get back to Panajachel tonight!" I shake the beer foam from my hand and stand, wishing my humble five foot two carried more clout. "So very funny, play a trick on a geeky girl. *Fine.* But did you ever think I might have a roommate, and no way to tell her I won't be coming back tonight? She might be a stupid tourist, but that doesn't mean her trip isn't just as important as yours. Not to mention—"

"I don't think you're geeky," Rowan says.

"That wasn't the *point!*"

"Bria, honey," Starling says, "why don't you give your hotel a call? Or your group mother or whatever?" She waves her phone in my face. "You can use mine—it's international. Hal's got a directory at the bar."

"But . . . ," I begin. "Oh."

I accept the phone. Starling slides off the tabletop and follows me to the bar. "Hey," she says. "Nice work there. Being concerned about your roommate, I mean, but also telling off Rowan. He really needs it from time to time." She grins. "Maybe we should keep you around."

I smile weakly, my head still throbbing from the force of my rant. Who knew I had it in me? If only I had the nerve to confront my parents like that. Or Toby.

Especially Toby.

Toby came to our school at the end of junior year. I remember exactly what Olivia said when she leaned over the lab table in second-period chemistry.

"There's a new guy! Jessa says he's hot."

Hot new guys are always interesting, but I didn't give too much weight to it, since Jessa Hanny's and my ideas of hot differ significantly. She's Olivia's backup best friend when I'm hanging out with Reese. Once the four of us went out to lunch, and it was nuclear.

While Reese and I bonded as kids over a joint enthusiasm for arts and crafts—me the arts part, her the crafts—and double dates with our coworker moms, Olivia's always been a different kind of friend: one who knows exactly how to coax out my edgy parts. Nobody else could have gotten me to sneak a Sprite bottle of vanilla vodka into homecoming (Olivia drank most of it herself), or to wear fake eyelashes, wedges, and a glittery halter top to Disneyland (I think I'm *still* blushing). And nobody could deliver news about a new guy like Olivia Luster, who always saved the best part for last.

"I hear he's an *artist*," she said.

Instantly, my stomach spiraled like a firecracker. She knew me well. I'd crushed, but never hard. I'd dated, but never seriously. When we joked about Bria's Dream Guy, he always carried a paintbrush. I hadn't even seen the new guy, and already it felt like he'd been casted just for me.

I didn't have to wait long. Moments after I found my seat in Life Drawing, he came over and sat beside me. "Bria, right?"

"Right," I said, kind of nervously.

"I'm Toby. I hear you're the artist."

It's hard to reply to a comment like that without sounding vain. I eyed him as I strung together my next words. He had curly blond hair, blue eyes, a few faint freckles. He wore a white sweatshirt and normal guy jeans. He didn't look like an artist. But then, neither did I. "I guess," I said at last. "As much as you can be in high school."

"Mr. Chiang said you're his best student. Where have you shown?"

"Excuse me?"

He shook his head. "Never mind. I'm an artist too. I'd love to see some of your stuff."

I'd never been shy about sharing my drawings. But for some reason, this guy's confidence intimidated me. "Only if you show me yours."

His grin made my stomach free-fall. "Then it's a date. It's great to meet you, Bria."

The next day, once I managed to pry a squealing Olivia from my wrist, I met Toby in the empty art room at lunch. We were both armed with sketchbooks. The same brand. The same size. But that's where the similarities ended.

I looked first.

Maybe it was Toby's grin that hooked me, but his drawings undid me. The detail. The dimension. City scenes I wanted to examine with a microscope. Landscapes. Portraits. And so many naked people I found myself blushing like crazy, even though usually I'm cool with that. They arched and twirled and stretched in a Cirque du Soleil of poses, dynamic enough to acrobat off the page.

"These are two-minute gestures," Toby explained, motioning toward a page of figures better than I could draw in an hour. "From the academy."

44

"The academy? You mean the Southern California Art Academy? You take *classes* there?" SCAA wasn't my top choice for college, since I loathed the idea of sticking around the city where I'd grown up. But it was an excellent school, nationally ranked. It was where I'd seen the art school girl.

"Well, I just drop by for life drawing in the evening. It's open to everyone. You should consider it—it's really worthwhile to get in some time with a live model." He grinned again, and I practically had to grab the sides of the table. "You know, they're starting a fast-track competition for incoming freshmen next year. If you make it, you don't have to deal with all the traditional lower-division bullshit."

"Really? I—"

Toby reached for my sketchbook before I could finish my sentence.

I'd always thought of myself as a serious artist, but at that moment, I knew it was a crock. I'd only studied anatomy from the book my father gave me—never figure abstractions, or rhythms, or any real methodology. And my subject matter . . . oh God. You see, I liked to draw fairies. And angels. Woodland creatures. My cat, Athena, who has since passed away, may she rest in peace. Sea monsters. Elves. Cherubs looped with ivy.

The whimsical. The fantastic.

Maybe my drawings were *good*, but they certainly weren't *serious*. You understand why, as Toby opened my sketchbook, I prayed to dissolve into a Wicked Witch puddle.

He didn't speak as he flipped through the pages. I felt each tiny gust of wind like a slap. Then he paused at one drawing: a fairy, of which I'd been particularly proud. I'd studied swallowtail wings on the Internet, rendering the veins of

45

color with my finest-tipped pens. "This one's got some depth," he said. "Androgyny, yeah?"

"Huh?"

"It's not a hermaphrodite? Isn't that a man's head on a woman's body?"

I stared at my drawing, horrified. "No! It's not supposed to be. Maybe I made her jaw a little big, or her neck, but—"

"Oh no!" Toby exclaimed. "Aw, Bria, I'm sorry. It's really nice. All of them are." He handed my sketchbook back to me. "But if you want, I can show you a little bit about mannequinizing your figures. It really provides a framework for rendering three-dimensional mass. You have so much potential."

It's hard to find fault with comments like that.

Well, in retrospect, it's not *too* hard. But Toby's backhanded compliments were easy to disregard in the radiance of the months that followed—months spent poring over art books with crumbling covers, tramping Malibu Canyon to paint the views plein air, making out against the door of the art room closet, talking on the phone for hours instead of calling back Reese and Olivia. Sketching caricatures of other students. Sketching teachers in drag. Sketching our fantasy trip to Europe.

All summer long, Toby and I prepared our portfolios for SCAA's fast-track admissions, swearing that whoever made it, whoever didn't, we'd still attend the school together, no matter what (because naturally, we'd both be admitted the regular way). Even if the Southern California Art Academy wasn't the East Coast atelier I'd dreamed about, the idea of attending art school with moody, intense, brilliant Toby

Kelsey—the first person who I felt really *got* me, or at least the me I thought I wanted to be—was too good to be true.

And yet it was coming true.

We were *planning* it.

Some of my old sketchbooks the ones I stashed under my bed right around the time art school acceptance letters arrived—held drawings of Bria's Dream Guy. He wore tiny black glasses and Converse shoes, with that legendary paintbrush tucked behind his ear. Then there was his archnemesis, the Bad Guy. In a series of two-dimensional encounters, Bria's Dream Guy rescued her from the Bad Guy—via surfboard, hang glider, and white stallion—paintbrush moonlighting as a sword.

Back then, I thought Mother Nature split the good guys from the bad with a fat black line.

But the thing is, in real life, they're often the same guy.

In the kitchen, the backpackers circle a table piled with food. Scrambled tofu, fruit salad, tortillas marbled with black beans, barbecued ears of corn. Guatemalan food with flower child flair. Everything is vegetarian—though not vegan, Starling warns me, like I care.

Okay, so maybe I've misjudged these people. It's hard to feel standoffish crammed shoulder to shoulder on picnic benches, eating with forks and fingers, while a red-haired Canadian guy strums David Bowie on a dented guitar. Several people get up and dance, hoisting their beers in the air. I laugh. And I eat. And I try not to think about how angry Marcy's going to be when I get back to Panajachel tomorrow morning, despite the message I left at our hotel's front desk. Or about Glenna, professional beadworker, sitting alone in our room just the way I left her. As long as I stay right here, in the present, I have to admit: I'm enjoying myself.

Then Starling ruins everything.

"Know what time it is?" she shouts. She chucks her beer bottle into the recycling bin and climbs up on the table. Her bejeweled toes are inches from my plate. "It's skinny-dipping time!"

A cheer erupts from the other backpackers. Benches scrape back as everybody hops to their feet. I stay put, hoping no one will notice.

"Come on, Bria!" Starling says. "You're the guest of honor—you've got to go."

"It's only cold at first!" calls a French girl.

Everyone's looking at me, but there's no freaking way in hell I'm getting in this or any other body of water, naked, clothed, or in a clown suit. I shake my head.

"Too shy?" Starling taunts.

"*Starling*," says Rowan, who has traded his apron for a gray button-down shirt. He steered clear of me all through dinner, presumably in case I turned violent. It's probably a good idea, even though I'm not really angry anymore. I shoot him a grateful look. Starling rolls her eyes before bouncing from the tabletop and out the door. Others follow, some of them already shedding clothes.

Rowan shrugs at me and heads outside.

Soon anyone who's not skinny-dipping has wandered away, including Hal. I'd head to bed, but I don't know where bed is. For a while, I hang around the empty room, skimming books in German, stacking dirty dishes. When I find myself

48

staring at a trail of ants on the floor, I decide I've had enough of myself.

The moon is out, doubled by the water. The silhouettes of the woolly black dogs stand guard on the dock. Shrieks and splashes carve the night. Since sitting on the dock above the swimmers might make me look like a pervert, I walk along the shore until I find a grassy patch beside the lake. From there, I can see the sparkle of wet limbs, glistening heads skating along the surface of the water, but no actual nudity.

I sigh.

It's not that I *want* to join in. It's just . . . I *want to* want to, if that makes any sense. My time with Toby taught me to look both ways before attempting anything new. Until now, when even the *suggestion* of joining in makes me resist.

"So you don't like getting naked with strangers?"

Rowan has materialized beside me. Entirely clothed and dry, I note. I shake my head and shrug at the same time. "Why, do you?"

"On occasion," he replies. He hesitates a moment, then settles beside me at a respectable distance. "Of course, it depends on the naked strangers."

"How about Starling?"

He wrinkles his nose. "My sister?"

"Oh, she's your *sister*." I clear my throat, silently thanking God that relief isn't something another person can see, like a blush. "You don't look anything alike."

"Different mothers. She's about a year older."

"Oh," I say again. I sift pebbles through my fingers until I find a flat stone to fling into the water. It skips three times before sinking, breaking up the moon.

"Anyway, it's not the nudity," I confess. "I don't swim."

"Don't, or can't?"

"Either."

"It's shallow here," Rowan points out.

I fling another stone into the water. "Doesn't matter."

"It's really about the nudity, isn't it?"

"Just quit it, okay? It's getting irritating."

He laughs. "That's quite a statement, considering those roly-poly people you're touring with. Why aren't you backpacking?"

I consider making up some kind of complicated explanation. But then I remember—cringingly—getting caught in my lie on the plane. By both Starling and Glenna. Horrors.

So I tell the truth. "It never even occurred to me."

Rowan runs his palm up and down his forearm, the dragon's eye winking in and out. I'd never admit it to his face, but his tattoo disappoints me. You'd think a guy like him would choose something more esoteric. Like a quote from a favorite book. Or maybe a mysterious religious emblem from somewhere special he's traveled. A dragon seems so . . . *frat boy*.

"It must drive you crazy," he remarks. "To have your entire trip planned out for you. No choices of your own. As soon as you begin to get acclimated somewhere, it's time to move on."

"At least I'm here."

"True. Most people don't get this far in their whole lives."

I hide my smile by pretending to search for more stones. "So what are you really doing here, Rowan? Straight answer."

"I teach scuba diving."

No wonder my aversion to water made him all itchy. "In the lake?"

"Sure. But all over the place."

"Like where?"

"Besides here?" He stretches. "Well, I've been in Guatemala almost three months—the longest I've been anywhere for ages. Before that, the Bay Islands in Honduras. Little Corn Island in Nicaragua. All over Costa Rica. I spent some time backpacking Thailand, Laos, and Malaysia. Not many other places, but I'm still young."

"How young, exactly?"

"Nineteen. Twenty in September. You?"

"I'm eighteen. But wait—you're saying you traveled that much in how long? How long have you been traveling?"

"I left home a couple weeks after I turned eighteen."

I shake my head in disbelief. He's been traveling for almost two years. I try to wrap my brain around it, but my mental arms won't reach. "What about college?"

"College is overrated. I'm already doing what I want to do: travel and dive. I don't need a degree to do it." He shrugs. "Although I've taken a few online courses for fun. Like Cognitive Psychology. And Oceanography. And Intro to Portuguese—I thought I'd visit Brazil someday."

He tries to skip a stone in the water. It sinks.

"Pathetic. You've got to find a flatter one." I find a perfect stone and hand it to him. He tries again. It sinks too, and I laugh. "So . . . where are you headed next?"

"Northeastward."

"What's northeastward?"

"More money, for starters. And more beauty, of course."

"More beauty than this?" I hold my hands at arm's length and form a rectangle with my thumbs and forefingers, a viewfinder. I miss my camera—it was the perfect excuse *not* to draw. Now my sketchbook's the only record I'll have of this trip. If I can ever bring myself to draw in it.

"It's different. There's rain forest. And the Caribbean. I have a dive gig off the coast of Belize, on an island called Laughingbird Caye. They're having a festival soon, and that's when the money comes in."

Laughingbird Caye. I like the sound of it. "And after that?"

"No clue. I'll head south, I guess."

Over Rowan's shoulder, I see Starling approaching. "Brazil?" I ask.

"Who knows?"

Starling heaves herself beside him. Her clothes stick to her damp body. "Forgot towels! The least sexy part of skinny-dipping is getting dressed." She leans back on her elbows and winks at me. "So how's it going, Bria Sandoval? Let me guess—you're thoroughly enchanted by *la vie bohème*, and you're ready to exchange that clunky suitcase for a backpack and join us on our journey."

She can't be serious. I hurl another rock at the water and it skips four times.

"You don't think I'm serious," she continues. "But I am. Listen: you've made it to Central America—hooray! But now that you're here, why don't you use this opportunity to travel? Like, to *really* travel? With people who know the right places to go?"

I glance at Rowan, who is busy examining his stack of string ankle bracelets. I'm starting to feel nervous. "Ha," I say. "You guys are crazy."

Starling chuckles. "It's not like we're inviting you to an

orgy! Although I hope you haven't taken a vow of chastity or anything—that might be a problem for my brother here."

Rowan shoves Starling's shoulder. "Hey! Who said I was even interested?"

"You're *always* interested."

"You know that's not true—"

"I have a boyfriend, anyway," I blurt out.

Where the hell did that come from? My face catches fire. Silently, I thank the darkness for hiding my burning cheeks. It's like something out of a bad romantic comedy. I *hate* that kind of movie; the liar always gets caught. But it's too late. I can't take it back. *Oh no, really, I was kidding. I'm single and ready to mingle!* Kill me now.

Starling, however, is grinning. "Perfect! You'll be our other sister. Entirely platonic. So there's nothing stopping you. Come on, Bria . . . be impulsive for once!"

I stare at the stone in my hands—and discover it's not a stone; it's an avocado pit. I roll it down the slope into the lake.

I want to argue that they know nothing about me—I *am* impulsive. Didn't I steal away to Santa Lucía? Sprint off in Chichicastenango? Journey to Central America in the first place? I even almost ate a street-cart tamale!

I have the feeling Starling won't be impressed.

Toby liked to say he chose not to be impulsive. As if being impulsive were something you consciously decide. When I look at Starling, with her turquoise turban and wet knot of hair, and at Rowan, with his stack of cheap string anklets, I think: *Impulsive isn't something you* choose. *It's something you* are. Like gay, or freckled, or bipolar.

53

Something I pretend to be but am not. Not really. Not deep down.

I try to find an easy out. "But I've got no money."

"None at all?"

"Very, very little."

"We're not talking like twenty dollars here, right?"

"Just a couple hundred . . ."

Starling waves her hand dismissively. "That's more than enough when you travel like us. When's your flight home?"

"I leave from Guatemala City in eighteen days."

"It'll be hard to get her back in time," Rowan says quietly. "I need to be in Belize for a whole week."

"But that leaves, like, eleven extra days," I say. "Doesn't it take just a couple days to get there? Why are you allowing so much time to travel?"

"Because it's the whole point—"

Before he can finish, the rest of the skinny-dippers—some of whom haven't even bothered to put on clothes—mob us, and in the resulting anarchy of wet limbs and dreadlocks, the moment's lost.

4

Day 4, Morning
My Walk of Shame

I wake the next morning to roosters screeching. My first
sensation is surprise: so I managed to fall asleep after all.

My bed at La Casa Azul turned out to be a second-level
bunk in a filthy dorm room shared with seven backpackers
stinking of lake water and armpits and worse. All night the
bedsprings gouged my back. A chill wind moaned faintly
through the fissures in the walls: La Llorona, sensing my
distress, seeping in to offer me her place. Out of pure disgust,
I tried to avoid using the bed's gray sheet. But too soon I was
shivering beneath it, my eyes on the ceiling rafters, searching
for moving things.

What's worse, I couldn't stop thinking about what I'd

overheard last night on my way back from the shared bathroom—Starling and Rowan, talking about me.

"What the hell were you thinking?" Rowan said. "She's never even traveled before."

"I like her."

"It's a terrible idea, Starling. I don't want to be anyone's babysitter."

"Come on! It's only for two weeks. And she's got so much potential. You remember what it was like. If you hadn't met Jack when you were eighteen—"

"I'd have saved myself a whole lot of grief."

I hurried back to bed, cursing that stupid word. *Potential*. It's exactly what Toby said about my art. *Potential* signifies almost-there-but-not. *Potential* means I'm lacking.

And anyway . . . potential for what?

The rooster screeches again. What time is it? I seem to be the only one awake, though I don't know how my roommates can sleep with the glaring daylight and shrieking poultry. I scrape myself out of bed and slide my dirty feet into my sandals. My skirt looks like a crumpled napkin. Holding one hand over my eyes to shield them from the light, I push open the door and slip out.

The common room is empty. Down by the water's edge, several villagers in bright clothes are slinging burlap bags onto the dock. I hear a buzzing sound, like a chain saw starting up. I squint across the lake. A boat is heading toward us, leaving behind a trail of white. The volcanoes complete a perfect picture.

I glance over my shoulder at the common room. Still empty.

If I leave now, no one will stop me.

The buzz grows more urgent as the boat approaches. I can

see the inconsistencies of rock on the distant volcanoes, iced with light. Everything looks different in the morning. When the sun rises higher, it will all fade to blue. My throat feels tight.

"*Veinte quetzales,*" says the boat driver, the same guy as last night.

It's easier this way, I tell myself as I fumble in my pocket for a bill. Damned if I'm not dying to fulfill my so-called potential, but I'm not going to do it with people who don't want me around. Rowan will be delighted to know he dodged babysitting duties. And while Starling might mourn her loss of a travel project for a second, I bet she'll be just as relieved.

"*Tienes otro?*" The boat driver points to a tiny tear in the bill I gave him.

"Sorry, I don't understand."

"*Necesito otro.* Is no good."

"What, because it's torn?" I touch the rip.

He nods.

"But this is all I've got."

Suddenly, a hand jams a crisp fifty in front of me. "*Por dos,*" Starling says. She's wearing red-framed glasses and a souvenir Nicaragua T-shirt over drawstring pants, her hair in a messy braid hanging nearly to her waist. "You sneaky bitch," she mutters at me, even though she doesn't sound angry. "I haven't even had my coffee yet."

"What are you doing here?"

She climbs into the boat and sits beside me, scooting closer as a Mayan woman squeezes past her. "I'm saving you."

"From *what?*"

The boat engine starts, and she has to shout her next words over the roar: "From regret!"

"I don't get why you care so much," I shout back.

"I can't stand to watch an opportunity for travel transcendence wasted. It would ruin *my* trip too." I narrow my eyes at her, but she just laughs. "Come on, Bria! We want you to come along. I mean it."

She's lying. Or half lying, at least. But I can't bring myself to tell her what I overheard late last night. It's too humiliating. Instead, I point to my ear and shake my head with a grimace, like I can't hear her over the sound of the engine. Then I turn away, rest my arms on the edge of the boat, and do my best to conjure up a kraken.

As soon as Starling and I enter the hotel lobby in Panajachel, Marcy pounces. "You ungrateful kid!"

All the things I planned to say scatter. I stand there, agape, while Marcy yammers on about decency and responsibility and respect. A few feet behind her, the rest of my tour group gawk with eyes the size of snow globes.

"You know I'm responsible for your welfare, and then you take off for the night without telling anyone, leaving nothing but an incoherent message at the front desk. Eight other people paid the same amount you did, and you had every single one of us worried sick. How can you be so self-centered?"

Self-centered? For going to a party for the first time in months? For being a normal teenager for a few hours?

I want to be offended. But . . . maybe she's right.

That's what this trip is about—doing what's best for myself. Becoming independent. Obviously, Global Vagabonds isn't helping that cause. Tagging along with Rowan and Starling isn't a perfect alternative—really, I'd just be leaving one game of follow-the-leader for another. What's more,

Rowan doesn't want me along. And even if he did, both he and Starling think I have a boyfriend, so I'd be dragging a stupid Toby-faced lie behind me the whole time.

There are a thousand reasons not to go with them.

The question is, what will I regret more—daring to go off with Starling and Rowan, or spending the remainder of my trip watching Dan violate maps?

It's not even a question.

"I'm sorry," I say. "I really am. I know I'm not making this easy on you. But I really do think it's better this way. Now you don't need to worry about me."

"What are you talking about?"

"I'm going off on my own. Kind of. Actually, I'm going off with her."

Marcy glances at Starling, who winks.

"Are you kidding? I won't allow it! You're just a teenager. Your parents entrusted Global Vagabonds to take care of you—"

"I'm *eighteen*. My parents had nothing to do with this trip."

It's true. Mostly. When I told them I was traveling this summer, my dad muttered about losing his paperwork help. My mom bellyached about my squandering my college funds, even though she's the one who put that title on my savings. But in the end, I think they were glad I got my mopey self out of the house. I'll bet my mom's going through my closet right this second, selecting shirts with a maximum boob-stretch factor to borrow.

Now Marcy's shouting. "But you already paid for everything! If you leave the group, your money's wasted. You're not getting one penny back."

59

"A bargain for the lesson learned," I say.

Okay, it wasn't really. But it sounded good.

When I rejoin Starling, my heart pounding, she claps me on the shoulder. "Holy cojones! Damn, girl, that's the second time I've watched you rip somebody a new one. Color me impressed."

I can't help grinning.

We start for the staircase to gather my things, but suddenly I stop. "Hey, would you mind going on up without me?" I hand her my key. "There's someone I need to talk to."

The Vagabonds are already in the street by the time I catch up with them. Dan sees me first and pokes Marcy in the side. She faces me and plants her hands on her hips. "Having second thoughts? After that display, I don't know if the group's comfortable enough with your presence—"

Ignoring her, I head for Glenna Heron, professional bead-worker. I tug her a few steps from the others and, in a low voice, thank her.

"For what?"

"For not telling Marcy where I went." I pause. "Did you tell her?"

She shakes her head. "You'd have done the same for me . . . that is, if I'd ever had the opportunity. I missed that part of being young."

"What part?"

"The *exciting* part." She smiles at me from under her floppy hat. "I'll send you a beaded necklace. So you can refer all your friends."

Starling West's unPacking List
AKA Things you should not bring to
Central America, or anywhere else you
go, ever, as explained to Bria Sandoval,
travel virgin

Full-size bottles of tea-tree conditioner
Shoes with heels higher than one inch
Ergonomic travel pillows
Strawberries & Champagne body spray,
    or any other kind
Purple leggings
Anything with spangles

By the time I get back to my room, Starling has completely ransacked my suitcase. Clothes are scattered all over both beds, draped over the backs of chairs, piled on the dresser. Underwear dangles from the bedpost. Cosmetics are strewn across the floor. My sketchbook sits on the bed, the elastic strap still wound around it. I hope Starling's not the type to snoop.

"I called Hal to let Rowan know you're officially a member of the family," she says. "For two weeks, at least."

I smile weakly. My boldness from moments ago is dissipating by the second.

"But this . . ." Starling spreads her arms. "This is *disastrous*. The worst case of overpacking I've ever seen. I've managed to pare it down. But you're not going to like it."

I push aside a pair of denim shorts with the tags still attached and sit on the bed, one hand on my sketchbook. "Which pile do I get to keep?"

"The one beside you."

"And what am I supposed to do with all my other stuff?"

"In theory, you could mail it home. But it might not get there. And it would be really expensive. The noble thing to do is to give it away—though I don't think the villagers will want anything to do with this." She twirls a glittery halter top around her index finger.

"That's not mine."

"Yeah, sure."

"No, seriously. It's my friend Olivia's. I've never even worn it."

"Olivia must be an interesting girl." Starling stretches the top between her fingers and shoots it into the trash. I picture Olivia's reaction and smirk. I'd love to see Olivia and Starling stuck in an elevator. As long as I wasn't stuck inside with them.

"How about we shove your extraneous shit in your suitcase and leave it on the sidewalk? With a sign: FINDERS KEEPERS, in Spanish. Then we'll locate a backpack."

"Can I at least look through the stuff I'm giving away?"

Without waiting for a reply, I shove aside my pink quickdry capris and swipe the white sweatshirt from Glenna's bed. "This stays."

"Not a chance! It would take up half your backpack. And you'll never need it. Where you're going, even the rainiest days are warm."

I unfold the sweatshirt and hold it at arm's length. I have it memorized: the ragged cuffs, the front pocket worn coarse inside. It reaches all the way to my knees when I wear it to sleep.

I know Starling's right. And it's humiliating that I kept it in the first place, let alone brought it all the way to Central America. So I screw up my face and force myself to remember. Not the good parts, the parts that made me stay with Toby long past our expiration date. But the shitty parts. The betrayals.

Like the way we ran into this girl from Toby's old school, and he gripped the back of my neck a little too tightly so I wouldn't say anything stupid, and after, got mad when I asked who she was.

The way my mom thought he was *just so cute*, and acted way more enthusiastic about my having a boyfriend than she ever did about my drawings.

The way he wouldn't even get out of the car the only time I took him to my favorite beach. *It's way too cold*, he said. He only opened the door to toss out the condom wrapper.

The way, when we talked about attending school together, he said *no matter what*, over and over, like a promise. Maybe I was stupid for believing, and even more stupid for wanting to believe. But either way, he fooled me. When it all fell apart, I was genuinely surprised.

With that, I shove the sweatshirt into the trash can so forcefully it tips over, while Starling looks on, her expression impossible to read.

5

Day 4, Afternoon
Wanderlove

I follow Starling down Calle Santander with a garbage bag containing the fortunate few of my belongings slung over my shoulder. Not a single spangle desecrates the lot. The bag still weighs a ton, but that's partially my fault. I insisted on including a second pair of jeans.

"You're going to swelter," Starling says, tugging up her drawstring pants.

"I'd rather swelter than look like a belly dancer."

She snorts, then links her arm through mine. Apparently, talking shit is the key to Starling's good graces. As we walk, she tells me we'll spend one more night on the lake, and then we'll leave for Guatemala City. A necessary way station, she calls it, like Bangkok or Delhi—unsavory, yet unavoidable. I can't help suspecting she's just name-dropping foreign cities, but whatever. After that, we'll head to somewhere called Río Dulce. My imperfect Spanish can translate that much: "Sweet River."

I wonder if you can drink from it.

By the time we reach the dock, the boat has arrived. Unexpectedly, Rowan stumbles ashore like a lopsided turtle, an army green backpack slung over one shoulder. He nods at me unsmilingly, and I nod back, trying not to let my sudden startled-mouse panic show on my face.

Alone with Starling, I'm fine. Add Rowan to the equation, and I regain an appetite for my fingernails.

"What the hell are you doing here?" Starling demands. "We're supposed to meet in Santa Lucía!"

"Too many people back at the hostel. A second boatload arrived. I was starting to feel agoraphobic. Or claustrophobic. Even xenophobic."

Starling laughs. "You could never be xenophobic."

"So I thought we could have lunch here instead." He shrugs off the backpack and gives it a shake. "Bria, I found this for you."

My expression must betray my disgust. The backpack looks like it's been through a war. A war in a swamp. A war in a swamp involving fireballs and monsters with fangs.

"Think of it this way," Starling says. "If backpacks are like stuffed animals, years of love and backpacker sweat have magicked that one to life."

"We can sew straps on your garbage bag, if you prefer," Rowan says.

What an ass. "It's just so small," I say, as if that's the issue. "How do you guys carry everything? Especially when you've been traveling so long?"

Starling shrugs. "Mine's even smaller. Too much stuff's a hassle."

"And it's heavy," Rowan adds. "Plus, small backpacks up your backpacker cred. The most hard-core shoestring types have an unspoken contest to see who can travel the lightest. Isn't that right, Starling?"

"While you lug around all sorts of junk you can't make yourself get rid of. Just look at that stack of bracelets on his leg, Bria. Whenever a little kid tries to sell him one, he buys it. He can't say no!"

We all stare at Rowan's leg. "There's over sixty of them," he says proudly.

"He thinks he's helping the economy."

Rowan's first travel rule:
*The smaller the backpack, the bigger
the ego.*

"Anyway, so many American luxuries are just that— luxuries," Starling continues. "You don't need them. They drag you down, and not just physically. I mean, isn't that why we travel in the first place? To renounce all those things?" She glances at Rowan. "*We*, I mean. Not other people."

"It's some sort of escapism, anyway," Rowan says.

They smirk at each other, as if sharing some private, sibling joke, while I am so far removed from this conversation, I might as well zoom off in a tourist-shaped flying saucer. I watch a yellow dog trot by, swollen teats swaying. Spaying

66

and neutering are probably some of those so-called American luxuries.

"But by renouncing Western culture—or by trying to escape it, whatever—aren't you also spreading it?" I ask. "Like the first European settlers coming to America? Bringing their European diseases and infecting the natives? Even if you don't mean to, something always sticks."

They both look taken aback.

"Well," Starling begins.

"I mean, isn't there a McDonald's in Chimaltenango now? With home-delivery service?"

"So I've heard," Rowan says.

I pretend not to notice their expressions as I unzip the backpack and prepare to transfer my stuff. If they think I'll be a docile companion, a travel pet, they're in for a surprise.

"I'm a big fan of *la comida tipica*," Starling says. "But sometimes, you just need some tempeh. You know what I mean?"

She looks at me, and I shrug. The three of us are sitting around a table, jammed against a wall papered in vintage maps. In that unspoken way of theirs, Starling and Rowan strolled straight to the restaurant, a colorful hole-in-the-wall specializing in vegetarian global cuisine. They selected the table without discussion, fell into the seats as if they were overstuffed recliners, snapped open the menus with indolent flicks. I guess it's cute in a sitcom sort of way. But their synchronization keeps reminding me that I'm still a stranger. A whim tacked on to their colossal history. It makes me want to hug myself.

"Actually," I say, "I'm allergic to tempeh."

Starling glances at me. "Oh yeah?"

"It makes my face itch."

"That's too bad. It's good stuff." Starling's pocket starts to jangle. She pulls out her phone, checks it, and stands. "I've got to take this call. Ro, can you order for me?"

"That depends on who's on the phone."

"Oh, come on," Starling says. "It's my boss in Flores! Not Jack, if that's what you're worried about. Besides, you're the one who's started buddying up with him again, not me."

Rowan glares at her. "Marius has strep throat. I *told* you. There's no one else available on the island to cover his dive class. Everybody else is booked because of Lobsterfest. And the shop pays better than La Casa Azul."

"Wow, you're so *practical*! Now you've made me miss my call. If you'll excuse me."

I feign interest in my fork as Starling storms off. Rowan doesn't explain anything, even though their exchange was packed with questions. In fact, he doesn't say anything at all, except when a woman comes to take our orders. As he watches the traffic on Calle Santander—the cyclists, the tourist vans, the tuctucs, like red ladybugs—I scour my brain for an electrifying conversation topic. "So who's Jack?" I ask finally.

Rowan blinks at me, like I've yanked him from a nap. Remarkable—he's already forgotten I'm here. "Who's what?"

"Jack."

"Oh," he says dismissively. "Just a dive buddy."

I count to ten, then try again. "So what's the deal with all the maps?"

"Maps?"

Is he dense? "All over the walls."

68

"Oh, right. Take a closer look."

I swivel in my seat and focus on the world map behind me. On closer perusal, I discover it's wildly distorted, like planet Earth on acid. Indonesia and Papua New Guinea are as large as a vertically swollen Africa. North and South America are tiny. A swarm of Asian islands crush a shrunken Europe. There's a legend, but it's in another language.

"What *is* this?"

"It's in Swedish," Rowan says. "The sizes of the countries correspond to the number of different languages spoken there."

"Eight hundred and sixty in Papua New Guinea," I read. "Wow—that's ridiculous."

"They're all like that."

"Like what? Linguistic?"

"Unique."

I cross the room to examine a map of the United States. "Leading church bodies by county," I read out loud. With my finger, I find Los Angeles County, colored blue for Catholic. I move to a second map of the United States This one features UFO hot spots, predominantly concentrated in the Southwest. I assume another world map depicts Pangaea, the ancient collective continent, but the caption explains it's the opposite: a NASA rendering of the earth 250 million years in the future. Other maps are designed to look like mythical creatures or political figures.

When I glance back at Rowan, he's smiling. Finally.

"Pretty neat, right?" he asks.

"They're incredible!" I join him at our table. "Who owns this place?"

"He's a Guatemalan world traveler."

69

"Is he here?"

"Not now. He's traveling, as usual." Rowan nods at the distorted map above our table. "I always thought I'd decorate my home with maps like these. If I ever settle down, that is."

"I heard that!" Starling shouts, tossing herself into the chair beside me.

"Heard what," Rowan says flatly.

"You admit that you'll *never* settle down."

"I didn't say '*never*.' I said '*if I ever*.'"

"It's all in the subtext."

"I'm sure he will someday," I say helpfully, "when he's ready."

Starling shakes her head. "Not when you're a whore like Rowan."

My jaw drops. Rowan, however, just looks exasperated, like he's dealt with this before. "Starling, give me a break! That's in the past, and you know it."

"If you consider a few months ago the past! Bria, tell me what you think." Starling leans against the wall, looking like a smug Sunday school teacher about to share a moral fable. "Imagine being eighteen years old. A fledgling dive instructor in one of the most beautiful places on earth—"

"Assistant," Rowan says, correcting her. "Assistant instructor. Can we quit this?"

"With no strings holding him back. From the very first minute, surrounded by a crowd of charismatic hooligans. *Influential* charismatic hooligans. And an ever-changing smorgasbord of backpacker chicks, all awaiting his *instruction* . . ."

Rowan's had enough. "Starling, come *on!*"

With perfect timing, our server arrives with our food, distracting Starling from her oversharing session. Rowan looks relieved, but I'm not sure how I feel. Part of me is dying to know the details. But if the details describe another guy like Toby Kelsey—because if the rumors are true, Toby definitely got around toward the end—I think I'd rather travel in ignorance. I scoop chili powder onto my pad thai, wondering if my meal is hypocritical, since I thought eating Paraguyan food was so ridiculous.

"Careful," Rowan warns me. "That stuff's really hot."

I shrug, take a bite, and try not to cry.

"So where was I?" Starling says, chewing. So much for distraction.

"Trespassing," Rowan replies.

"Trespassing? What do you . . . Okay, I get it. Fine. Fine! Forget the girls. I won't go there. But there's something else Bria should know if she's going to travel with us. With you, especially."

"You don't mean . . ." Something like panic passes through Rowan's eyes. It's gone as soon as Starling shakes her head, but takes lodge in the center of my chest instead. I'm getting the distinct impression there is something they're not telling me, and it's starting to seem sinister. It better not have anything to do with black markets and body organ harvesting.

"I'm talking about your religion," Starling says.

Or cults.

"May I tell her about it, Rowan? Pretty please?"

Rowan leans back in his chair. "You're going to, whether I want you to or not. Anyway, it's not a religion. More like a philosophy."

"Or an affliction."

I glance at him nervously. "An affliction?"

Starling spreads her arms grandly. "He's afflicted with Wanderlove!"

"Don't you mean wanderlust?"

"No. Not lust. Wander*love*."

"Wanderlove." I try out the word.

"See, wanderlust is like itchy feet," Starling explains. "It's when you can't settle down. But Wanderlove is much deeper than that . . . it's a compulsion. It's the difference between lust and love. Have you ever been in love? Maybe with that boyfriend of yours?"

Thoughts of Toby bubble up, like acid reflux. I force them down with a shrug.

"Well, have you ever been in love with any*thing*? Not a person, necessarily." I shrug again, helplessly, and she shakes her head. "Poor baby."

Indignant, I keep searching—sifting through the months, back and back—until I find it: the most obvious thing of all.

"I used to love to draw."

I expect Starling to roll her eyes, and feel thankful when she doesn't. "Okay. Do you remember how it felt? In your gut?"

I recall the rasp of charcoal on newsprint, the chewing-gum stretch of a kneaded eraser, the precarious bite of a razor blade in a new pencil. The vibrancy of fresh watercolors squeezed from a tube. A new sketchbook, cracked open to flawless white. The way the smell of turpentine made me feel simultaneously sick and excited. On this trip, I brought mostly pens and number-two pencils—much easier to shove into my bag. I think about the way I've squeezed my pencils so hard over the years my middle finger has a permanent bump where the wood presses against it. I run my thumb over it now, trying to calm the thrill in my stomach, the sudden, overwhelming urge to draw.

"Now," Starling says, "imagine that feeling amplified, and projected all over the place, like a beam of light. Brightest in front of you, glowing everywhere but behind you . . ."

"That's stupid," Rowan says.

"Then *you* define it better."

"Pointless. You'll never get it."

"I'm the one who invented it in the first place!"

"That's like saying you invented electricity."

Instead of retorting, Starling stands a quetzal coin on its edge with one finger. She flicks it with her other hand. It spins in a blur of gold. All three of us stare at it until it starts to tremble. Then Rowan slaps it flat with his hand.

"How about this?" Starling says. "The abridged version. Wanderlove is about forgetting the bad things and focusing on the good. Out with the old and in with the new."

Silently, Rowan slides the coin across the table to Starling.

"No matter what he says, that's Wanderlove," she tells me. "That's how he lives it. Isn't that right, Rowan? The only way to escape the past is to keep moving forward."

Starling slides the coin back to Rowan. Harder, so it makes an audible scrape. But Rowan doesn't touch it; he just lets it sit there on the table, unclaimed.

Art: The Wonder Drug

When I was little, drawing wasn't just for fun. It was
my panacea, my cure-all for all kinds of heartsickness.
My dependable happy-maker.

Like if my mom bawled me out for something—spilling pomegranate juice on my dad's papers, or running through the house with muddy sandals—I fled to my room and curled around a notepad, the repository for all my grief. If I got an answer wrong in class, I scrawled on a scrap of paper hidden in my lap. By junior high, those papers had turned into knockoff Moleskine sketchbooks I kept in my backpack. When I waited for Reese to join me at lunch, or when Olivia got talking and talking, I pulled it out and sketched. I was the sketchy girl. You know the one. But I wasn't showing off—I was making myself happy. It was like a magic power.

And then I gave it up.

With a pathetic whimper instead of a bang. It wasn't this great big temper tantrum I threw, or a resolve I made, or anything even slightly so dramatic. After we got the results of fast-track admissions, art slowly shifted from the light of my life to the bane of my existence. It meant fights and shame. It hurt to talk about. It hurt to think about. Before Toby and I broke up. And after, when I told my parents I wasn't going to art school after all.

So for months, I didn't draw, and didn't, and still didn't. Until I found I couldn't—even when my heart was the saddest and sickest it'd ever been.

Giving up my art made me need it more than ever. That's the worst part of all.

~ July 16, Santa Lucía, Guatemala

In the evening, I sit in a striped beach chair in front of La Casa Azul, my sketchbook on my lap. It's been ages since I've drawn, but the absence of my art has never felt this physical.

A longing that aches like a Pacific cold-water swim. I blame Starling and all her talk about love.

I just can't understand why it's so difficult to do the thing I've done an infinite number of times, especially when I'm surrounded by sketchworthy scenes. The colossal black dogs Osa and León. An anonymous backpacker girl dozing in the shade. The glazed blue bowl of the lake.

But something stalls on the journey between my eyes, my brain, and my fingers. I don't even know what to call it. Fear isn't quite right.

I left my new/old backpack in the common room, along with the smaller daypack I bought in Panajachel. Though it's barely dark out, the hostel buzzes with shouts and laughter, clinking bottles, the mournful plink-plunk of a mistuned guitar. Everyone's gearing up for another evening of rooster beers and skinny-dipping. Everyone except me. I'm sure I'm damaging my backpacker cred—as if I have any to start with—but I want to be alone right now.

I've only been sitting for fifteen minutes when I see Rowan approaching. I slip my sketchbook between my thighs. He has a novel under his arm: *Atonement.*

"Oh," he says when he sees me.

"Hi, Rowan!" I say cheerfully in an attempt to offset his hostility, which is starting to get on my nerves. "What brings you out here on this gorgeous evening? Have I stolen your seat?"

He blinks at me a moment, then recovers. "It's not mine unless I'm sitting in it."

"Great! I thought we'd have to battle it out. I may be small, but I can kick some serious ass."

Half smirking, Rowan ruffles the pages of his book with

75

his thumb. "Actually, I thought I'd go read down by the water. There's a new group here tonight, I think I mentioned, and they're dead set on a karaoke competition. My eardrums already ache in anticipation. Also, just too many people."

"You're not big on people, are you?"

"I wouldn't say *that*. Just . . . when faced with the choice between small talk with strangers and peace and quiet, I'll choose the latter every time. You know?"

"It depends. Are we talking naked karaoke?"

Rowan pauses a second and then cracks a smile. "Could be. But I assume naked karaoke with strangers isn't your thing?"

"Depends on the naked strangers."

We grin at each other for a moment past stupid, and it's really decent, and I'm so proud of myself I could backflip. Finally, Rowan starts for the lake.

"Are you coming?" he calls over his shoulder.

I'm so surprised it takes me a second to reply. "Um, I don't have a book."

"Did you say . . . no book? No *book?*" He pretends to pull a knife from his chest. "We've got to remedy that. Just grab one from the book exchange inside. Hal won't care. If you're feeling overly ethical, leave a few quetzales."

My first impulse is to decline. Because—admit it—there's something perversely appealing about sitting all alone, feeling sorry for yourself, especially when the scenery's stunning and there's a party going on behind you.

But that's not what this trip is about. It's about jumping in. Making up for all the times I held back. And if I'm not quite ready to rip off my clothes and sing "Livin' La Vida Loca," I should probably go read by the lake.

I'm about to stand up when Rowan shrugs. "No big deal. See you in the morning, then."

Apparently, I took too long to decide.

I watch him trudge down the slope toward the water, allowing myself to feel shitty for exactly ten seconds. Then I open my sketchbook. I pick up my pen.

And for the first time in months, I draw.

PART
2

The Jungle

Every act of creation is first of all an act of destruction.   *~Pablo Picasso*

The secret to so many artists living so long is that every painting is a new adventure. So, you see, they're always looking ahead to something new and exciting. The secret is not to look back.   *~Norman Rockwell*

6

Day 5
Breakdown

Guatemala City, Guatemala
Guatemala City is one of the most dangerous
cities in Latin America. Petty theft is rampant,
as are violent crimes. As a result, we will not
be spending any more time than necessary in
Guatemala City after our airplane lands.

I crumple up my Global Vagabonds itinerary and shove it
into my daypack. Most of the destinations differ from ours,
but it's the closest thing to a travel guide I've got if you don't
count Rowan and Starling. I'm sitting beside two strangers on
my first chicken bus ride, with half my ass hanging over the
seat, one leg braced in the aisle.

As far as I can tell, there are no chickens.

I'm profoundly disappointed, but I suppose the name is metaphorical. Though the ride is cheap, I've quickly learned any money saved is eclipsed by liters of sweat, kicked ankles, malodorous human beings, white-knuckled feats of highway navigation, and other forms of discomfort. Maybe it would be bearable if I had a window seat. All I've seen during our three-hour journey are hips, backs, and the undersides of bosoms. And we had to sit through four . . . entire . . . *hours* of this before our arrival in the supposedly savage avenues of Guatemala City.

Okay, so they *do* look kind of savage. When my plane landed, it was late, and the Global Vagabonds shuttle rocketed straight to Antigua. Now, as I stagger down the bus steps and attempt to find my land legs, my eyes are whirling in every direction. The streets swarm with schoolchildren, businesspeople, cowboys, Mayans. I see uniformed guards with machine guns flanking the entrance of a bank. Another guard stands a couple of doors down, defending an ice cream parlor. Overhead, menacing-looking tangles of wires crackle with electricity.

As Rowan strolls off to collect our backpacks—they were riding on the roof of the bus—Starling turns to me. "Is it just me, or is your bladder about to explode?"

"Ew," I reply.

We each pay a quetzal for a wad of toilet paper at the bus station bathroom, otherwise known as the Chamber of Stinking Horror. It seems more women missed the toilet than made it. Breathing through my mouth, I hover over the seat until my legs cramp.

When we make it out alive, Rowan is waiting in front of

the station entrance, our backpacks gathered around his legs like good little children. Mine's the largest by far. I'm already considering ditching that second pair of jeans I insisted on packing.

"That bathroom reeked like hot death," Starling says. "But for some reason, I'm starved. Can you guys grab some snacks while I get our tickets?"

"We need tickets?" I ask. On our last bus, we just climbed on.

"Sometimes you do, sometimes you don't."

"But how do you know?"

"Experience. Meet me inside in ten, okay?"

I watch her dark blond bundle of hair glide over the crowds. Her confidence must be a result of all that experience, because I feel utterly helpless. A little more Spanish comprehension would probably help.

Reluctantly, I follow Rowan to a row of street carts outside the station and attempt to select a snack, but the chaos all around us keeps stealing my attention. An orange dog brushes my leg, startling me. Its face is peppered with scars. Why are creepy Guatemalan dogs always brushing against me? I realize I'm standing a little too close to Rowan.

"We'd better hurry," he says.

I turn back to the carts. The meats heaped on crusty black grills don't tempt me. Neither do the wobbly towers of flan. I hesitate in front of a fruit cart. Everything looks spotty, dented, bruised.

"It all looks like it's been in a battle."

"Maltreated mangoes," Rowan says.

Is he actually joking with me? I smile tentatively. "Abused avocadoes," I try.

83

"Warmongering watermelons."

"There aren't any watermelons."

"That's because they lost the war."

Still smiling, I pick up a small green fruit. "What's this?"

"It's a guava."

"Is it? My friend Reese had them on a tree in her yard. They looked different, though." I recall how we tossed them in the golf course pond by her house, along with oranges and persimmons, testing to see which would float. I learned to skip stones in that same pond, during the drowsy summer before ninth grade. Not long after, I met Olivia at freshman orientation and started dividing my time between the two of them. Until I met Toby and didn't have time for either.

"*Cuánto queso?*" I ask the vendor.

Rowan stares at me, obviously impressed by my Spanish fluency. Except the fruit vendor is staring at me too. "Oh," Rowan says, starting to grin. "You meant '*Cuánto cuesta?*'"

"That's what I—" I pause. Oh no. Oh God. I totally asked, *How much cheese?*

"*Dos por uno,*" the vendor replies, shaking her head.

Dying of humiliation, I hand her a quetzal and take two guavas. I dig my fingernails into one and break it open.

It's crawling with bugs.

I scream and throw it into the street. It explodes in a blossom of juice, like a tiny smashed jack-o'-lantern. I hop around, alternately shaking my hands and wiping them on my jeans. Rowan looks like he doesn't know whether to comfort me or crack up.

"I feel like they're all over me! What *are* they?"

Rowan goes over to inspect the splatter. "Some sort of beetle . . . Ooh, maggots."

I hurl the other guava into the trash. That takes care of my hunger.

Rowan buys a bag of candied peanuts for Starling, and we head inside the crowded bus station. The space stinks of perspiration and sour fruit, of bus exhaust and dog pee and probably human pee. A toddler screams at the top of his lungs, but his weary-looking mother does nothing to calm him. Stray dogs weave in and out of people's legs. A few yards away, a pair of teenage boys stare at me with their arms crossed. I try not to make eye contact.

Starling meets us at the station's single empty seat. While we wait for our bus, we play musical chairs, and it's my turn to sit first. Rowan leans against the wall and tinkers with his dive watch. Starling stands in front of me, knock-kneed, with her hands in her pockets.

"Whenever I'm in a crowded place like this," she says in a low voice, "I always think the floor's going to cave in."

My blinking is audible. "Why's *that*?"

"Didn't you hear about the giant sinkhole?"

Giant sinkhole? "I have no idea what you're talking about."

"The Guatemala City sinkhole. It just opened up beneath a bunch of poor people's homes, and the houses and everyone in them fell into this underground river of sewage and got swept away."

I glance at Rowan in disbelief.

"True story," he says. "Though I heard it was just one home. Three people."

"It was, like, five hundred feet deep," Starling says. "Can you imagine? What a way to go—death by sludge!"

If I really concentrate, I think I sense a rumble beneath my feet. Probably from the buses. But I can't help imagining a

85

sweeping ocean of sewage, brown and loathsome, rushing beneath a fragile crust of asphalt. I pull up my feet onto the chair, as if that will save me. "Could it happen again?"

"This is Central America," Starling says darkly. "Anything can happen. Put your feet down; you're getting our seat dirty."

Our bus breaks down in the late afternoon. I have my head tipped against the window, wishing there were enough privacy to draw. After last night, the urge is a bundle of heat in my chest, like a swallow of too-hot tea. But the idea of drawing in front of Rowan and Starling makes me shy. I'm tracing a face on the wall with my finger when the driver slams the brakes.

"What the hell," I say, rubbing my clunked forehead.

There's a metallic screech that sounds like an orgy of bats, and the smell of exhaust clouds down the aisle. After a moment, the bus squeals to a stop beside a cliff spray-painted with advertisements: Alka-Seltzer, Fanta, *aspirin rápido*. I could use some of all three. On the other side of the highway, pastureland stretches into the darkening hills.

Without the wind rushing in the windows, the temperature seems to shoot up ninety-nine degrees. Someone curses in Spanish. Starling, who sits across the aisle, curses in English. Rowan, who's sitting behind me, sleeps through the whole thing.

"What's happening?" I ask Starling.

She closes the travel journal she's been skimming. From her volunteer time in Nicaragua, she told me earlier. The most volunteering I've ever done was competing in a charity art show at age thirteen. I sold three greeting cards for two dollars each. Pretty weak when compared to spoon-feeding Nicaraguan orphan babies. "You should be thrilled," she says with a yawn. "It's a discount tour of the authentic Guatemalan lifestyle."

Without announcement, the driver cranks open the bus door and heads outside. From my window, I see him dial on his cell. He listens for a second. Then he bangs the phone against the heel of his hand.

"Shit," I say.

The other passengers slouch in their seats and stare out at the empty pastures. I remember our backpacks on top of the bus and hope they're safe. "So this is pretty typical?"

"It's not uncommon." Starling wedges her knees against the seat in front of her. "Ugh, it's hot. I wish we had cold drinks."

And food. My appetite has forgotten the wormy fruit. Well, until just now. "How long will it take to get going again?"

"Depends on how quickly a mechanic gets here." She returns to her journal.

The minutes struggle along like damaged insects. I attempt to read my book from La Casa Azul, a novel called *Bel Canto*, but I can't concentrate. The muted light strains my eyes. I flip to the blank last page and draw invisibly with my index finger, loopy, whirly figure-phantoms, until even that gets boring. Out my window, I see the bus driver light a cigarette.

"Just be glad the bus isn't full. Imagine if we were sitting three to a seat," Rowan says. I turn to find him stretching, his fingers grazing the overhead racks.

"Or even two," Starling says, crossing the aisle to sit beside her brother. She pulls the elastic from his ponytail. "You stink."

"What, you think you smell like roses?"

"Roses? How boring. I smell like jasmine and citrus blossoms." She turns Rowan's head to the side, then, using her fingernails as a comb, begins to french-braid his hair. He lets it happen, seemingly unconcerned. I'd laugh, but I don't think I have enough oxygen.

"Damn it all to hell," Starling says, patting the top of Rowan's head. "Let's play a game."

I stick my book in my daypack, a little wary but mostly intrigued.

"Let's tell scary stories. Really scary stories. None of that crap from third-grade scout camp. Never mind, scratch that." She grins ghoulishly. "We're not going to tell *scary* stories. We're going to tell stories about times we were scared."

I glance at Rowan. He shakes his head, but I can't tell whether he's rejecting the game or just amicably disapproving. Starling gives his braid a yank.

"When were we scared?" she asks him. "Think back."

"Not *we*. This is *your* story."

"But what about that time in San Pedro Sula? Before you went to live on Utila? You and Jack tried to convince me to take that puddle jumper to La Ceiba because Jack knew the pilot, even though you knew he was smuggling a few pounds of—"

"Christ, Starling!" Rowan swats her hands from his head.

88

"What's the big deal? Nothing happened, in the end."

"No."

I examine my fingernails, pretending not to see the cartoon storm cloud hovering between them. Pounds of what? *Pounds of what?*

"What about that time in Puerto Sol?" Starling asks Rowan.

Until I hear otherwise, I'm just going to assume she meant pounds of bananas.

"Whatever. You don't need my permission. As long as the story's yours."

She kicks off her sandals and pulls up her knees. She has at least three toe rings on each foot. I wonder if they pinch her skin when she walks.

"So I was living in Puerto Sol. That's on the Caribbean coast of Nicaragua. Really hard to get to, or at least it was two years ago. I was staying at this volunteer camp in the summer, helping implement renewable energy in the village. Did you know like fifty percent of Nicaragua's population doesn't have dependable access to electricity?"

I shake my head.

"It's a tragedy. Anyway, one day I'm heading back to the dorms in the late afternoon and I turn down a side road. It rained that day, so there are puddles along the gutters. Mud in the street. Right away I get this creepy feeling, even though I've passed this way a million times before, and it isn't even night yet, but the feeling's impossible to ignore.

"Then this arm comes around in front of my face. And suddenly, I'm on the ground.

"I fight like a wildcat—which is exactly what you're *not*

supposed to do. The majority of injuries during muggings happen when the victim fights back, did you know that? But the kicking, the screaming is involuntary—I can't stop."

She drops her feet.

"Then, over my mugger's shoulder, I notice this man standing there with his motorbike. And so I direct my screams for help toward him. But he just stands there, watching. Finally, the man wrenches my bag from my hands. And then—get this—he goes and climbs on the back of the other guy's motorbike, and they speed away. They were in it together."

"So all he wanted was your bag?" I ask.

Starling nods animatedly. She's standing now, leaning over the seat between us. "If I'd known that's what he was after, I'd have given it to him! Hell, I would have curtsied. I fought because I thought he was going to—well, you know what I thought. A big mistake. I didn't even know I was bleeding until I stood, and I saw it in the dirt." She pulls out her bottom lip with two fingers. "I bit all the way through it. See the scar?"

So it wasn't from a piercing. "I would have been on the first plane home," I say.

"Well . . ." Starling seems to realize she's standing, and sits back down in her own seat. "I thought about it. But I'd moved out of my last apartment. I didn't have anywhere to go home to, other than my friends' couches. I hadn't spoken to my parents for ages, so I didn't want to call them. I couldn't even bring myself to go to work. For a week, I just hid in my room."

"What made you stay?"

"Rowan."

I glance at him. He's looking out the window.

"He'd come to visit me twice before, for a week each

time," Starling explains. "The first time, he got his Advanced Open Water certification. The second time, he got his Rescue Diver certification. The third time, he never left. He traveled to other countries, of course. But never home."

Two years. I still can't wrap my brain around it. I wonder what he was like before he left for his perma-vacation. Less than a week into my own, I already feel changed. Although not nearly as changed as I'd like to be.

"Rowan reminded me that those muggers were just two bad people out of millions of good ones. Great ones, like my host family. And that it had happened to me—well, it was just luck of the draw."

"Having hot-pink streaks in your hair didn't help, though," Rowan says.

"Victim-blamer! You should be ashamed of yourself." Starling nods at me. "Your turn, Bria."

I take a deep breath. I listened to her story, but at the same time I was deciding what I wanted to tell. "When I was fourteen, I almost drowned," I begin.

Starling looks disappointed.

I tell them how I woke up underwater with no idea how I got there. I could see the place where the wall met the bottom of the pool. But it didn't occur to me to kick. I just hung there, unmoving, suspended in silence. Then a pair of hands grabbed my arms, and with a sucking splash, someone lifted me into the world of noises again. I'd learn later that I'd hit my head on the diving board. Blacked out for just an instant. Drank half the pool into my lungs. I'd slipped, Olivia said.

"Luckily, I didn't need help breathing," I add. "I coughed up all the water as soon as they pulled me out. We decided not to tell our parents. My friend Olivia took me home."

Starling wrinkles her nose. "The girl with the spangles."

"I have a scar, but it's hidden under my hair."

"Like that little Antichrist boy in that old movie *The Omen*? With the 666 tattoo?"

I stick out my tongue at her. "Exactly."

"So that's why you don't swim," Rowan says quietly.

Wrong. Sure, almost drowning was scary and all, but I've swum dozens and dozens of times since, maybe even hundreds of times. But if I told Rowan the truth—that swimming has made me sad ever since I stupidly gave my virginity to my jackass ex-boyfriend at my favorite beach, the beach where I used to draw and swim, and he totally didn't get the importance of it, of any of it—he would think I was pathetic. And probably also a little insane. At least the swimming pool story makes a good excuse. "Your turn," I say in lieu of agreement.

"Pass."

"Pass?" I repeat. "You can't pass." I glance at Starling, waiting for her to object, but she doesn't. I turn back to Rowan. "Rowan, you must have been scared before."

"Sure. But I choose not to share it."

"Then . . . I don't know, tell about a time you were mildly apprehensive."

Rowan just shakes his head.

"Rowan . . . ," Starling begins. "Never mind. Forget it. There's no arguing when he gets like this. I'm taking a nap." She slips her hands into her sandals and curls up on her side, her bare feet sticking into the aisle. "Wake me when we're moving. Better yet, when we arrive in Río Dulce."

"This is crap," I say, louder than I meant to.

"Just go to sleep, Bria. It was a stupid game."

Fine. I avoid looking at Rowan as I take out *Bel Canto* and pretend to read, like I don't mind in the slightest. I know mine wasn't too outrageous of a memory. I've got worse ones, and better ones. And Starling's story probably beats them all. It's Rowan's refusal to participate I find frustrating. Like his memories are too precious to share with the likes of me.

I've scanned the same paragraph sixty times when Rowan touches my shoulder. "It's too dark to read," he says. "Want to go stretch our legs?"

I glance at Starling, who's sleeping. Since I have nothing better to do, I follow Rowan outside.

We jog across the highway to the pasture. In the midst of the long grass and roadside junk, there's a solitary cement pillar tipped over on its side. Vines grow up all around it like alien tentacles. I tap it with my sandal. "What do you think it held up?"

"Probably an ancient Mayan coliseum," Rowan replies.

"The Mayans had coliseums? Wasn't that the Romans, or the Greeks or whoever?"

"Sure, but the Mayans built them too. Or tried to, at least. See, they made them too big—they thought they could hold up the sky. It's in all the history books." He says this with a straight face. I don't know him well enough to know whether he's joking. But then one corner of his mouth twitches.

"You are one hundred percent full of shit," I say.

Smiling, Rowan sits on the pillar, facing the dark expanse of farmland. I sit beside him, facing the highway. I think I can make out my backpack on the roof of the bus.

And then . . . silence.

And more silence, until his unvoiced thoughts start

making me nervous. Which is annoying, because he was the one who ruined Starling's game, not me. I wait for him to speak. Thirty seconds. Forty. One minute. I'm actually counting.

"Have you ever seen *Easy Rider*?" he asks.

"Huh?"

"The 1969 movie by Dennis Hopper? You know, the road movie? It's about a couple of bikers thundering all over the U.S. They end up in some kind of hippie commune. No?"

I shake my head.

"I saw it as a kid." He pauses. "Probably wasn't the most age-appropriate film—I was seven or so—but my dad hardly monitored that kind of thing. It was just me and him most of the time. I remember watching it on my stomach, in the living room of our shitty apartment, and promising myself I'd never be like that. My dad moved us around all the time: chasing work projects, running away from one-night stands. I *hated* it. And wouldn't you know it . . ."

"Your life became a road movie?"

"Kind of. But this time around, it's me calling the shots. It makes all the difference—being the one in control."

I think about how liberating it felt choosing La Ruta Maya from the Global Vagabonds pamphlet. But it was a momentary thing. I could have chosen differently. I could be sitting in Thailand right now. Maybe that's where my caravan of beautiful people from the pamphlet went.

"Isn't that what your memory was about, Bria? Losing control?"

I pause. "I never knew memories were *about* anything. Besides the obvious. You make them sound like dreams—subject to interpretation."

"I think the two are more related than we realize. It's all in how our minds frame them. How we decide what—and how—we remember."

A phantom insect pricks my shoulder. I slap, but I'm too late. On the other side of the highway, a man climbs off our bus. As I watch, he unzips his pants and begins to pee against the cliffside. "I don't know if I can handle this," I say.

"What?" Rowan turns to look. "We can find you a bush if you've got to go."

"No! That's not what I meant," I say, laughing. "I meant I can't handle . . ." My smile fades. I'm afraid to say it, but I've already begun. "I feel like you guys see all the layers in everything I say. Even when I don't know they're there myself. It's too intense."

"Really? Because I think you're the intense one."

I'm not sure what to say to that. At first, I feel kind of flattered. But as I think about it, I realize *intense* can mean a limitless number of things, many of them opposites. Like thoughtful, or reckless. Calculating, or overeager. I guess I can be any of those things, depending on the situation. I wonder how many more sides of me I'll encounter on this trip.

"I think I kind of get it," I say. "Your Wanderlove thing."

"Oh yeah?"

"It's about always looking toward the future. You can appreciate the good things all around you, but the best part is imminent, just out of reach. Like . . . perpetual anticipation."

"Perpetual anticipation," Rowan repeats. "Nice. That's about right."

I shrug. Because really, I'm only starting to understand. The appeal of leaving and never looking back. No end point to your journey.

How gloriously terrifying.

From a great distance, I hear a dog barking. It almost sounds like it's coming from the sky. And at that moment, the bus engine starts. Rowan and I jump to our feet at the same time.

"I guess they didn't need a mechanic after all," he says.

"You know," I say as we cross the highway, "your hair's still french-braided." Rowan touches the back of his head, and we grin at each other, and for a moment, I allow myself to hope he's thinking the same thing as me—that the three of us traveling together might not be so bad after all.

7

Day 6, Morning
Río Dulce

The next morning, Starling shakes me awake. "Bria, come with me."

Groggily, I sit up. Judging by the weak light shining through the curtains, we've only slept six hours, tops. We didn't arrive in Río Dulce until midnight. The first budget hotel we found had only one room left. Fortunately, it had three twin beds; any shuffle of mattress-sharing between the three of us would have been awkward.

I glance at Rowan, who's sleeping on his stomach. The sheet has come away from his back. I recognize the muscles from my art anatomy book, the one I used to study nightly, tracing every part, mouthing every name.

The trapezius. The deltoid. The latissimus dorsi.

I realize I'm staring.

"Okay, I'm coming." I attempt to pat down my wild hair. I probably look like a member of the Cure. I slip on my shoes and join Starling outside, shutting the door gently behind me. The first thing I notice is her backpack, leaning against the stairs.

My stomach plummets. "Wait—you're *leaving?*"

"I got called in early." Starling heaves her backpack onto one shoulder and slaps down the stairs in her leather sandals. "I thought you could walk me to the bus."

"Starling, you can't just *leave!*" I hurry after her, feeling sicker with every step.

"I don't have a choice, Bria. You've still got Rowan. You'll be fine."

"But . . ." I don't know how to object without sounding helpless. "I'm not . . . Aren't you going to say goodbye to Rowan?"

"Rowan and I don't do goodbyes." She pulls out her phone and checks the time. "I've still got twenty minutes. How 'bout I buy you a *licuado?*"

I don't want Starling's *licuado,* whatever that is, but I follow her anyway.

Under the overcast sky, Río Dulce is just waking up. Vendors fasten beach umbrellas to the fronts of their shops, angling them over their wares. Like the back alleys of the Chichicastenango marketplace, most of it seems geared toward locals, not tourists. Starling leads us to a café by the water and chooses a table. Just a few yards away, the river labors along, reflecting the gray clouds.

I can't believe she's leaving. It's not like we're the best of friends or anything, but there's something reassuring about her presence. Maybe because the alternative—my traveling alone with Rowan—frightens me into convulsions. I barely know the guy. Our conversation from last night seems like a dream, his forthrightness an exception to his real feelings—that he doesn't want me along.

And Starling *knows* that. Even if she doesn't know I do.

My distress is starting to feel more like anger. "So where the hell are you going, exactly?"

"Flores. It's still Guatemala—in the Petén region, up north." Starling turns to the server, a young, skinny girl in a Mickey Mouse shirt. *"Dos licuados de piña, por favor."*

"Actually, I'll have mango. *Mango, por favor.*"

"Pineapple's better."

I shake my head. Really I want pineapple, but I'm feeling contrary. Eyeing me, Starling props her knee against the table and wraps her arms around it. The morning light catches the hair on her arms, making it glow golden against her tan.

"Why can't I go with you?" I ask.

"Technically, you could. . . . But for two weeks? You'd be bored out of your skull after two days. Flores is about the size of my thumbnail. It's a tiny island in the middle of a lake—and I don't mean the boisterous Laughingbird Caye sort of island. There's stuff to see around the lake, but . . . honestly? It'd be kind of sketchy, a girl like you tramping around on her own."

My werewolf hackles rise. "A girl like me?"

"You know what I mean."

"I'm not sure I do." Okay, I have an idea, but I want to make her say it. The roar of a blender masks her next statement. "What did you say?" I shout.

She waits for the blender to shut off. "I said, you're a *good* girl."

Coming from Starling, it sounds like an insult. "I'm not that—"

The blender turns on for the second time. We sit there in silence until it feels like the whirling blades have *licuado*-fied my insides.

"What I mean is, you haven't traveled much," Starling explains, looking more and more uncomfortable. "You're not a party girl, as far as I can tell. You're . . . a hanger-back. An *observer*."

"You don't know me." Ugh. I sound like one of those Jerry Springer teens.

"There's nothing wrong with that, Bria! There are two types of people, I've found. People who jump in with their eyes closed, and people who watch others flail—then swim as soon as they hit the water. I'm fairly certain you're the second kind. Your near drowning notwithstanding. But that quality is why Rowan needs you around."

"What? Rowan doesn't need me."

"He does."

"Starling, what are you talking about? Of course he doesn't." I take a deep breath. "Look. I overheard what he said back at the lake, okay? The first night, after you invited me."

Starling pauses, as if trawling through her mind for what was said. Too late, I realize I've only perpetuated her opinion of me as creepy observer. "What exactly did you hear?"

"That Rowan doesn't want me along."

"Is that all you heard?"

"It was enough."

"But that's out of context. I don't just mean in our conversation, I mean in our entire history. Rowan's history. It's only natural that he'd hesitate, after what he's gone through. . . . I mean, he doesn't travel with companions anymore. Especially girls. He's reformed. Mostly."

"Then why in the world is it a good idea to drag me along?"

"Because you're not like those other girls. You and Rowan are a perfect match. As in, you're not a match at all. Even if you didn't have a boyfriend, Rowan wouldn't hook up with you—well, he *probably* wouldn't—because you're the exact opposite of his type."

"Whatever." I pause. "What type is that?"

"Like . . . autonomous. Nonconformist. With tons of life experience. But even if you were that type of girl, you're solidly in the friend zone. Plus, the two of you are stuck together for more than a couple days. Rowan doesn't mess around with anyone he can't escape."

The Mickey Mouse girl brings our drinks, served in frosted milk shake glasses with reusable twirly straws. I jam mine into my mouth. I hate the sour yogurt taste, like rotten mango. But I drink it down, ignoring the brain freeze, swallowing and swallowing, as if stuffing my throat will stop my hurt feelings from filling it instead. It reminds me of all the times Olivia ditched me at parties to dance with Jessa Hanny. My fault for refusing—I can't dance without feeling like I'm standing out-side myself, watching—but I felt rejected just the same.

It's like I become whatever people presume me to be. Toby called me clingy, and in protest, I dug in my claws. Marcy and Rowan called me naïve, and just like that, I became gullible, silly. Starling thinks I'm helpless, and even while my adult self objects, the little girl inside me bawls. I want to demand: *If it's not personal, then what is it?* But I can't, because I know it *is* personal. No matter what she says, Starling invited me along because she thinks I'm unlikable.

101

No wonder Rowan doesn't want to travel with me.

But it's too late now. I don't have a choice. I'm not about to track down the Global Vagabonds and catch up. I could camp right here in Río Dulce for two weeks, but that's just too sad for words.

"How do I know Rowan won't just ditch me?"

"He would never do that," Starling says fiercely. "*Never*. Not Rowan. He's honorable in all the important ways. You'd have to, like, do something to betray him—and even then, he'd have to be completely certain you could take care of yourself. Because as long as you need him, he'll never, ever abandon you. Ever. I promise."

She seems like she's trying awfully hard to convince me. I watch as she pulls out her journal and tears out a scrap of paper.

"Here's my phone number, if it makes you feel better. Now you can call me if he abandons you in the rain forest. Just kidding!" she exclaims when she sees my face. "He won't leave you. I promise promise promise." She slides the scrap of paper to me. "Also, call me if . . ."

The Mickey Mouse girl takes our empty glasses, scowling at the teeth marks on my straw. Apparently, I've been gnawing. "If what?"

"I'm trying to think of the best way to put this. I don't want to scare you."

What. The. *Hell*.

"Remember back in Panajachel, when we were talking about Wanderlove? About Rowan running from his past?"

Rowan's second travel rule:
The best way to escape the past is to keep moving forward.

Nervously, I nod.

"Well, let's just say the island you guys are heading to for Rowan's dive job is part of that past, and if you ask me, it should remain there."

"This is supposed to make me feel *better* about traveling alone with him?"

"Look. Rowan's a great guy, I swear to God. One of the greatest people I've ever known. Not just saying that because he's my brother. But he's gotten into some dodgy stuff in the last couple of years—that's all I should say. It's over now, he swears. And I want to believe him.

"But then again . . . see, Rowan thinks all his Wanderlove junk is about love. But it's not about love—it's about hate. Hating his past. Hating himself. Even though he'd never admit it. He might seem like a strong-willed guy, but really he's so vulnerable. Without me around, I just don't trust him. Not this soon. Especially on that island, with his old dive crowd. Specifically, his old dive partner. And during Lobsterfest—it's the biggest party of the year."

She digs into her pocket and clinks a handful of coins onto the table.

"He needs someone to look out for him, just for a couple weeks. Someone to be his friend. His travel sister, since I can't be there." She reaches for my hand. "Listen, you're still going to have an incredible time! Rowan's the ultimate travel partner, especially for a new traveler. And if he's responsible for someone, he'll be much more likely to do the right thing."

"And if he doesn't?"

"Then you have my number. You can call me from any hostel or Internet café on Laughingbird. If you need me, I'll drop everything and come. Flores is about a day's journey

103

from the island. Shorter if I take a plane. How does that sound? Are you in?"

No! I want to shout. I can't handle that kind of responsibility; I'm having enough trouble handling myself. And that Rowan *needs* me? Unfathomable, even when I recall what he told me last night about his selfish, roving father, the childhood that catapulted him abroad. Because I'm pretty certain the past Starling's alluding to has more to do with . . . *pounds of bananas.* A more dangerous past, and one far more recent. Which means a much more recent reform.

That's what should be scaring me. But for some reason, it isn't. My brain's still preoccupied with the idea of traveling alone with a guy who dislikes me. At least, the *me* Rowan and Starling take me to be—the introverted hanger-back with a boyfriend. The girl I'm trying to escape.

"I can do it," I hear myself say. "But . . ."

Then I blurt out the only excuse that might make a difference.

"But I don't really have a boyfriend. We broke up."

"I guessed that." Starling slips her arms through the straps of her backpack. "But let's keep it our little secret, all right?"

When I arrive back at the hotel, alone, I find Rowan in the courtyard, reading in a tangerine-colored hammock. He doesn't see me approach. So I hang back for a moment, watching him, sketching him with my mind.

One arm is folded behind his head, the other propping up his book. His bare foot dangles off the end of the hammock, and I can see his left gastrocnemius muscle flexed above his stack of bracelets. He looks content, composed—not a hint of the screwed-up, wounded baby bird Starling made him out to be.

He also looks like a stranger.

I try to imagine us standing together on a Caribbean island beach. It just doesn't work. Sure, I can picture Rowan there: with his rope of black hair and tanned skin, he seems designed for an island lifestyle. And I can picture myself there too: wearing my billowy white skirt and silver necklace, gazing at some far-off horizon, like a girl in a cruise ship ad.

But when I try to imagine us together . . .

I have an impulse to flee. But I have no idea where to go. And besides, my backpack's still in our room.

I need to face the truth—that for now, Rowan and I are shackled together. As long as he's the non-ditching good guy Starling swears he is. Maybe it won't be that awkward. All our best exchanges occur when Starling's not around, talking over both of us and brandishing her philanthropic backpacker badges. I can take back my art while Rowan guides me through extraordinary places. If I'm supposed to act like some kind of private investigator—not to mention a romantic force field, repelling an onslaught of backpacker skanks—fine. I can do it. I can pretend to be badass.

And maybe I can learn to do a little less observing and a little more jumping in.

Taking a deep breath, I walk over to Rowan and give his hammock a nudge. "You read more than anyone I've ever met."

Lazily, he tips his head my way. "Morning. I didn't used to."

"Read?"

"It's like I just discovered it in the past few months. I can't get enough." He closes his book. "Where's my sister?"

Here goes nothing. "Starling's gone."

"Gone?" Rowan swings his legs over the edge of the hammock and sits up. "What do you mean—she left for Flores?"

"That's what she said."

"Damn her! She knows I don't . . ." He shakes his head. "This is just like Starling. It's not the first time she's pulled a stunt like this."

"What, made you a babysitter?"

He stares at me.

"Because I'm not any happier about this than you are, all right? Maybe it sucks to be chained to a travel newbie like me. But how do you think it feels to be dependent on someone who doesn't want you tagging along?"

"It isn't . . ." He pauses. "That's not— Did Starling tell you that?"

I tuck my hair behind my ears, wishing for more length. "It doesn't matter."

"It isn't you," he says, and I think, Yeah, right. "It's just that . . . I usually travel alone. Unless I'm with Starling. And even then, we can only last a couple weeks before we want to murder each other. She should have told me she was leaving."

"She said you don't do goodbyes."

Rowan sighs. "Well, we try not to, anyway. Something we developed in our last couple years of constant comings and goings. It's easier."

"Why's that?"

"They're a drag. I mean, seriously—they just drag out painful moments."

I shrug, still feeling all sorts of unpleasant. "I suppose."

"Think about it. Think about your last big goodbye. Both

people are searching for the right thing to say, and both are uncomfortable because there *is* no right thing to say. Best to just leave and be done with it. Shut the book as quickly as possible."

I try not to think of how long I dragged out my breakup with Toby. Isn't that what a breakup is? A painfully protracted goodbye? At least, it was in my case. "You make it sound easy."

"It's worked for me so far." Rowan clears his throat. "Anyway. I'm sure we can handle each other's company for a few days. Once we get to the island, we can do our own thing. Sound okay?"

I stuff my hands into my jeans pockets to refrain from punching him in the latissimus dorsi. "I suppose we'll manage," I mutter.

"So . . . Onward, I guess." He slides out of the hammock onto his feet. "Have you had breakfast? I've been dying for a pineapple *licuado*."

8

Day 6, Afternoon
Into the Forest

"Just under two hours late," Rowan says as the motorboat bumps against the cement pier. "Are you getting used to Central America time?"

"Hardly," I reply, stretching my bench-shaped back. I snap shut my book, realizing I unintentionally sketched in its margins. My fault for using a pen as a bookmark.

We're about to head down the Río Dulce to Guatemala's Caribbean coast. To a village called Livingston, Rowan told me matter-of-factly. It's not mentioned on my Global Vagabonds itinerary. Before I threw it away, I memorized it in its entirety, including:

Copán Ruinas, Honduras
Travel via charter plane (approx. 30 min) to
the town of Copán Ruinas, the gateway to the
Mayan ruins of Copán. Experience architec-
tural tour of the Maya site and stopover at
Macaw Mountain Bird Park.

Cancún, Mexico
After Chichén Itzá, enjoy margaritas and salsa
dancing lessons at all-inclusive Mexican resort Grasa del Mar, aka "Bounty of the Sea,"
before flight south to the Tikal ruins.

I'm trying not to mourn missing salsa lessons alongside
Glenna Heron, but it's hard.

"So are we off the beaten path yet, or what?" I ask Rowan
as we hand our backpacks to the boat driver. I'm immediately
embarrassed, but he takes my question seriously.

"Depends on what kind of traveler you're talking about.
For the people in your tour group, yeah, sure. For your average
backpacker . . . not really. For someone who's been traveling
forever . . . well, anywhere that accepts U.S. dollars—like
most of these places—is pretty well trod."

"Got it," I say.

Rowan's third travel rule:
*The more you travel, the more all the
paths seem beaten.*

A quarter inch of river water sloshes in the bottom of the
boat. The driver wraps our packs in tarps before stuffing them

under the benches. Eight people accompany us for the journey: a trio of backpacker boys, a couple with a humiliated-looking preteen daughter, and a pair of middle-aged birders who screech like parakeets when they see anything with feathers. I rest my chin on my hands, searching for manatee-shaped shadows in the murky water.

As soon as the engine starts, the tallest backpacker boy clambers over to our end of the boat. He sits beside me and offers his hand to Rowan.

"Nice to meet you, bro. I'm Pete."

Rowan shakes the guy's hand. "Rowan," he says. "This is Bria."

Pete ogles me for a moment. I adjust the straps of my tank top.

"So listen," he says to Rowan, "we're new to this budget-travel thing: me, Sammy, and Carlos—that's them over there. We saw you on the pier and decided you looked like the kind of guy who knows his way around, who knows the score."

"The score?" Rowan repeats, in a tone that says, *Are you for real?*

"You know what I mean—you look experienced. Tough."

I bite my knuckles, stifling a laugh. Not as if I know "the score" myself, or what the competition is in the first place, but it amuses me that somebody appears even more clueless than I am.

"We're heading to Belize," Pete says. "Do you think you could give us a few pointers?"

"What kind?"

Pete glances at the family, then leans in close. "Like, which places are the most stoner-friendly?"

I glance at Rowan, who yawns, like he's seen guys like

110

Pete a thousand times before and can't be bothered. In contrast, you'd think Pete wants to be boyfriends, as excited as he is to talk to Rowan. It reminds me of two nights ago, at the lake. Once Rowan came in from reading, the other backpackers latched on to him like bloodthirsty flies. I wonder what it is that makes him so irresistible. His quiet confidence? His unmistakable status as a veteran traveler? His ponytail? Or does he just seem like a nice guy? Little do they know what a judgmental ass he can be.

"Not just weed," Pete clarifies, "but other stuff? We heard Belize is the place to go, as long as we keep a low profile. Yeah?"

Pounds of bananas, I repeat to myself. *Pounds of bananas.*

"Drugs aren't legal anywhere, *bro*," Rowan says.

"Sure, we know that. But we heard about this one island . . ."

"What island?"

"Bird Cay something. Dancing Bird Cay."

Rowan sits up, suddenly interested. "Oh, you mean Laughingbird Caye," he says. "Pronounced like *key*, by the way."

"That's it! You know about it? We heard it's like booze, pharmaceuticals . . . and easy backpacker chicks. Yeah?"

Rowan shakes his head. "Laughingbird's not where you want to go."

"It isn't?"

"That island's dead. The American tourists killed it. It's all retirees nowadays: muumuus and dentures and silver chest hair. Sometimes all three at once."

Pete winces.

"Carambola Caye . . . now, *that's* what you're looking for.

It's even closer to here than Laughingbird. But still remote enough that you can do whatever you want." Rowan leans in and lowers his voice. "*Whatever you want.* You know that book *The Beach?*"

Pete's practically salivating. "Book? You mean the movie with Leonardo DiCaprio?"

"Sure."

"The island's like that? Holy shit—how do we get there?"

"First thing tomorrow morning, take the boat from Livingston to Punta Gorda. Then catch a bus to Dangriga. From there, you can find a boat to take you out to the cay. Ask a fisherman or something. They might try to convince you there's nothing there, but don't listen. It's all part of the game."

Rowan scribbles directions on a scrap of paper. As soon as Pete rejoins his friends on the other end of the boat, I squint at Rowan. "Isn't Laughingbird Caye where we're going?"

"That is correct."

"And you didn't want that guy there."

Rowan shrugs one shoulder. "It won't make much of a difference. Plenty of his type make it there anyway. Spring Breakpackers, Starling calls them."

I think of Olivia, who spent spring break in Cabo San Lucas with Jessa Hanny. They certainly hadn't brought backpacks. "So does Carambola Caye even exist?"

"It sure does—it's a wildlife refuge. Completely uninhabited. I think there might be a bathroom hut. Maybe a couple hammocks."

"You're kidding."

He looks pleased. "They can learn about nature."

Nice guy, my ass. I shake my head. I should feel sorry for

Pete and his pals, but anyone who approaches strangers asking about easy chicks kind of has it coming. "You and your damned pranks."

Rowan has the decency to look contrite. "In my defense," he says, "when I invited you, I was sure you wouldn't come."

"Invited me here? Or to dinner at La Casa Azul?"

"Well, both. But in this case, I'm talking about marooning you on the wrong side of the lake. I'd forgotten about boat times when I asked you to dinner." He pauses. "I was just . . . tossing a stone on the water. Trying to see if it would skip."

"That's a really bad analogy."

"I don't want you to think I'm a jerk. I usually only play tricks on people who deserve it."

I guess it's progress—that he doesn't think I'm a deserving victim of his travel pranks. I can't help wondering what kind of trick Rowan would play on Toby, who takes everything so seriously. It sounds boring, but that's what drew me to Toby: his intensity. His certainty, when it came to his art—and to our relationship. In contrast, Rowan doesn't seem to take much seriously at all.

Except for his past. I might joke about the pounds of bananas, but I'm dying to know the details. For example, how many bananas? Are we talking Chiquita or Dole?

"Rowan," I begin, "on the bus, when Starling said you—"

"Hey!" he exclaims, interrupting. "Look behind you!"

For how excited he sounds, I expect to see a manatee, maybe skipping on its tail all Flipper-like, but it's almost as good. The boat has drifted into an undulating sea of white: a floating carpet of water lilies that extends all the way to the far shore.

Rowan comes over and sits beside me. Side by side, we lean over the edge, gazing at the flowers.

"It's like *The Voyage of the* Dawn Treader," he says.

"I've read that book!" I exclaim. "I remember the lilies. Right before the ship reaches heaven. And the ocean was sweet in the book, just like the water here. The name of the river, I mean. Río Dulce."

Rowan's grinning at me. *"Mar dulce."*

"Sweet sea." Our arms are pressed together, but neither of us moves until the boat driver revs the engine. It snaps us out of the moment, and Rowan takes his seat on the other side.

For forty-five minutes, we roar down the river with the wind in our faces, along with our motley crew: the birders frowning at the folly of speeding through such bio-wealth, the preteen girl gripping a pink hat over her eyes, the back-packer boys verbally abusing each other at the top of their lungs. When the driver cuts the engine again, the return of normal sound is a shock. And somehow, so gradually I didn't notice, we've entered the rain forest.

Both riverbanks ascend into canyon walls of impenetrable green: piles and piles of trees, dripping with vines, ivy, lacy sheaths of moss. All around us swells a tangible orchestra of jungle noise that rises and recedes, rises and recedes. Even the Spring Breakpacker boys shut their mouths. Something neon green streaks though the water. I gasp, breaking our collective silence.

"Iguana," the boat driver says, grinning at me through an impressive mustache. *"Joven."*

"They swim?"

The preteen girl is craning her neck to see. "There," I say, pointing. She blushes ferociously and turns away. I forgive her, since I remember how mortifying life was at that age. Even without the compounded shame of parent-daughter travel. Not that I've ever experienced it. My dad always talked about taking the family to Barcelona to visit his cousins, but it hasn't happened yet.

"Oh, eek, it's a lizard!" I hear Pete shout. "Quick, let's run over it."

It takes me a second to realize he's making fun of me. Now I'm the one blushing. Rowan glances at me, then says something in rapid-fire Spanish to the boat driver, who nods.

As we round the next river bend, we're greeted by a small dock. Next a rooftop, blanketed with banana leaves, emerges among the trees. "This is it," Rowan says as we pull up. "Get your stuff."

"This is Livingston?"

He brings a finger to his lips.

"What?" I say. "I don't—"

He shakes his head.

"I think we need a code word," he says once we've hoisted ourselves onto the dock and the boat has sputtered away.

"A code word?"

"How about *geckos*? As in 'Did you hear those barking geckos last night?' Or maybe it should be some kind of hand signal." He wiggles his fingers in my face. I grab his hands to make him quit.

"Rowan, why'd we stop if this isn't Livingston?"

"It's just for the night."

"But why? How far is the coast?"

"It's just around the bend."

I stare at him.

"It's best to greet the Caribbean in the full light of day," he says. "Also, this place is cheaper. And really, it's a life experience. You'll see. But mainly, I wanted to ditch those guys."

I follow him onto the muddy bank. Tiny flies glance off my ankles.

"So about this code word thing," he continues over his shoulder. "I know you haven't really traveled before, but we might get into some *situations*. . . . We'll need an easy way to remove ourselves from them. That's what the code word's for. Signaling the other person to pay extra-close attention. Or to get up and follow, no matter what."

"Oh . . . I didn't get that."

Rowan hops onto the wooden walkway leading to the guesthouse. "That's my point."

The lobby of the Rainforest Retreat is basic, to say the least. Overhead, a vast palapa roof seems like a haven for fauna of the way-too-many-legged variety. I keep my eyes on the desk. "*El matrimonial?*" asks the woman behind it.

I glance at Rowan. "Did she just say what I thought she did?"

"There aren't any cabins with two beds?" he asks the woman. "*Hay cuartos con dos camas?*"

She shakes her head. "*No más.* Is booked."

Rowan and I glance at each other again. I swear he's blushing beneath his tan. "It's okay," I say hurriedly. "I'll pay for my own room."

I can tell he's relieved. "You sure?" he asks.

"I'll just drink a couple fewer *licuados. Dos cuartos,*" I tell the woman. "*Por favor.*"

A network of wooden walkways and plank bridges connects the cabins to the open-air common area, suspended over several inches of water. When I look over the edge, I see tiny crabs scampering over a submerged landscape of tree roots and slime. After a lengthy trek, Rowan leaves me at my cabin and heads to his, only twenty feet from mine, but obscured by trees. At least he's close enough to come save me if I scream. I unlock the tiny padlock on my cabin door. Crookedly, it swings open.

The room is almost bare, except for a mattress topped by a gray sheet. A canopy of mosquito netting floats over it. There's a row of grimy shelves. No bathroom. When I turn on the bare lightbulb, a zebra-striped cockroach as long as my thumb skitters across the floor and through a crack in the wall.

I stand there for a long time—hugging my daypack, staring at the crack, and trying to imagine all the diabolical creatures that could find their way in.

Crabs.
Snakes.
Spiders with chopstick legs.
Flies with pea-sized eyes.
Those Jesus Christ lizards that run on top
     of water on two legs with their mouths
     open and really freak me out.
Ebola.

Ebola is sufficiently ridiculous to get me going. I make sure all the zippers are shut tight on both my daypack and backpack and tuck them inside the mosquito netting. Then I hurry out.

Back in the common area—surprise!—Rowan has already made friends. He sits in a striped hammock beneath a sign that reads KEEP OUT AT NIGHT: BATS! (Bats. I didn't think of bats.) In front of him stand a girl in a beige linen skirt with wild black hair and a stout, shirtless guy with a hairy chest.

"That's not it," the girl says, her English heavily accented.

Rowan shook his head. "It's also known as Cochino Grande. I promise."

"But our book says Cayo Mayor."

I watch them argue good-naturedly until the girl spots me. "Is that Bree-*yah*?" she crows, rushing toward me. Startled, I let her grab my hand and drag me over, feeling kind of amazed Rowan's already told these strangers about me.

It's just . . . nice. That's all.

Rowan's new friends are Tom and Liat. Tom's British, Liat Israeli. They met last year at a hostel in La Paz, Bolivia, Liat tells us, along with about nineteen hundred other factoids; clearly, she loves to talk. During dinner, Tom lets Liat do most of the storytelling, breaking in occasionally to comment on the jungle sound track.

"Grackles," he observes stoically. And later, "Tree frogs."

Rowan's pretty quiet all through the meal. But when Liat suggests a round of Scrabble, he finally speaks up. "Now that," he says, "that's a barking gecko."

"Really?" I listen. Finally, the sound comes again: a high-pitched chirping, five times in succession. It doesn't really sound like barking, though—more like laughter. I catch Rowan staring at me meaningfully. *What?* I mouth.

He shakes his head, as if I've disappointed him. "Some other time, maybe. It's getting late, and I need a shower. Bria, you ready to go?"

We leave a pocketful of change for our server and say good night. There are no lights on the trails, but Rowan whips out a tiny flashlight to guide us through the dark. Once we're far enough along to be out of earshot, he sighs. "Bria, you failed my test."

"What test?"

"Barking geckos. Remember?"

"Wait a second—geckos? No fair! We didn't decide on that."

"You're right. From now on, though, it stands." He pauses. "If that's okay with you."

"Why wouldn't it be?"

"No reason. Just trying to be democratic."

"Oh." A stick cracks beneath my sandal, and I jump. "Well. So why'd you want to get away?"

"I really do want a shower. Also, too much tension."

"What are you talking about?"

"Come on. It was like ice water. . . . I give them three weeks."

"Tom and Liat?" I'm astounded. "You're crazy! They're completely in love."

"You're an optimist."

"I am not—you're just jaded."

Rowan doesn't reply, and as we walk, I start to wonder whether I've offended him. I clear my throat but can't think of anything to say. We arrive at the crossroads between our cabins. He hands me his flashlight.

"Take it," he says. "I've got eyes like a cat."

I take way too long meeting him, because I can't locate a single thing in my backpack. When I pull out my arms, clothes explode all over the mattress. "Damn," I say, raking everything into a pile. It feels damp, as if the jungle air has already saturated it. I locate my gym shorts and a white tank top, then refold the items, piece by piece, before stuffing them back into my bag. Best to be safe—just in case any chopstick-legged spiders seek a warm nest while I'm gone.

The outdoor shower stalls resemble stone cells: stone floor, stone walls inlaid with mosaic tiles in shapes like cave paintings. Wooden doors latch shut with metal hooks. There's no ceiling, just a web of black branches against the sky.

"Rowan?" I call. "Are you here?"

"In the next stall. Don't come in, I'm not wearing anything."

I have the foolish urge to peek over the wall, but I hold back. "Where's the spigot?"

"There isn't one. Just the bucket. It's lukewarm, but at least it's not freezing."

"Bucket?" I stare at it. It's hot pink, with balloon stickers all over the outside.

"There's no running water here, only well water."

"Well water?" The bucket's only partially full. I suspect others have used it before me, and I'm unsure what level of disgusted I should be by this. "You're lying," I said hopefully.

Rowan steps around the corner, a striped towel wrapped around his narrow hips. Pectoralis, my art brain thinks. Iliac crest. At least, I think it's my art brain. Disastrously, I feel myself blush. After so many months of nothing but Toby, I've turned into a prude.

"I wish I were," Rowan says, oblivious. "You'd better hurry, before the water cools completely."

"But I don't even know what to do. Do I splash water on myself? Dump it on my head?"

"Whatever works." He grins wickedly. "I can help, if you like."

I blink at him. It's the closest he's come to hitting on me, the closest to implying anything slightly sexual.

"But then that boyfriend of yours might hop on a plane and kick my ass."

Before I can reply, he disappears into the jungle.

Shaking my head, I lock my door. Then I strip to my underwear and stand with my arms crossed over my chest, staring at the plastic bucket and trying not to think about hot showers back home. Something howls in the treetops—bird or monkey, I don't know which. Or maybe it's a ghost. Like La Llorona. A crab dances across the floor, narrowly missing my bare toes.

Enough stalling. I kick off my underwear and plunge my hands into the water. I splash my face, my hair, my body, using a fragment of yellow soap to wash as best I can. When the water's almost gone, I upturn the bucket over my head.

I stand there just a second longer, eyes closed, water streaming down my face. If I cover my ears to keep out the jungle sounds, I could be anywhere.

9

Day 7, Way Too Early
Swingers

I have to pee.

I roll onto my back, trying to give my bladder as much room as possible. I have only a vague idea where the outhouse is in relation to my cabin. Why, why, why did I drink that second orange Fanta at dinner? To make matters worse, I gave Rowan back his flashlight before bed. Although I'm pretty sure I can find his cabin in the dark, I don't want to knock on his door. What if he thinks I'm trying to . . . you know. . . . Yeah, no way. I'll just have to hold it until dawn.

I last about five more minutes before an imaginary red light starts flashing in the darkness.

Emergency. Emergency.

Then I remember my phone. I fumble through my daypack

until I find it, and turn it on. It glows weakly, a blue specter in the dark room. At least I'm getting some use out of the thing; the international roaming charges are something like nine hundred bucks a minute. I uncrumple my crispy gray Windbreaker from my backpack and slip it on. Then I wedge a rock in my door and step onto the trail.

"Left, left, right," I whisper to myself, following the hazy map in my brain. The night forest screams back at me.

When I round the third turn, I see a dim hulk against the trees: the bathroom? I sprint forward, then halt. It's just another cabin. That can't be correct—I'd gone left, left, right. Right?

I backtrack, counting my turns. Once, I accidentally step off a walkway and splash into the black water. Jungle slime oozes between my toes. Leave it to me to attempt to navigate the rain forest barefoot. I follow one trail until it dead-ends against a mossy tree. Another leads back to the river, inky and sinister-looking. When I hear something yowl in the forest on the opposite bank, I want to cry. I have no idea how to get back to my room, let alone a bathroom, and now I'll probably be devoured with my bladder still bursting. Finally, I squat beside a cabin wall.

A pterodactyl-sized insect flies up in my face, and I almost fall ass-first into my own puddle. Maybe it would be funny if I wasn't feeling so miserable. And if stupid Toby's stupid face didn't keep appearing in my stupid head, laughing like a maniac.

You're not the traveling type.

When I called Toby a few weeks ago to brag that I was traveling, I was certain he'd be impressed. Especially since I knew his summer plans consisted of the usual: art, more art, and putting in hours at his uncle's paint shop to support his art. Maybe he was envious. I remember the time my father explained the difference between envy and jealousy. Envy is when you want what someone else has. Jealousy's when you also don't want them to have it.

Jealous. Toby was jealous.

"Well, I'm here now," I say out loud.

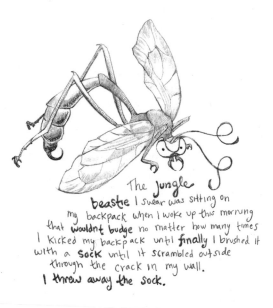

The jungle beastie I swear was sitting on my backpack when I woke up this morning that wouldn't budge no matter how many times I kicked my backpack until finally I brushed it with a sock until it scrambled outside through the crack in my wall. I threw away the sock.

It'd be more empowering if I wasn't squatting with my shorts around my ankles. I yank them up. Time to embark on the journey back, which I hope is less eventful. I follow the wall around the corner and discover it doesn't belong to a cabin: I've found the guesthouse's common area. Empty, except . . . there's a shadowy form in the hammock across the room.

"Rowan?" The hammock jerks, and I giggle, my misery forgotten.

"Bria? What are you doing here?"

Like I'd ever tell him I was too inept to locate the bathroom. "I was . . . taking a walk."

"In the dark? Why?"

"I couldn't sleep."

"Me neither. I thought maybe I could sleep better in here, with more air coming through, but . . . here I am. Still sleepless."

I'm feeling spine-meltingly shy, but I make myself go and stand beside his hammock. He has a new book on his lap: *The Omnivore's Dilemma.*

"Aren't you scared of the bats?"

He flicks on his flashlight and aims it at the ceiling. "I'm telling myself they've all gone for the night. Doing whatever bats do. *Echolocation*—I think that's the word. Nice jacket, by the way."

Oh damn. The dreaded crispy Windbreaker has been exposed. I make a face.

"No, I'm serious. It's such an . . . *attractive* color."

"I call it gutter water."

"I was thinking more like . . . baby possum."

"Or oatmeal gone rancid."

"Or stormy sky. After the apocalypse."

"You know what it's really like? It's the exact shade you get when you're painting with watercolors, and you're too lazy to change your cup of water, and all the colors blend together into a great big glass of ugly."

Rowan looks at me with interest. "You paint, too?"

I stuff my hands into my crispy pockets. "When I was younger."

"How much younger?"

125

"Younger."

For a moment, we seem to run out of things to say. The jungle is so loud I can almost sift the sound waves through my fingers, but it's better than the gracelessness of total silence.

"Well," I begin. "I guess I should—"

"Climb in?"

"The hammock?"

"If you sit facing the other way, we should be okay."

He sticks out his hand. I stare at it just long enough to crank up the awkward-meter to eleven. Finally, I crawl in beside him, clumsily, my Windbreaker crisping and crackling until I tear off the damned thing and hurl it over the side. The wood columns anchoring the hammock creak angrily at our combined weight.

"Don't worry," Rowan says. "I've got an emergency plan. If the hammock breaks, I'll just roll on top of you so you can break my fall."

"Oh, thanks."

Rowan flicks off his flashlight, and our conversation fizzles out again. Now Rowan and I are folded together, in the dark, and the silence is awkward enough to peel paint.

"I'm sure *Starling* would approve of this," I joke. *Curse my mouth.*

Fortunately, Rowan just laughs. "She *is* awfully protective of me."

"Why?"

He coils his fingers through the hammock's multicolored webbing. "She thinks of me as her little brother. And technically, I am. She's seen me at my worst. She's seen me at my best, and that's what she wants for me."

"I guess."

"She really does. I know she can be . . . overbearing, but she's always trying to do right. Compared to her, I'm a selfish jerk. You've heard some of her stories. She does these immense, philanthropic things, volunteers for months, works for pennies in tiny villages, and honestly? I'm just not that good."

"What about . . ." I tap the bracelets on his leg. Then I fold my hands on my stomach, just in case they feel like getting grabby again.

Rowan nudges a chair with two fingers, making the hammock sway. "I guess I work in small ways. It's kind of like this story someone told me, about a guy on the beach in Mexico throwing starfish in the sea. Thousands had washed ashore. Someone asked him why—'Why are you wasting your time, when there are so many? You can't possibly make a difference.'"

"I know that story! The man threw another one back, and said—"

"'Made a difference to that one!'" Rowan finishes. "Where'd you hear it?"

"I read it, actually."

"Where?"

"I think it was my mom's old copy of *Chicken Soup for the Soul*."

He laughs. "Oh great! I thought it was some ancient Zen proverb. Something respectable."

"Are you saying my mom's not respectable?" I tease him.

"Not if she reads *Chicken Soup for the Soul*."

"Apparently you do too."

He grins. "Touché."

It's all I can do to seal my lips around my own grin. We

127

seem to have no trouble talking in the dark. It's during the day when things get uncomfortable.

"Anyway," he says, "I started buying the bracelets a couple months ago. And just kept buying them. Starling calls them my ring of guilt. I'll probably take them off soon."

"When?"

"When I'm not feeling guilty anymore, I guess."

I nudge the side of a table, making us swing again. "Can I ask you something?"

Rowan seems a little wary but nods. He probably thinks I'm going to ask about his guilt, but I'm not. Here's what I want to ask: *Don't you ever get homesick?* It's the question that has come to me every time I've considered the scope of Rowan's travels. But my actual wording is less sappy. "Is there anything you miss about . . . home?"

"Sure. Lots of things."

"Like what?"

Rowan looks thoughtful. "Well, clothes that fit, for starters."

"Your clothes do fit."

"That's because Starling brings them for me from the States." He pushes off the chair. "Also, I really miss knowing the hot water's going to work when I get in the shower. And certain foods. Like fresh berries—especially blueberries. And raspberries. Real cheddar cheese. Fortunately, once you've been traveling long enough, your appetite makes compensations." He thinks a little more. "Also, I haven't driven a car in ages. I used to really like that . . . going for a drive."

"I do too. Long drives."

"Yeah?"

"Like sometimes I take the 2 up through La Cañada, into

the mountains. Or the 14 into the desert. Not too far—just far enough to be someplace different."

"By yourself?"

He looks surprised. I guess it *is* strange, coming from me: the undertraveled. Driving was something I did after Toby and I fought—which was often, especially just before we broke up. I'd fill my tank with my savings. Get in the car. And go, and go, and go. I never drove longer than an hour or two, so my parents wouldn't notice I'd been away. Just enough for the scenery to change into something unexpected, to remind me there was another world outside my bubble. Unfortunately, the feeling never lingered. As soon as I reentered the Los Angeles city limits, I was back to my usual antics. Calling Toby. Telling him I was sorry. Compacting myself into the backseat of his Honda before our next fight drove me to the road.

It occurs to me that maybe I'm doing the same thing right now, this very minute—just escaping by plane, chicken bus, and boat instead of by car. Maybe I've been a Wanderlove wannabe all along without ever knowing it existed.

"I always wanted to go to college somewhere else," I say suddenly. "Somewhere far. New York or Chicago or San Francisco. Or even Rhode Island."

Instantly, I'm embarrassed. Because why go to Cambodia or Croatia when you can visit Rhode Island? States don't *get* any smaller!

"The school of design, right? You said you used to love art."

I gape for a second, then hinge my jaw shut and nod. RISD is a famous school and all, but I'm still surprised Rowan knows about it. And even more surprised he remembers what I said about loving art.

"What stopped you from going off to school?" he asks.

"My parents had something to do with it," I reply. "Art school's expensive, and we're right in that middle-class bracket where there's not enough money for private school, but too much for any real financial aid." I cross my arms. I wish I had a jacket, but I'm not about to reach for my Windbreaker. "Anyway, their reasoning was pretty solid. Why would I ever leave Southern California? The best climate on the planet. Urban suburbia. Culture, beaches, nightlife. All the things young people migrate to find, L.A. already has. Including art schools. And then, of course, there was Toby. . . ."

"Toby? Is that your boyfriend?"

Shit. My throat starts to ache: the advent of tears. I didn't mean to mention Toby to Rowan. Not now, and maybe not ever. Rowan's insight makes me careless; it's only a matter of time before all my skeletons clamber out.

"Yeah," I say carefully. "That's him. He said he wanted to stay in Los Angeles. Attend a particular art school in town. A good one—just too close to home for my liking. But I thought I wanted . . . Well, we haven't had what you'd call the healthiest relationship." Not a lie when put like that. "Sorry. I just—"

Rowan puts his hand on my arm.

"Stop right there. You don't have to make excuses for your experiences—how can you? They already happened. And you don't have to dwell on them either. Just look to the future. Like we were talking about. You can't control the past, but you can control where you go next."

I nod. "That's why I'm here."

He nods back. "Me too."

We swing for a while in silence. My throat still aches, but I don't want to cry anymore. Rowan said just the right thing,

130

even though he barely knows me. He seems interested in everything I have to say. It makes me want to cover my mouth with my hands and spill my guts at the same time.

Now he's looking sleepy. And me, I'm exhausted. But I know I won't feel this bold tomorrow— in the daylight, when we remember we're companions by happenstance, not choice.

So I ask the other question I've been considering ever since Starling told me about Wanderlove.

"Do you ever think about going back?"

Rowan reaches for the chair. But instead of pushing off again, he uses it to steady himself as he climbs out of the hammock. He holds it for me, smiling thoughtfully, almost sadly.

"Every day," he replies.

10

Day 7
Livingston

We're standing on the beach with our backpacks on, facing the ocean. A faint drizzle—what my dad calls a Scotch mist—makes the gray sea and sky bleed together like wet-on-wet watercolor. Even the waves seem sluggish, heaving toward shore. "So this is the Caribbean?" I ask.

"Sort of."

"Either it is or it isn't."

"Then it is," Rowan admits. "But it gets better the farther north we go. Once we get to Belize, you'll see the real Caribbean in all its turquoise glory."

The paths of tiny sea snails twirl across the sand, like writing in another language. I set down my backpack and my daypack, kick off one sandal, and touch the water with my toes. "At least it's warm."

"Want to go for a swim?"

"No way."

"Oh . . . I forgot. I promise. But really? There's no chance you'll get in the water this entire trip?"

"I don't think—"

"What about on the island? Even if you don't dive, the snorkeling's ridiculous. Imagine rays the size of kites sailing beneath you . . ."

"*Rowan.*"

He glances at me. "Right," he says. "Sorry."

Silently, I slip my sandal back on, feeling like a jerk.

We head toward town. Livingston curves around a C-shaped harbor, backing into a fortress wall of jungle that stands starkly against the clouds. Despite the crappy weather, the streets bustle with activity. I see Mayans and mestizos, but most of the people are Garifuna: descendants of castaway African slaves and Caribbean Amerindians, Rowan explains. The men are tall and thin with burnt-gold skin; the women are curvy, dressed in skirts, scarves, and dusty plastic sandals. They speak Spanish, English, and the rollicking Garifuna language, which sounds like laughter. I can't help wondering what they think of us, strolling through their downtown as if we belong. Especially since the majority of backpackers I've seen are white. Or at least half white, like Rowan.

Rowan walks a couple of feet in front of me. Not because he's hurrying, but because I'm hanging back. The more I think about it, the more annoyed I am at myself.

It's not that I don't want to swim in the ocean. Not that

long ago, I loved to swim. But now that I've made swimming into this great big thing, I feel nervous. Especially alongside someone like Rowan, who's probably got salt water flowing through his veins.

I'm drawing in my sketchbook as I wait for Rowan in our room. Our *shared* room. Our twin beds stand just a hand's width apart. Mine has Dora the Explorer sheets—except they say *Door the Explore*. The room's walls are painted light blue, and I can see lumps in the paint where the brush trapped insects everlastingly. Pretty revolting. But at least there are two beds.

When I hear Rowan coming down the hall, I slip my sketchbook under my pillow. He leaves the door open, which makes me wonder if he's trying to be a gentleman. Or if he doesn't want to be alone with me, on account of the undeniable moodiness that's plagued me ever since we left the shore.

"Well," he says, "we won't spend much time here."

"Of course."

"I think you'll find Livingston a really fun place."

"As long as the rain holds back."

"It will."

"How do you know?"

"Because I'm magic like that, and I thought we could go hiking tomorrow. There's this group of waterfalls in the forest called Seven Altars. I haven't hiked there before, but Starling went along with this crew of peace corps kids once. . . ."

He's looking at me tentatively, like he thinks I'll refuse. But hiking, I can do.

"Why not today?" I ask.

"Are you crazy? It looks like rain." He pauses. "Hey, what's that?"

I glance over my shoulder, afraid to see the corner of my sketchbook poking out. But Rowan's pointing at my hand. My hand, upon which I have unconsciously drawn. I shove it into my pocket. "Nothing. It's nothing."

"But—"

"So what are we going to do today, if we're not hiking?" I push past him into the hall.

Rowan hesitates, then follows. "I don't know. Wander around." He closes our door and slams the padlock shut.

This is what we do.

We drink fresh pineapple juice in a café overlooking the fishing boats in the bay.

I pay a little girl two quetzales to put a single skinny braid in my hair. Rowan does the same when she begs him, but pulls it out as soon as we leave.

In an office the size of a tollbooth, Rowan introduces me to Sandu, our Garifuna guide for tomorrow's hike. He wears little John Lennon sunglasses. Outside, we take turns on a pair of drums, owned by a man with a gold front tooth.

We feed rolls to stray dogs. Some are purebred—mostly German shepherds—but others look like a dozen breeds pasted together. They remind me of a game Reese and I have never outgrown.

The Monster Game
1) Take a piece of paper and fold it
   horizontally, into fourths.

135

2) *The first person draws a monster head.* Then she folds the top fourth over to hide it.*

3) *The second person draws a monster chest. You have to leave a couple of lines overlapping into the next fourth, to guide each other.*

4) *Next come the monster hips and thighs. If you're a pervert, you can draw monster naughty bits.*

5) *Last come the monster knees and feet.*

6) *When you're finished, you unfold the paper together and crack up at the ridiculous beast you created.*

*Once, after we'd had a fight, I drew Toby's head in the top fourth. Reese and I laughed so hard we cried.

Unexpectedly, the novelty I feel hanging out with someone like Rowan seems to go both ways. With each new spectacle—a fishmonger selling live crabs on sticks, two old women playing some version of patty-cake on the church steps, a moth with a wingspan wider than my hand flattened against a stucco wall—he seems genuinely fascinated by my reactions. As if my companionship just might be one of the strangest countries he's ever visited.

Our day's not all pineapples and patty-cake. We argue. A lot. Like when Rowan has a little too much to say about Southern California. Or when I won't try his *elotes*, because mayonnaise just doesn't belong on corn on the cob. Worst is when I ask about Lobsterfest and the island, which Rowan isn't very eager to talk about.

"We're going to be spending a week there," I complain, "and I know nothing about it."

"Google it," Rowan retorts. "You know how, right?"

Asshole. I guess I should have known better.

Mostly, though, Rowan and I have fun. So much fun it's easy to forget how little I know him. When I remember, I feel a sudden shyness wash over me.

Over the course of the day, I try to piece together what I do know. Rowan has a half sister named Starling. He watched *Easy Rider* as a little boy. He skipped college and traveled instead, spinning the world like a top, teaching diving wherever he landed. Sometime in the last couple of years, he screwed up, and he's trying to get over it, trying to forget.

I can't help wondering about the details.

I know what Starling implied, about the smorgasbord of backpacker chicks and the dive partner and the pounds of bananas that in all likelihood weren't bananas, but Rowan doesn't seem eager to share the details. It's frustrating, but I can't blame him.

We're sitting at a restaurant, picking bones out of fish with the fins and heads still attached, when Liat ambushes us. "Bree-*yah!*" she crows, throwing her arms around me. She's wearing a long purple dress with a fuchsia flower in her crazy hair, which is so big I could practically hide inside it. "Why didn't you guys wait for us at the Rainforest Retreat? You *knew* we were going to Livingston." She glances over her shoulder. "Tom, come!"

Tom of the Jungle shuffles over obediently, glowering into

a beer mug. His eyes are red. I wonder if they've been fighting. I glance at Rowan, who's already getting to his feet.

"Nice to see you guys," he says, "but unfortunately, we were just leaving."

"You're *always* leaving." Liat turns to me. "He *always* leaves. Bria, why don't you stay a while? Have a Cuba libre. Let the good boy go to bed."

I glance from Liat to Rowan. I think my decision-maker's broken. Part of me wants to go with Rowan, and the other part—let's call it the Olivia Luster on my shoulder—is compelling me to stay out. I wish Rowan didn't seem so averse to meeting people. Maybe he's met too many; I don't know. But I do know I'm never going to reinvent myself if I don't at least pretend to be the girl I want to be: the independent party girl who seizes the day, all day, every day. And a Cuba libre seems like a painless way to start. "Maybe for a little while," I say.

"Really?" Rowan says. "You sure?"

His eyebrows reach cruising altitude. I try not to feel insulted, but it's hard. "Yeah, really."

"Yaaayy!" Liat hugs me again.

"Bria . . . can I talk to you a minute?" Rowan asks.

Liat rolls her eyes.

Once Rowan and I are outside, he clears his throat a couple of times. I wait, feeling annoyed. "Don't stay out too late," he says finally. "This isn't the safest place in the world."

"I'll be fine," I insist, though now I'm a little spooked. "That's all?"

"Just knock five times when you get to our room."

"Or I could just say, 'It's Bria.'"

He looks like he's trying and failing to smile. "Okay . . . See you later."

Still feeling annoyed and spooked and now weirded out besides, I rejoin Liat and Tom at their booth. Things only get weirder. Liat doesn't scoot over, and I'm forced to sit by Tom, whose posture resembles a fist.

"So what's Rowan's deal?" Liat asks.

"He's tired, I guess."

"Tired?" She begins a story about the time she fell asleep on a nude beach in Crete. I keep waiting for some kind of punch line, but the story just rambles on and on. Then, without any warning, she jumps up and skips off into the crowd. I'm left sitting beside Tom, who mumbles something into his cup.

"What did you say?" I ask, leaning in.

He nods out the window. "Bats."

I listen hard. Sure enough, I detect a high-pitched squeaking. At long last, Liat reappears, clutching a new cup. Instead of sitting across from us, she tosses herself onto my lap, hurling one arm around Tom's neck and one around mine. "Tom didn't tell you about the Czech chicks, did he?"

"Huh?" I glance at Tom.

"Because we promised," Liat says.

"Um, he didn't say anything. Really."

Liat looks placated. "So where's Rowan?" she asks as she slides into the gap between Tom and me. I use the opportunity to switch benches.

"I told you. He's in bed."

"You didn't. You only said he was tired. Did he tell you I knew him in Honduras?"

I almost knock over my cup. "What?"

"On Utila island! *Everyone* knew him. Rowan's crazy wild. You should have seen the shit he got away with. It was like a nonstop rave when he was there."

I hide my face by taking a sip of my drink.

I can't believe Rowan didn't tell me he knew Liat. He had tons of chances, last night and today. Why wouldn't he tell me? It's too damn weird. Is it because this so-called knowing is the nudge-wink kind? Ugh. Rowan's not my property—I barely know him—but it bothers me more than I care to admit. And a nonstop rave? *Seriously?*

"Where are you guys headed?" Liat asks, unaware of my discomfort.

"Some island," I say vaguely. "He's teaching a class."

"With the giant?"

"The what?"

"The giant! That Scandinavian beast, what's-his-name. Rowan's business partner." She winks exaggeratedly. "Come on, girl! You know the diving's just a front. You should have seen him the time he—"

"I don't want to talk about it," I say quickly.

And I don't. Not because I'm not dying of curiosity. Or because I feel particularly bad talking behind Rowan's back, especially now that I've discovered he lied about knowing Liat.

No, it's because, all of a sudden, I'm having trouble breathing, and I suspect what I hear might result in full cardiac arrest. I remind myself of how Rowan turned away those drug-seeking Spring Breakpacker guys on the boat. And of how Starling seems so certain he's reformed—*mostly* certain. Liat is referring to the past, not the present, and the past is something for Rowan to tell me about when he's ready. I owe him that much, even if I'm pissed off.

"So what are you guys doing tomorrow?" I direct my question toward Tom, whose silence is starting to fester.

Liat interjects. "What are *you* doing?"

Oh, great—she took it as an invitation. I'm not sure if she's trying to get closer to Rowan, or if it's entirely innocent and she just wants to be my friend. Or maybe she and Tom are swingers. And I don't mean the hammock kind. Whatever her motive, I want to escape.

"We're supposed to hike." I start massaging my temples. "But I'm getting a killer headache, so it might not happen. To be honest, I should probably head for bed. . . ."

"What hike?" Liat perks up even more.

Without waiting for my reply, she launches into a story about a time she went trekking up Mount Sinai with a group of American Birthright kids. She's still talking as I squeeze myself out of the booth, nod uneasily at Tom of the Jungle, and back out of the bar.

Here's the thing about SCAA's fast-track competition: we both were certain Toby would make it.

By all conventional rules, he was the better artist. He'd always taken art more seriously, at least. If it came down to the two of us, they'd choose him, not me.

And I was *fine* with that. Really.

The day fast-track admissions were announced, Toby and I were lying on my bed. He held my laptop, his other hand on my stomach, which was aflutter with mutant moth-creatures. Toby never got nervous—outwardly, at least. Casually, he ran his fingertips over my skin as he clicked *refresh, refresh, re-fresh*, waiting for the list of names that was already twenty minutes late.

"I'm telling you, you shouldn't have stuck in that fairy

drawing," he said, teasing me. "They're going to think you're ten years old."

Twelve students would be admitted to the fast-track program. It was exciting, but honestly, it didn't offer all that much over regular admission: some extra professor mentorship, a few general education units waived. Mostly, it signified what Toby called gloating rights. But nothing too monumental, I told myself, or too divisive. If either of us didn't make it into fast track, we'd both still attend SCAA anyway. Nothing would change between us. I filled out the general application to California's state schools to appease my parents, but I didn't apply to any other art schools.

I'm still trying to figure out why.

Refresh, refresh, refresh. "What about that fat man you drew?" I teased back. "He looked like he had tires around his thighs."

"The foreshortening was excellent, I'll have you know." *Refresh, refresh, refresh.* Then, suddenly, he sat up. "There they are!"

I peered over his shoulder as he curled around the laptop. In bold black letters, a list of names and locations. One jumped out instantly.

Bria Sandoval, Los Angeles, CA

"Oh my God!" I exclaimed. "I made it! And . . ."

I trailed off. Because none of the eleven other names was Toby's.

In silence, we stared, and we stared, and then, finally, Toby slammed my laptop shut hard enough to make me flinch. "They must have mixed up our portfolios or something."

He was joking—he had to be—but his voice was absent of

142

humor. The thrill I'd felt on seeing my name started to congeal in my stomach. "Are you okay?"

"Of course I'm okay."

I put my arms around him. "It won't change anything, you know? Like we promised. Who cares if I'm on fast track! You're the better artist, you know that."

Toby didn't confirm or deny it. He shrugged off my arms and stood. "I've got some stuff to take care of at home. We'll hang out later, okay?"

"Don't go," I begged, but he was already pounding down the stairs.

In the days and weeks that followed, Toby withdrew even more. He wasn't mad, but he needed space. Nothing had changed; he just needed a breather. That's what he said, anyway.

But here's the other thing about the fast-track competition: Toby's hurt was real.

He might have dealt with it wrong. It might have been overblown, his actions overreactive, but it killed me to see him hurting like that. It took months before I understood Toby wasn't envious—he was jealous. He'd treated fast-track admissions like a contest. And it wasn't his loss that angered him so much.

It was his loss to *me*.

A few weeks after that, I sat in front of my sketchpad. The blank pages had never looked so glaringly white. White enough to make me squint. Or maybe that was the tears in my eyes. I shut my sketchbook, shoved it under my bed so I wouldn't have to look at it, and grabbed the phone to call Toby, to try to fix something art had inexplicably broken.

11

Day 8, Morning
Geography

I huddle with the other hikers under the overhang of a café, watching the rain fall in the Livingston graveyard. The tombs look like candy-stained teeth. Our hike began with a tour of the village, and that's as far as we've gotten. We haven't even reached the forest, let alone the waterfalls.

"Sorry," Rowan says, coming up beside me.

I glance at him. He's wearing a pair of patterned drawstring pants, the kind I saw for sale all over Panajachel. On anyone else they'd look stupid, but not on Rowan. He wears them low on his hips, under a dark blue shirt with the sleeves torn off. A silver stone with some kind of Mayan symbol on it hangs on a black leather cord. Altogether the look is disastrously attractive, but its appeal is mostly lost, since I'm still upset about last night. Rowan has to suspect Liat told me the truth—some of it, at least. But he hasn't asked, and for now I'm fine with letting him wonder.

"You don't control the weather," I say.

"The hike was my idea, though."

"Only because I never have any of my own." Wait a second. "I mean, I don't know Guatemala like you do."

"I wouldn't say I *know* it, exactly. Just parts. And almost everything I know is on the Internet."

"I suppose I could have Googled it."

Rowan winces. "Look—all I meant was as long as travelers have visited a place, there's information about it available. How to get there, what to do, where to stay. It's not like some big secret. How do you think all these people heard about Livingston?"

I glance around. There are seven hikers total, including the couple from the riverboat, their terminally humiliated preteen daughter, and an older woman from Belgium with a walking stick. Sandu is attempting to entertain his wet, miserable flock with a Garifuna fable about a monkey and a stolen loaf of cassava bread. Because his accent's so heavy, I don't understand much more than that.

"But I'll still bet you've been *some* places other people haven't been," I say. "You've traveled more than anyone."

Rowan laughs. "More than anyone? No way. I met this guy last time I was in Belize, this novelist, who'd been traveling nonstop for almost a decade. Africa, Asia, the Middle East. Living in Bedouin tents. Laughingbird Caye was like Cancún for him."

Rowan's fourth travel rule:
No matter how well traveled you are,
you'll always meet someone who's
traveled more than you.

"The rain's slowing," Sandu says after he finishes his story. "Are we ready to go?"

Rowan and I glance at each other.

"I said, are we ready?"

"But the storm might *come back*," the preteen girl whines. Behind her, the Belgian woman sits sipping a mug of coffee. Sandu's John Lennon glasses droop. He probably sees his livelihood washing away in the rainwater.

"You and I can still go," Rowan says. "It's your decision."

My decision. I glance at the muddy trail, the saggy-diaper sky. The mud doesn't sound like fun, but neither does staying in town, where I might run into Liat and Tom.

Maybe I understand why Rowan didn't tell me they'd known each other way back when. The idea of Rowan meeting a gossip like Jessa Hanny and hearing a condensed, probably misshapen version of my past makes me shaky. At least Rowan didn't flat out lie, like I did about Toby.

So I'll forgive him, I decide. The past's in the past. But that doesn't mean I'll trust him.

"Screw the rain," I say. "Let's go."

As expected, the going's slow. In a number of places, the trail's grown so sloppy with mud our feet stick. Once I even lose a shoe, and Sandu has to pry it from the muck.

The trail narrows as it squeezes between the trees. I hike

146

ahead of Rowan and Sandu, the backs of my calves tightening, a stitch pinching my side. Their voices fade behind me until all I can hear is the chain saw noise of bugs and quaking leaves. When the trail ends at a shallow stream, I tie my sneakers to the drawstring of my shorts and step into the water barefoot, biting my lip as the gravel gnaws my heels. The first waterfall's a baby one, less than three feet tall. I dip my hands into it before I trek onward.

I hop over tree roots bigger than my waist, with skittering, vicious-looking ants. Once, I startle a gigantic iguana, which crashes off into the brush. My scream brings Rowan and Sandu running. "Are you all right?" Rowan asks. "What was it?"

I'm still trying to catch my breath. "It's gone now."

"What's gone?"

"A hyena," I reply, widening my eyes.

Sandu looks around wildly. "What's this hyena?"

Instead of hurrying ahead again, now I stay beside Sandu and Rowan. We pass waterfalls two through six, each larger than the last. We have to climb over the tops of a couple, the water tugging at our ankles like an angry naiad.

Even though I hear the roar of the seventh long before we reach it, the sight of it makes my jaw drop. Fifteen feet tall and thirty feet wide, the waterfall tumbles into a pool colored blue by minerals, dancing with fractured light. The air in the clearing somersaults with mist and noise.

"The seventh altar," Sandu says proudly.

I turn to Rowan. "It's . . . ," I begin, but stop as he strips off his shirt.

"It's what?" he asks as he tosses it on a rock.

"Never mind."

147

"Let me guess. You're not getting in? Come on, it's just a pond—a perfect primer for the ocean."

I shake my head. Before I left the country, Reese warned me jungle streams can contain amoebas, flesh-eating bacteria, and these evil little fish that swim inside your urethra when you pee in the water and become lodged there forevermore. I don't know if this is true, but I really, really don't want to risk it.

"It could be polluted," I say. "And there might be . . . water snakes." I decide not to bring up the pee-hole fish.

He sighs. "That means I'll have to make up for it. To balance out the universe."

"What the hell's he doing?" I ask Sandu as Rowan starts scaling the rocks beside the waterfall. Sandu just chuckles and shakes his head, like, sorry, he can't control the crazy. "Are you sure that's a good idea?" I call to Rowan.

"Sandu told me he's done it a bunch of times!"

"When?"

"Back on the trail, when you were speeding off ahead."

"How do you know he's not lying?"

"Hey, Sandu," Rowan calls, crouching atop the highest rocks. "Did you hear that? She called you a liar!" And then, without even glancing down, he leaps.

I can't believe he did it. With my heart thudding in my throat, I crawl to the edge of the pool and stare into the water until he surfaces. Unless he's bleeding internally, he's survived the plunge intact. He paddles over to me and leans over the stone surface where I'm sitting.

"Told you there are water snakes." I point to his tattoo. "Actually, it looks more like the Loch Ness monster. You know—Nessie."

148

"I'll ignore that statement if you jump next."

"There's no way."

"Won't you get in, at least? You can hold on to me."

"Not happening."

He touches the top of my foot. It's the farthest place from my head, but I still feel the jolt. "Come on, Bria. What's it going to take to get you to jump in?"

The water looks cool and blue, like an electric-raspberry Popsicle. I want in. And Rowan knows it. Dive instructor, my ass. He's a psychic. He can see right inside my brain—how much I want to give up, slip in. I just hope that's all he can see. Because I swear to God, *his* brain's impenetrable, and it's starting to drive me insane.

"I don't know, all right?" I snap, pulling back my foot. "It'd happen a lot more quickly if you'd stop pressuring me."

I brace myself for a stinging comeback. But instead, as Rowan backpaddles away, his dark blue eyes have gone all wounded puppy on me, and I feel like an asshole all over again.

On our way back, we pass a slope overlooking the yard of a primary school. The rains have turned it to mud, but that doesn't stop a group of boys from scampering around with a soccer ball. They're barefoot, their school uniforms streaked and dirty. A nun watches the mayhem alongside a cluster of little girls. The feminist inside me is turning purple.

"I remember that," Rowan says. "Back when sports were fun. Before high school, when you couldn't play unless you were on a team. Took all the joy out of it."

I look at him, glad he finally broke the silence we brought back from the jungle pool. "I take it you're not an athlete?"

149

"Actually, I swam."

I shouldn't be surprised. I open my mouth to reply, but with comic timing, an errant kick sends the muddy soccer ball right into my hip. "Son of a—"

"Are you okay?"

"I'm fine." I stick my tongue out at the boys, who are laughing hysterically.

Sandu scoops up the ball, and they all clamor to receive his throw, shouting, *"Aquí! Páseme!"* Instead, he tosses it to me, resulting in a second muddy splotch on my clothes.

The boys change their tactic. "Lady! Pretty lady, give it here." I pick out the most uncoordinated-looking kid of the bunch and hurl it his way. Too bad I can't throw. A bigger boy kicks it away with a happy yell, sending the other kids scrambling.

"Hey," Rowan begins. He's got that maniacal Peter Pan gleam in his eyes, the one that danced there all through yesterday. In this context, it makes me nervous.

"What?" I ask warily.

"Do you think they'd let us play?"

Sandu grins. "I know these kids. They go crazy for it."

Without another word, Rowan hops over the low concrete wall and skids down the slope to the field. The kids shout and swarm around him. "He's batshit insane," I tell Sandu.

"Bria?" Rowan calls. "Come on!"

Make that hyenashit insane. For a split second, I imagine the feeling of the mud between my fingers, gooey and grainy, like chocolate frosting. But I don't know how to play soccer. And I don't want to look any clumsier than I already do.

So I invent an excuse. "I've got a sore ankle!"

"I don't"—Rowan stops to kick the ball—"believe it for a second!" The boys run after it, shoving each other and skidding in the mud, while he looks up at me even more wounded puppy–like and guilt-trippy.

"It's true."

He shrugs and turns back to the game, but I still catch his expression: disappointment. But not surprise.

I don't know why it's so important to me: proving to Rowan I'm worthy of being his travel companion, a stand-in for Starling and Liat and those other girls—the autonomous, nonconformist, life-experienced girls who stood at his side in other places. It's almost like if I'm accepted by Rowan—the pinnacle of pickiness, the travel ideal—Toby Kelsey and art school won't matter anymore.

I'll have won. This time, for always.

But it's never going to happen unless I close my eyes and jump.

The element of surprise is on my side. Rowan doesn't notice me until I come up behind him and whisper in his ear: "I'm open."

It sounded less suggestive in my head.

He's so startled he drops the ball. I grab it and hop away, the mud slurping at my bare feet. From the hilltop, Sandu cheers, waving my shoes. The boys gather around me, hollering. They haven't yet learned to be shy around women. Luckily, they don't seem to care that I've got no idea how to play soccer. Playing with grown-up foreigners shatters all the rules.

I hold the ball over my head for just a moment before a boy slaps it from my hands. I scream and run after him, which is a bad idea, because I slip and fall flat on my back.

Unfortunately, the mud doesn't swallow me up. So I am

not protected from the humiliation of Rowan leaning over me, the gray sky framing his concerned face.

"Are you okay?"

Concerned—but maybe a little amused, too.

"Fine," I mutter.

"Nothing broken?"

"Not that I can tell."

I hold out my hand. As soon as he grabs it, I yank hard, sending him tumbling into the mud beside me. I have to laugh at his stunned expression. "Oldest trick in the book!" I tease.

Rowan reaches for me, but I roll away just in time. There's something refreshing about being so caked in muck you just stop caring. Until he scoops up a glob of mud and aims.

"You wouldn't. . . ."

He does. It hits me square in the chest, and I yelp as the mud oozes down my shirt. I try to scrape it away with my forearm, but it only flattens, forming a mud pancake in my cleavage. Which is even *less* hot than it sounds. I lunge at him and shove him onto his back, pinning him with my knees on either side. He's laughing so hard he doesn't resist, even when I paint his face with my muddy fingers. Cat whiskers. A clown nose. A unibrow.

All of a sudden, we realize we have an audience. The boys are standing in a forlorn cluster a few yards away. They don't find us amusing—we've ruined the game.

A slight rain begins to prickle our dirty faces. And in that second, it's like we both become self-conscious. Or maybe it's just me. Because I'm the one who has the imaginary boyfriend, straddling a guy I barely know before an audience of children.

152

Ahem.

We both stagger to our feet, scraping mud from our shirts. Sandu's waiting for us at the top of the hill, shaking his head and grinning.

"Don't say anything," I tell him.

He holds up his hands, like, *I wasn't about to!*

On our way back to the guesthouse, we stop by the beach so Rowan can wash off in the ocean. When I refuse to join him, he makes up names for me—like Mudsicle, Frankenslime, and Mudusa—until I tell him to quit.

"Did you know *medusa* is the Spanish word for 'jellyfish'?" he asks.

I pry a flake of dried mud from my neck. "Since I know about twenty Spanish words, no."

"If you're lucky, I'll teach you." He pulls off his shirt and tosses it on the sand. He's got to stop doing that. Abdominal oblique, I think, and there's a flit of wings in my chest.

I turn away.

Maybe I can't control what Rowan thinks of me, but I've got to control how I think of Rowan. He's off-limits. Might as well be straitjacketed in barbed wire. And Starling made it clear he could never be interested in me, even if I let myself be interested in him.

I think of Tom and Liat, the soupy friction between them. The way they discussed everything except what itched, until Tom devolved into a man-shell who could only mutter about bats and insects.

I think of my parents and their relentless wars. They care enough to stay together but have paved their marriage with battles and bickering, and now they don't know any other way to be.

I think of Toby and me. The tension I never noticed in those joint sketching sessions, before it became so abruptly evident I couldn't believe I hadn't noticed it all along—like waking to a cacophony of screechy birds, or becoming suddenly aware of an embarrassing song playing on a store's speakers (usually "I'm Gonna Be [500 Miles]" by the Proclaimers). I should have noticed that Toby's art lessons tapered off the moment I started to get really good. If I had, all the fallout after I made fast track and he didn't wouldn't have surprised me.

Rowan and I have at least two days before we reach the island. And if anything, the tension keeps getting worse. I don't want to travel like that.

That means he and I will have to open up, at least a little bit.

And if he doesn't start, I'll have to.

12

Once I finish showering, I douse my arms and legs with 35 percent DEET bug spray. I despise DEET. It stings the cuts on my ankles from shaving. And it stinks. Plus, it always seems so counterproductive drenching myself in insecticide seconds after I've washed. But Rowan—who can be worse than Reese—terrorized me with tales of mosquito-borne malaria, yellow fever, and dengue, which I'd never heard of. Apparently, it's also known as breakbone fever, because when you've got it, bending an elbow or a finger feels like snapping a bone.

It's pretty much the most frightening thing I've ever heard of.

Actually, it's the second-most. First is botfly larvae, which I can't even think about without wanting to cry.

I wrap my towel around my shoulders like a shawl and look at myself in the scratched-up mirror. My hair's a dark, wet tangle, and my cheeks are lollipop pink from the frigid shower. Hot water seems to be a luxury on the budget back-packer circuit.

Finally, I open the door. The night billows with sound. I linger by the doorway, noting all the layers.

> *A ceaseless chain saw buzz.*
> *A low, mournful whistle.*
> *A shrill shriek.*
> *The rustle of leaves.*
> *A sound like a car engine turning on*
>   *and off.*
> *A sporadic, chirpy bark.*

Because I am not Tom of the Jungle, I can name only the last one.

I sigh. Despite my nervousness, I know it's time to con-front Rowan. My only consolation is that our talks always seem to go better at night.

I find him sitting in a battered director's chair on the hotel porch, reading a book by flashlight. He's draped his wet hik-ing clothes over the picket fence behind him. I should prob-ably do the same. "Hey," I say.

Rowan glances up. "You look like a superhero."

I twirl, making my towel fan out like a cape. Then I take a deep breath. "Rowan . . . I think we need to talk."

He clutches a hand to his heart. "Are you breaking up with me?"

"Ha," I say. "I'm serious."

"I know." He sets his book in his lap; this time it's *The Handmaid's Tale*. I can't believe he's already finished his last. His eyes must scan the pages like lasers.

I slide down the wall until I'm crouching in a towel-covered bundle. "Do you want to start?" I ask hopefully, even though I haven't told him what this conversation's about. I'm not really sure myself.

Rowan tips his head, as if examining me. "You make me nervous."

I squirm. "Sorry. I just thought we should talk, considering—"

"I didn't mean right now. I mean in general."

"Huh?" I say, surprised.

"You're just so secretive. You're always writing in your journal. You're like that spy girl in that kids' book. Do you think I don't notice?"

"Why does it matter?" I protest. "Lots of travelers keep journals."

"It's not the journal that makes me nervous—it's the way you slam it every time I glance over. And hide it when you think I'm not looking."

I guess I'm less stealthy than I thought. "But *you're* the secretive one, Rowan. I've told you more than you've told me. I don't know anything about you. You could be, like . . . an international spy. You could be a serial killer." One I hope isn't provoked by accusations.

Rowan rolls his flashlight in his hands. "It's not that I'm trying to hide my past. Not exactly. It's just . . . I'm over it. You could say I've been born again."

"Like a virgin?"

"Right!" he says. Then he sings it.

When we stop laughing, he continues. "There's a reason I'm like this. When I first started traveling, I was always looking behind me. Walking backwards, with my face in the past. And that meant I was always trying to compensate. Trying to make up for everything that happened to me—like my mother running off, my father being such a fuckup—by *doing*."

He runs his thumb over the edge of his book, strumming it like a deck of cards.

"All that overthinking—that over-remembering—almost destroyed me. Now I've got to get over that part of my life too."

"And that's why you won't talk about it?"

"I don't even talk about it with Starling. To tell you the truth, I'd flat out rather you didn't know. Really, it's all kind of cliché. *Precocious youth with messed-up past finds refuge in immorality. Abroad.* Boring, right? The colorful backdrop notwithstanding."

It doesn't sound all that boring to me.

"Remember a few days ago, when the bus broke down?" he asks. "Sitting outside in the dark? We agreed not to dwell on the past. I thought we were on the same page."

I pull the damp towel around me tighter, a cocoon. "It's just . . ."

"Just what?"

"It's just *strange*."

Rowan laughs. Then he shines his flashlight under his chin, making a demon face. "*Strange* I can deal with."

"It's like . . . you want to erase your whole life before this trip."

"But isn't that the way it should be?"

"What do you mean?"

"*Now* is what's important." He sweeps his flashlight over the trees. The beam illuminates the branches in two-dimensional detail, like flash photography. "Just look around us. Look where we are. What's the good of loitering in unpleasant places when the *here and now* is so incredible?" He aims his light at me.

I scrunch up my face. I see what he means, but then again . . . "I don't want to keep walking on eggshells. Worrying about what we can ask and what we can't."

"I don't want that either." Rowan clicks off his flashlight. "How about we think up some ground rules?"

I rub the apparitions of light from my eyes, then rest my chin on my knees. "How about this: if I say a topic's off-limits, no questions, no jokes, nothing."

"Like swimming?"

I shrug.

"I can respect that. But the same goes for you."

"Of course."

"We need a list." He pulls a tattered, water-stained scrap of paper from his book and hands it to me. I can make out the words *Utila Bay Express*.

"Is this from a boat?"

"Yep. Sometimes I forget to throw away receipts. They make perfect bookmarks."

"Are you sure you want to write on it?"

"It was a terrible trip. I got seasick. Go ahead."

I write: *Swimming. Old boyfriends.*

"Old boyfriends?" he reads.

My pen freezes.

Earlier, when I was freezing my ass off in the shower, I was determined to tell Rowan the truth about Toby. Not

159

everything. But enough to shine the light away from my stupid, stupid lie, the one I swore I'd admit, tonight: that I don't have a boyfriend.

Now's the perfect moment. But I just can't do it.

"All boyfriends," I say, correcting what I wrote.

"I meant, can we make that 'relationships'? I know I said my past was rowdy, but . . ."

My face heats up. "Got it."

"Not that there's anything wrong with that." He pauses. "Add *family*."

I glance up at him. "But that includes Starling. Which means you can't talk about anything more recent than when—two days ago?"

"Then write *parents*. A big tangled knot I'd rather not unravel."

I write *Rowan's parents*, and then, beside it, *Fears. Art.*

"Art? Really?"

"It's personal."

"Is that why you wouldn't show me your hand?"

My hand. Resting on my leg, exposed for the world to see. I sigh. I know how silly it is hiding my drawings. I never used to care. I was practically an artistic exhibitionist.

I look at Rowan. He's so casual, unruffled, with his arms crossed over his book, his flashlight against his knee. I know I agreed to this list in my hand, which already seems kind of dumb. But I came out here tonight to find out more, not less. And that's what I'm going to do.

"If you show me yours," I say, "I'll show you mine."

"My hand?"

"Your tattoo."

"Up close? No problem." Rowan pushes the arm of his

T-shirt over his shoulder, displaying the entire piece. I hobble over on my knees to get a closer look, leaving my towel behind. It's quality art, thank God. Shitty tattoos make me stabby.

"So why a *dragon*?"

"Why do you have to say it like that?"

"Like what?"

"With a sneer."

"Sorry," I say, trying not to giggle. "It's just . . . it's part of the stereotype, isn't it? A dragon's such a tough-guy tattoo. It could be worse—like a lopsided tribal armband. Or something written in Chinese with an entirely different meaning than what you thought."

"Like 'helicopter'? Or 'mock duck'?"

"Or worse. Example: my friend Olivia wanted the word *free* in Chinese tattooed right here." I touch my hip above the hem of my shorts. "So she went to this glammy Chinese restaurant in North Hollywood and asked the host to write it down for her. Unfortunately, she didn't tell him why. Turns out there are two different Chinese characters for *free*, with different definitions: One means, like, liberated. The other one—the one she got—means *free of charge*." I pause. "Kind of fitting, though, if you know Olivia."

"Ouch," Rowan says. "My tattoo's not like that. I promise."

He extends his arm, holding it aloft until I catch it in my hands.

"Look close."

With my eyes, I trace the dragon as if I'm drawing it: the scallops of its scales, its slanted eyes and trailing whiskers, it claws, splayed out like talons. Rowan's skin shows through a gleam of light left inkless along the dragon's torso. Underneath its belly scampers a row of tiny human feet.

"I don't get it," I say.

"It's not just any dragon. It's the one they use to celebrate the Chinese New Year. Specifically, in San Francisco's Chinatown."

"Is that where you're from?"

"I lived there at one point. The city, not Chinatown. But my dad took me to the New Year's parade when I was six. I thought we were having father-son time. . . . Really, it was just an excuse for my dad to meet with some woman. So naturally, he lost track of me."

I'm still cradling Rowan's arm. I try not to move or do anything that might suppress his story.

"You can't imagine how terrified I was," he says. "Everything was commotion. Clanging bells and firecrackers bursting in my face. I didn't recognize anything. I wasn't much of a reader then, but it wouldn't have mattered—all the signs were in these wicked-looking Chinese letters. At first I panicked, sobbing and pushing through the knees, but no one noticed me. There were just too many people. I even searched the shops. I remember this one place, some sort of pharmacy, with one wall covered in ugly withered things like shrunken heads."

I discover I'm squeezing Rowan's arm, but he doesn't pull away.

"Then, all of a sudden, it was like the smoke dissipated. I can't really explain it . . . but somehow, I realized my father wasn't going to find me, and it was up to me to get *un*-lost. It was up to me to take care of myself. And so I swallowed my tears, and quietly, calmly, I made my way through the crowd until I came to an intersection. And when I turned the corner, I recognized the street. I knew where I was.

"My dad didn't find me—I found myself. So that's when I figured out that the only person who could take care of me was *me*."

I wait to make sure he's finished. Then I release his arm and wrap myself in my towel again. "But you were just a little boy," I say, sitting back against the wall.

Rowan nods. "I was. But I'm glad I learned it so young. To depend on myself, and no one else."

"What about Starling?"

"Starling?" He shrugs. "Like I said, Starling means well. But she doesn't always know what's best for me, even though she thinks she does."

I think of my conversation with her at the Río Dulce café. How protective she is. How much she obviously cares about her brother. And despite myself, I feel an unwanted surge of loyalty for her. "Still, it must be nice to have someone in your corner."

"Believe me, I'm not ungrateful. I know what it's like not to have anyone."

I'm not sure if I believe him. Rowan's always had Starling;

when was he ever on his own? Even if they lived in different places, they must have exchanged phone calls or emails or something. I hug myself under my towel cape. "I need to take lessons from you, Rowan."

"You don't trust yourself?"

"Not really. I haven't been very . . . trustworthy in the past." I fold up our off-limits list and stick it in the pocket of my shorts, where I plan to forget about it. "Anyway. I'm sorry I called your tattoo Nessie. And thank you for your memory."

"*The Giver*," Rowan says.

"The what?"

"It's another kids' book. Dystopias, memory sharing—it's epic. You should read it." He reaches out and gently taps my shoulder with his flashlight. "It's your turn. Though I'd rather see the book you keep hiding from me."

"My sketchbook? You've got to be kidding."

"It's a *sketchbook?*"

I make a face. "Well, I write things in it too. But it's for Bria's eyes only."

"Okay, okay. Just your hand." He reaches for me.

I turn my face as he examines the butterfly I drew on the back of my hand, in the crook between my index finger and thumb. By now, it's almost entirely faded. Nothing much left but a ghost of wings. I wait for him to call me out, since I gave him such a hard time about the dragon tattoo. Aren't butterflies even more cliché than dragons?

But all he says is "It's beautiful." For a second, he laces his fingers through mine.

13

Day 9, Morning
Go Slow

We can actually *see* the storm moving toward our boat: a wall of water agitating the sea in a perfect line, surging in our direction. As the first fat drops strike our faces, Rowan kicks a tarp out from under the seat.

"Grab that side!" he shouts to the man sitting in front of us. *"Tome ese lado."*

We're swallowed in blue plastic, huddling so close we're practically on each other's laps. The wind yanks at the tarp, and I seize a flailing edge before it flips into the storm. There must be a gap somewhere, because the rain's streaming down my neck and into my shirt. At least I'm not wearing white. For someone who shuns water, I do an awfully good job attracting it. In just one week, I've voyaged through a lake, down a river, and now across the stormy sea.

It's just past eight in the morning. We barely made our boat, which is heading to Punta Gorda in Belize. If we'd missed it, Rowan said, we'd have had to proposition a fisherman.

There's a boom so loud I bite my tongue. Then a flash, way too close. I grip the tarp so tightly my hand cramps. As if a sheath of plastic could keep us safe from the fire gods.

"Can it hit us?" I yell over the roar.

"What?" Rowan yells back.

"I said, *can it hit us?* Can the lightning hit us?"

"No! Don't worry."

Another peal of thunder shudders the air. I close my eyes, thankful for the solidity of Rowan's body pressed against mine. I know I'm trying to act all brave and independent on this trip, but lightning's *scary*. I'm certain we've blown off course and are approaching Jamaica when the boat engine finally slows. The rain splatters vertically instead of sideways through the gap, which is a relief. I brave a peek, clutching the tarp around my shoulders like a poncho. Through the haze, I glimpse the dim, gray shore of Belize, along with the outline of several boxy houses. I reach under the tarp and pinch Rowan's side.

"We're here! Come out, come out, wherever you are."

He tickles me back. I double up, spilling more water down my shirt as Rowan emerges from the tarp. The boat chugs through the colorless water toward a gloomy pier, sort of what I'd imagine the dock on the banks of the river Styx to look like.

"So *this* is your Caribbean?" I ask.

"Wow," he replies. "I'm starting to feel like a fraud."

"I could be on my way to Mexico right now. Sipping mimosas on a white-sand beach. All of it prepaid, I should add."

"If it's raining here, it's probably raining there, you know."

A man in a yellow slicker hoists our backpacks as we climb out onto the pier. Earlier we tied garbage bags around them to keep out the rain, and it appears to have worked for mine. But when Rowan lifts his, water gushes from a rip in the plastic.

"There's karma for you," I tell him.

He stares at me for a second. Then he shakes his backpack in my direction. An arc of water slaps me in the legs. I'm already drenched, but I chase him down the dock anyway. I don't notice the pair of uniformed soldiers until I crash into one of them.

He grabs me by the arm. "Why are you in such a hurry?"

I forgot Belizeans speak English. Rowan turns and jogs back toward us, and I swallow nervously, wondering if I've just gotten us deported. "We're just . . . ," I begin.

"Happy," Rowan shouts, "to be in Belize!"

After a moment of silence, both soldiers begin to chuckle. The first releases me, and the other wipes his eyes. "Welcome," he says. "Customs is that way."

"And *slow down*," the other adds. "This is Belize. We go slow here."

"Belize smells like Christmas," I tell Rowan as we stroll down the wet road, trying to find an Internet café. Our bus to Belize City doesn't leave for an hour, and Rowan has some phone calls to make.

He stares at me, mystified. "How's that?"

I shrug. I'm not sure why I said it; it's not like this is Douglas fir country. "Maybe it's the rain." It continues to float down in gauzy sheets, making me feel lethargic. If it wasn't so oppressively muggy out, I'd long for a cup of coffee and a fireplace.

"California girl," Rowan says, grinning at me.

"You said you lived in San Francisco. Aren't you a California boy?"

"Sure. And a Montana boy, an Oregon boy, a Mexico boy . . . Want me to go on?"

"Yes," I say, but he doesn't.

He steps over a puddle. "This is the right weather for a seaweed."

"A *what?*"

"A seaweed. It's a classic Belizean drink. I'll make sure to find you one."

Even though Punta Gorda is on the water, there aren't really any beaches here. Just a strip of weedy grass lined with rocks, and then the foamy sea. Coconut palms lean into the wind. Their coconuts aren't tan or green, but macaroni-and-cheese orange. The village itself kind of resembles Livingston, minus the jungle and hilly landscape. And the Spanish. The same pastel paint on the concrete houses. The same muddy streets. The same muddy dogs. But there's a definite difference in the level of prosperity; the homes are larger, the public spaces better kept. The dogs all look like they belong to *someone*, even if they're not well bathed.

We pause in front of a woman selling coconut bread. Toffee-colored hair frames her face in immaculate hot-curler coils. One Belize dollar—locked at fifty U.S. cents—per wedge, about twice what we'd have paid in Guatemala.

"Belize is doing a lot better than Guatemala," Rowan says when I comment. "They don't have the same history of violence. Guatemalans have had a rough time of it."

Rowan's fifth travel rule:
Prices are relative. So is poverty. So is happiness.

Unfortunately, Belize's good luck means my money is going to run out more quickly here. When we stop by an ATM to withdraw Belizean currency, I'm glad the machine can't show me my balance.

In the café, I open a browser window on an ancient PC. I haven't been online since Panajachel, which is probably the longest I've ever been off the grid. I log in to my mailbox and am greeted with twenty-seven new messages. Both my parents' names, over and over. A thicket of exclamation points.

Great. I know I should read them. I should write back. But sifting through the messages sounds excruciating. My parents are probably angry—justifiably, since I haven't contacted them, not even to let them know I got here okay. But *I* know I'm fine. And a part of me wants to let them worry a little longer. In a messed-up way, it feels validating.

They're not *bad* parents. When I compare them to Rowan's dad, losing his kid at the parade, I know I should be grateful. Anyway, I'm the one who quit confiding in my mom, mostly because she hates unpleasant things. Volunteering the truth about Toby, about how I felt when I stopped drawing and she didn't comment, about the real reason I'm not going to SCAA—it would have been like closing the blinds on a sunbathing kitten. It's much easier to keep my mouth shut.

I've always felt closer to my dad. He's a numbers guy, sort of endearingly awkward. Very much a man of few words—often no more than a couple. Like when I found that old sketchbook of his in the bottom drawer of his desk. It was just after fast-track admissions came in, when Toby was acting like a jerk and I was flailing, and it could have led to a heartening dialogue, a fresh link in a connection that had grown fragile over the years.

But all he said was "It's nothing."

He probably thought he was being encouraging—like, *my art's nothing compared to yours*—but it instantly cauterized the conversation. Soon after, when I told him attending a nearby state school made more sense than SCAA, he asked if I was sure, and that was it. So that was that.

I skim the emails from my friends. Reese's are short, sweet, and concerned, while Olivia's are stream-of-consciousness, paragraph-free text bricks describing her latest promo modeling gig and her fights with Jessa Hanny, topped with not-so-subtle *no strings!!!* reminders.

I decide to write them back first.

To: "Olivia Luster"
<olivia.luster@gmail.com>
Subject: The Caribbean!

Hey,
Sorry I haven't written. So you know that tour group I was talking about? I ditched them. I've met some

amazing people, and we're having a crazy awesome
time. One of them's a guy. Calm down! It's not like
that. But he's not my only chance. We're heading to
this crazy party island, and I still plan to keep my
promise. You know the one.
You're totally missing out.
Love, B

To: "Reese Kinjo"
<reesekpiece@gmail.com>
Subject: The Caribbean!

Hey,
Sorry I haven't written. Remember when we used to
sit by your pond and skip all kinds of crap in the
water? I've gotten really good at it here. Even when
there are waves.
I'm not thinking about He Who Shall Not Be Named
at all, except when I typed that. It's hard for me to say
you're missing out without sounding like a jerk, but . . .
you are. I guess that just means we'll have to come
back someday, together.
Love, B

I can't bring myself to email my parents.

I wait outside, leaning against my backpack, while Rowan
finishes his call. Across the road, muddy-legged kids push
each other on a dilapidated swing set that resembles a crumpled paper clip. Through the open door, I can hear the rise
and fall of Rowan's voice.

"To dive," he's saying. "And that's it."

I try to imagine Starling and Rowan as children. Starling would have chaotic blond hair and skinned knees. Rowan's dark hair would flop in his face, his eyes unnervingly large. He'd be reserved, thoughtful, while Starling would be domineering, brash, the kind of little girl who elbowed her way up the monkey bars ladder and spit from the top. She's protected Rowan ever since the beginning. From schoolyard bullies. Bellowing cousins. Imaginary yeti. They spoke in a secret language that would impress Tolkien. They called each other Ro and Star.

I'm so enchanted by this history, I almost forget I'm making it up.

Rain starts falling again, and the kids scatter. I grab my backpack and drag it inside, where Rowan's still sitting in a wooden phone booth on the far side of the room. Impulsively, I buy a map of Belize from a stack beside the register. I didn't think of Googling the island, but at the very least, I can have some idea where we're headed.

I glance over as the tone of Rowan's voice changes.

"I told you, the money's not the issue. Of course I need the money. But if I finish my Divemaster cert, that won't be a problem." He pauses. "There's no arguing with you when you're like this!"

I thought he was talking to Starling, but now I'm not so sure. I don't know whether to approach him or act like I haven't heard anything. As I'm hovering there, indecisive, Rowan notices me. We lock eyes for a split second. "I've got to go," he says quickly, and hangs up.

"Are you okay?" I ask. When he nods, I can't help adding, "Who was that?"

He heaves his backpack onto his shoulders. "Never mind. We'd better catch our bus."

14

Day 9, Afternoon
Rainbows

"Do you know what highway we're on?" I ask Rowan, who's sitting beside me on the bus.

"Southern," he replies without glancing up from his book.

I stare at him a moment before turning back to my map. I'm still not sure who was on the other end of his phone call in the Internet café. But if I ask again, I'll sound like I'm pestering him. And when I go over what I heard, I decide there's not enough to go on—at least, not enough to risk breaking our hours-long argument-free stretch, which, for us, is a marathon.

With my little finger, I trace the Southern Highway northward from Punta Gorda on my map. Near a city called Dangriga, it turns into the Hummingbird Highway, which has got to be the best name for a highway I've ever heard—not that there's much competition. We'll probably be taking the Coastal Highway, which branches off of the Hummingbird Highway heading north. Both join the Western Highway, which leads from Belize City back to the border of Guatemala. I feel like a child enthralled by a sandbox universe. Hours and miles conquered by my eyes in an instant. I mouth the names of Belizean places, bouncing them on my tongue. *Cockscomb, Caracol, Orange Walk, Nim Li Punit, Crooked Tree, Gallon Jug.*

"'Community Baboon Sanctuary,'" I read out loud. "Baboons? I thought baboons were African."

"They're actually howler monkeys." Rowan sticks his thumb in his book. "Black howlers. The locals call them baboons."

"You know everything, don't you?" I glance again at my map. "It's not so far from Belize City."

"No, maybe an hour away."

"You've been there?"

"Sure. It's nothing fancy, but it's worth a trip. The guide goes with you in the forest and calls the monkeys down. If you're lucky, he'll have a howling contest with one of the males. I'll take you there sometime."

Rowan says the last part so matter-of-factly, it takes me a second to catch it. Despite how sketchy and secretive he was acting while on the phone, I break into a grin. "Is that right?"

"Fairy-child, if only you should take my hand, I would show you things beyond your wildest dreams."

My expression makes him laugh. "What's that from?"

"Some book I read."

"I should have known." I pause. "Did she follow?"

"How could she resist? Of course, she ended up devoured. But at least she saw some far-out sights beforehand." Rowan returns to his book.

Still feeling sort of fluttery, I locate Laughingbird Caye on my map. It's part of a constellation of islands off Belize's northern coast, shaped like a half-moon. I fold the map and trade it for my sketchbook. I flip to a blank page, consider drawing a baboon, and draw the Global Vagabonds hysterical giraffe logo instead. Rowan doesn't glance at me once.

I want to keep going, but I can't concentrate. Because of the rain, all the windows are shut. The bus is an oven of exhaled breath. I wedge my knees against the seat in front of me, like Starling does. The vinyl makes a ripping noise. I drop my feet.

"How do people *do* this?"

Rowan closes his book again. "Do what?"

"Get around."

"Belizeans? The same way we do. They drive or take the bus."

"I meant other travelers. Not travelers like *us*—I mean travelers with money. Somehow, I doubt they take chicken buses."

"They rent cars. Or they fly."

"There's a plane?"

"Sure. Belize has a couple local airlines."

"How long does it take?"

"From Punta Gorda to Belize City? Maybe half an hour. If the plane stops in Placencia or Dangriga, an hour. Flights are expensive, though."

I look out the window. Spindly, wind-bent trees dot the countryside, broken occasionally by rivers or canals. Gashes of red mud streak the roadside. A mountain range looms hazily in the distance. As I watch, we pass a solitary concrete house on stilts, with a black dog panting on the porch. "In a plane," I say, "you'd miss the scenery up close. The way we see it."

"Travelers like us?" he says with a grin.

I recall what I said and elbow him in the side. Still smiling, Rowan tips his head against the window and closes his eyes.

I try to sleep, but can't. So I make a list instead.

Annoying things about backpacking
Sleep deprivation.

*Backpackers who stink like old wet
    laundry.*

*Putting on your backpack. (It's fine once
    it's on, but slinging it onto your back is
    like using a single arm to lift an
    extremely fat seven-year-old, or maybe
    even a nine-year-old in my case.)*

*A constantly gurgling stomach, even if you
    just ate.*

*That permanently soggy place between
    your back and your backpack.*

*Something always aches. (Like your
    calves, or your shoulders, or the place
    where your shoe rubs your heel or
    your flip-flops gash the wedge between
    your toes.)*

Something always itches.

176

Below I draw an archetypal backpacker pair. I'm careful to make them anonymous, but the girl still looks a little too much like Starling.

At a bus stop in the middle of nowhere—seriously, I haven't seen a house for like half an hour—a mustached man in a suit and tie climbs aboard. He sets a briefcase on the front seat and stands in the aisle. His pants are too short, and I catch a flash of scrunchy white socks, the Hooters Girls kind from the eighties.

"Greetings, friends!"

He launches into a monologue so heartfelt I wouldn't be surprised if he dropped to one knee and started reciting Shakespeare. I assume he's some sort of salesman, though I can't understand 90 percent of what he's saying. I thought Belizeans spoke English. Finally, he opens his case and whips out his extolled merchandise: a stick of Halls cough drops.

Magic pills to cure all your ills! I stifle a giggle and glance at Rowan. He's sleeping. It reminds me of Glenna's incorrigible napping when I first saw the lake.

Glenna. I haven't thought of her in a while. I hope she's found some quality beads.

The monologue continues as the salesman brandishes product after product, distributing them through the rows of passengers. A portable sewing kit. A pack of neon orange circle stickers, the sort people use at garage sales. Notebooks with fake leather covers. Glitter body spray. A pair of those narrow wraparound glasses with prisms in the lenses, so everything you look at turns to rainbows.

On impulse, I wave him over.

"What would you like?" he asks in perfect English.

"The glasses." I dig through the pocket of my shorts for my easy-access cash. I haven't been wearing my money belt. I pull out a wad of paper, but it's not money—it's our list of off-limits topics. Soaked. Nothing left but a gummy wad of wood pulp.

"What language were you just speaking?" I ask the salesman as I search my other pocket.

"Kriol. The national language of Belize."

"The national language isn't English?"

"English is our official language. But it isn't *Belizean*."

"Oh." I finally find some cash, and we swap.

I put on my glasses and look at Rowan. He transforms into an expressionist painting. Rainbows bounce off his eyebrows. His hair shines in a halo of color.

I count back the days we've traveled together. Tomorrow is Sunday. If I include Chichicastenango—I'd never count the airport; let's erase that from the universe—it's been eight days. A little over a week. According to Olivia's older sister, college relationships count as double in dorm-time. That is, when both parties are living together in the dorms, a three-month relationship is really six months. If that's true, how accelerated are travel relationships? Or in this case, travel friendships? They have to be similar—people colliding at warp speed, sharing breakfasts and bedrooms and secrets. So what's a week, then? Three weeks? A month?

No matter how I multiply, it's no time at all.

I stick my map in my sketchbook and shut it. Maybe when I get home, I'll put maps up all over my bedroom walls like the guy in the Panajachel café—I'm sure my dad would approve. Actually, make that my dorm room walls. My boring dorm room, at my boring fallback college, where I major in something boring and make boring friends.

The walls of art school dorms probably resemble Jackson Pollock paintings.

I think back to what Rowan said about the monkey sanctuary: he'd take me sometime. He was joking, I'm sure. He knows I'm here only another ten days, and we'll be on the island for most of them. He knows I'm supposed to attend college in the fall.

We've never talked about that, though.

I've definitely never told him how uncertain I'm feeling.

179

How I gave up on attending SCAA, even after I knew Toby wouldn't be there. How I never mailed in my housing forms for state, so I might have screwed up my chances of attending any school at all. How I have no idea what's waiting for me on the other end of this trip—a thought that terrifies me but, in a strange way, exhilarates me too. I haven't told him much at all.

I wonder how that affects my calculations.

Outside, the storm is beginning to break. As the sun shifts in the clouds, the light coming through the windows makes Rowan shimmer. He's almost unreal. Even now, when I close my eyes, I can hardly picture him. And yet when I open my eyes, here he is—sleeping beside me, with his forehead against the bus window. So close I can hear him breathe.

The bus strikes a pothole. People curse, but Rowan doesn't wake up.

It reminds me of the time my dad forgot to take his insulin. You'd think he'd get one of those automated contraptions, but he's too stubborn. He passed out with his eyes open. After giving him his insulin, with remarkable composure, my mom pressed his eyes shut with her palm, as if he were a corpse in the movies. While she called an ambulance, I just stared at his eyelids, waiting for them to spring open again. He was fine. And it was one of the most tender moments I'd ever seen between my parents. But for a second . . .

My stomach knots up. It's enough for me to tap Rowan's shoulder. He jolts, like I've pulled him from a bad dream. "What? What is it?"

"I just . . . I thought we were here."

He glances out the window. Nothing but miles of empty beach forest. "Here?"

180

I shrug helplessly.

"I know what you look like!" he announces, as if he were contemplating it the entire time he was napping. "You look like the blind guy from *Star Trek*."

"You're just jealous," I tell him, adjusting my glasses. "I now see the world in Technicolor."

15

Day 10
Belize City

Rowan sits beside the taxi driver, a fat man who chomps jalapeño-flavored Pringles as he drives, periodically wiping his fingers on his seat. I sit in back with my head sticking out the window, until I nearly get decapitated by a stop sign.

"Hey, Bria," Rowan says, leaning around the passenger seat. He's been quieter than usual all morning, and his voice comes as a surprise.

"What's up?"

"I've been thinking. . . ."

I wait patiently.

"Do you want to stay another night in the city?"

"Another night?" I wrinkle my nose at the window. We spent last night at a crummy guesthouse where everything was wicker and floral: wicker chairs, wicker tables, floral curtains, floral sheets on our bunk beds. This morning, we wandered around town. I expected Belize City to resemble Guatemala City, with masses of people, clogged highways, skyscrapers, Pizza Huts. But Belize City's only a fraction of the size, which means a different kind of chaos. Everything's damp and windblown, slanting toward the sea. Instead of stoplights, there are roundabouts, crammed with honking vans and taxis, locals on bikes. It's fine. But the city's not somewhere I want to spend a second night, especially with *la isla bonita* and the legendary Lobsterfest just a short boat ride away.

"I'm just not in a huge hurry to get to the island," Rowan says.

"Why not?"

"No real reason." He's trying to look breezy, I think, but it's not working. "It's just—there'll just be loads of people there."

Our cab veers around a group of teenage boys on bikes. One of them knocks on the roof of the cab, and our driver brandishes a fat fist out the window.

"There are loads of people here," I tell Rowan.

"Strangers."

I stare at him a moment before I figure it out.

He's talking about all the island's *non*-strangers—people who know him. Who *knew* him. Maybe even people who participated in the unscrupulous crash landing Starling alluded to—like the notorious dive partner.

All right. I get that. But here's what I *don't* get: why in the world did Rowan take the island job in the first place if going back is such a hazard? We've traveled all this way. And now

183

that we're almost there, it's like he suddenly doesn't trust himself.

"Also," he adds, "there's a chance our boat will be grounded, if the storm's offshore. Lightning and all that."

I blink at him. "Lightning? I thought you said lightning couldn't strike a boat."

"That's ridiculous. When did I say that?"

"Yesterday morning!"

He pauses, then looks sheepish. "You're right. I just figured there was nothing we could do about it, since we were already on the boat, so why worry you?"

He didn't lie to be bossy—he lied to be sweet. I know this, because we're talking Rowan, not Toby, but my stomach clenches anyway. I was just starting to forget all that Liat stuff, and now here he goes again. The most frustrating part is I can't be mad.

Because I lied too.

The cab pulls up in front of the water taxi terminal. We pay our driver and haul our backpacks onto the sidewalk. I can hear the ocean slapping against the boats. A maritime funk hangs in the air, salt and fish and boat exhaust.

"Are you angry?" Rowan asks.

I hate when people ask that. Somehow, it makes your anger seem less valid.

"I'm just sick of you guys shielding me from things," I say. "I may not be as well traveled as you, but I can *handle* it. I'm not *entirely* dependent on you. It's just that I don't know a damn thing about these countries. . . ."

Rowan sighs exasperatedly. "Have you even tried? You can always read a guidebook, you know. I've seen them at every book exchange. Or go to an Internet café and Google it! I

184

told you, the information's out there. There's no excuse for ignorance when you travel."

A knot jerks my throat. "*Thanks*, Rowan. It's great to know how you really feel about me."

"All I'm saying is—"

"Don't worry, I *know* what you're saying—that traveling with me is a drag. It's a shame you didn't invite a street-savvy girl across the lake, but then again, a girl like that wouldn't have fallen for your stupid prank."

"It's not about you, Bria! I told you—I don't travel with anyone."

"Why?"

He shakes his head. "Not important."

"Of course. It's part of the past! Can't talk about *that*."

A car horn honks, and we have to cram ourselves up against the side of a building to let the vehicle squeeze by. Above us, there's a rambling billboard for Dano instant milk powder: PROBABLY THE BEST MILK POWDER IN THE WORLD. I wish I could laugh. At the milk powder. At all this lunacy, made so momentous. But right now, I just can't find the funny.

Suddenly, Rowan grabs my backpack and takes off down the street.

"Rowan!" I yell after him. "Come *on*!"

I kick his backpack, which he left beside me. It tumbles over. Immediately, I feel guilty: after a while, backpacks seem more like travel companions than inanimate objects. Rowan knew perfectly well that stealing my backpack would force me to follow him, and that I'm too nice to leave his backpack behind. At least it's lighter than mine.

I dodge pedestrians, cross a small park, and stop beside him at a promontory overlooking the sea. A red-and-white lighthouse looms overhead. Below us, waves burst against a wall of rocks. Rowan sets my backpack on the ground, and I quickly swap it for his. Just in case I need to make a quick getaway.

"You're only trying to make us miss the water taxi," I say.

"Not true . . . I just don't think we should go to the island angry."

"Why, is that some big no-no? Like going to bed angry?"

"Maybe it should be."

Way out in the gloom, a cruise ship disgorges passengers into ferries. I wonder if they're just as disappointed by Rowan's Caribbean as I am.

"I want you to trust me," he says. "Don't you?"

I look at him. In the stormy light, his eyes look dark, almost black. Toby's are pale blue. They couldn't look more different. They couldn't act more different. But there are similarities between them, too—ones I can't ignore any longer.

"I've caught you lying twice now," I tell him. "If you have trouble being honest about little things, how can you expect me to trust you with everything else?"

"What was my other lie?"

"Liat."

Rowan squints at the non-sun. "You're right. I'm sorry. I don't know why I did that. Although I didn't lie, exactly." He cuts me off before I can object. "But I didn't tell the truth, either, which is almost as bad. Did she tell you any . . . stories?"

"Not really. I stopped her before she could."

He stares at me. "You did? Why?"

"I didn't mean anything noble by it. I was just scared of the truth." I shrug. "But she did tell me your past was wild. . . .

186

I think she called it a 'nonstop rave.'" She also said diving was just a front, but I need proof before I accuse Rowan of something like that.

"See, that's exactly what I'm afraid of, Bria. I don't want you to look at me differently. And if you knew what a mess I was back then, you would."

"I don't know if I would," I say quietly.

"You would. Believe me. The Rowan you know is the good-parts version."

"Really? Okay, *now* I'm scared."

He smiles. "In all honesty, I thought we were doing okay. This is all new to me. I've never been forced into this situation before—I've never gotten to the point where anyone *wants* to know about me. Other than places to go, places I've been."

"No one's *forcing* you to do anything."

"That came out wrong."

"It's okay. After all, Starling signed you up for this. She did a great job of matchmaking, didn't she? Look at us: we're both screwed up."

He shakes his head. "I'm screwed up, you mean."

A massive wave bursts in front of us. Rowan grabs my waist and pulls me away, so we miss the worst of the spray. When he lets go, he seems to do it almost reluctantly, dropping his hands into his pockets and backing away.

"Know what the shittiest part about all this is?" he says. "It's that I'm making everything a bigger deal by keeping it quiet."

I know exactly what he means.

"If you really want to know, Bria, at some point, I'll fill you in. On everything. Just . . . not right now, okay?" He sweeps his hand over the horizon. "Looks like the storm's clearing. I guess it's now or never, right?"

He takes a step toward the road, but I grab his backpack to stop him.

"Before we go . . . there's something I need to tell you." I try to smile. I probably look like a Claymation monster, pinched into existence. "And by telling you, I don't mean it any way other than as a statement of fact. So you have to promise not to read anything into it."

"I'm not sure what that means, but okay. I promise."

"I lied," I say.

"You lied?"

"Because I wasn't over it. Lying was just another way to hang on to the past . . . like some kind of security blanket. But now I'm ready to put it behind me. The thing I lied about." I look away when I say it. "I don't have a boyfriend. Anymore. We broke up before the trip."

There's a silence. A silence that carries the weight of a thousand anvils. I feel myself cringing as I anticipate the crush.

"Oh," Rowan says.

He thinks I'm such a loser. I know it. What kind of girl lies about having a boyfriend? Or having broken up with one? I cross my arms over my daypack and start heading back toward the water taxi terminal, trying not to cry, because the only thing that could embarrass me worse is crying in front of Rowan.

Then I feel the tiniest pressure behind me. I glance over my shoulder. Rowan is resting his hand on my backpack. And somehow, it makes me feel better.

188

Then, right before we pass through the doorway of the terminal, he leans toward me.

"I get it," he says. "You're running too."

Things Toby said that should have made me dump him instantly:
"You didn't really include that fairy drawing, did you?"
"Maybe it was the diversity factor—Sandoval sounds Latino."
"I thought it was more of a professional school, is all."
"Isn't that a man's head on a woman's body?"
"You have so much potential."

Toby was sitting at his art table, leaning over an expensive pad of bristol board, when I arrived at his house. I rapped my knuckles on the doorjamb and he jumped, slamming the pad shut. Like I'd caught him cheating on me. It sure felt like it. He was supposed to be the wounded one, and yet *he* was having no problem drawing.

Almost two months had passed since fast-track admissions were announced. Acceptances were overdue. But every time I'd broached the subject with Toby, he'd changed it. Usually by groping me and trying to lead me out to his car. That day I was determined we'd talk, and nothing else. Even if I had to force the sentences out of him with a piece of charcoal to the jugular.

"I was just searching online," I began. "About housing at

the academy. We have a few choices. I thought we might want to stay in the same building. . . ."

Toby opened his pad of bristol again without replying. Why was he making this so awkward? Had it really been only a couple of months earlier we were laughing together? Maybe we never did, and I'd turned the past into a fantasy. Just like our future one, which faded with every second of his silence.

"There's something I should tell you, Bria."

In moments of half clarity, I knew my relationship with Toby was a sand castle pummeled by waves. I should have been the one to kick it over—to break up with him—a million times, for a million reasons. But instead, I kept scaling the walls to higher towers, trying to avoid its inevitable collapse. Which meant I set myself up for the fall that came next.

"I'm going to Chicago."

"For a trip?"

"For college."

I sank onto his bed. "What are you talking about?"

"I got into the Art Institute of Chicago. I'd be crazy not to go there—it's a great school."

"So's SCAA!"

He exhales. "Sure it is. But it's not Chicago. I'd be crazy if I didn't take the chance to live somewhere like that."

"But . . . that means you applied months ago. Why didn't you tell me?"

There was so much condescension in his smile I wanted to pry it from his face. "You're right," he said. "I should have told you earlier. But you were just so excited about going to the academy together . . . I didn't want to disappoint you."

I balled my fists so hard they cramped. He knew he was

190

wrecking me, and I knew he knew it, and still I couldn't make myself behave. "But I didn't apply to other art schools!"

"That's your fault, Bria. You can't blame me for your own self-sabotage."

And therein lay the shittiest part of all this: he was right. I gambled my future on a lopsided relationship, all because of a promise. It was the promise of a fantasy: two kindred spirits (okay, I despise that term, but you know what I mean) united by a love for art and—I thought—for each other. Exactly what my combative, incompatible parents never had. It wasn't that Toby was faking his feelings for me. But he wanted me only as long as he could believe he was better.

For the first time, I realized that.

And for the first time, I was *pissed off*. That he'd kept all this from me. Hid the truth so that every decision I'd made in the last few months I'd fumbled at blindfolded—without the knowledge I needed to do what was best for myself. Too bad it took my fantasy castle crashing around me to make me see clearly.

I stepped forward. Opened my mouth.

And before I could speak, *he* dumped *me*.

"Look," he said. "It's been fun, Bria, but it's obvious we're going our separate ways. We might as well not drag it out all summer, you know?"

There's nothing that can quite describe the feeling. All that power and fury boiling through my veins sealed up before I could vent it. I'm sure Toby had known what was about to happen. He'd seen the determination on my face. At long last, I'd been ready to do what I should have done ages earlier—dump the boy who'd helped take my art.

But he took that from me too.

I look up as the water taxi approaches the dock. It's the biggest boat we've taken so far. A substantial crowd has gathered around us, lugging suitcases, backpacks, and boxes of Tang and Quaker Oats. "Ready?" Rowan asks me.

I close my sketchbook—careful not to slam it—and tuck it inside my daypack while Rowan watches mildly. For once, I don't care. I'm not going to hide it anymore. That doesn't mean I'm going to show him all my drawings, but I'm not going to be ashamed, either.

Because I've decided this is it. I'm finished. I am closing Toby inside these pages. On the island, and every day after, for the rest of my life, I'll be new.

I'm done looking back.

"Ready."

PART
3

The Island

Art to me is seeing. I think you have got to use your eyes, as well as your emotion, and one without the other just doesn't work.

~*Andrew Wyeth*

A painting doesn't have to have a profound meaning. It doesn't have to "say" a word. We fall in love for simpler reasons.

~*Harley Brown*

16

Day 10, Evening
Laughingbird Caye

Something about the mainland must attract clouds. Because as soon as the water taxi pulls out of the harbor and into open water, they fall away. The ocean changes from gray to blue. Then, gradually, as the setting sun spears it and the sandy floor nears the surface, it brightens to a luminous turquoise.

"I told you!" Rowan shouts over the roar.

When I turn to grin at him, I find his face just inches from mine. We're sitting hip to hip with Belizeans of every variety: buff guys with tiny children, teenagers in booty shorts with manicured nails, a trio of white women with beads in their hair, an enormously fat man in a yellow Lakers jersey. When the guy to my left leans over to tie his shoe, I catch a peek of his boxers: red, with cartoon hamburgers and french fries.

There are almost as many travelers as there are locals. Rowan assured me Laughingbird Caye is primarily a backpacker destination, but some of the girls resemble Olivia more than Starling.

Island after island floats by in the distance, each a squat patch of green bordered by tiny threads of white. The wind makes my eyes tear up, but I can't stop looking.

"That's it," Rowan says. "That's Laughingbird Caye."

I'm a little confused, because all I see is a strip of mangroves. But as we speed alongside it, houses begin to appear: boxy structures on tall stilts, with decks, painted lemon yellow and purple and Caribbean green. Docks protrude like wooden fingers, and coconut trees tilt at precarious angles. Pelicans with tousled heads hover in the wind.

The young guys driving the boat cut the engine and the current surges around us. I lean over the edge and gaze into the clear water as we head to shore. The sandy floor is mottled with sea grass, and I can see every blade of it. Black-and-yellow fish dart in and out.

"They're like bumblebees," I say to Rowan.

He smiles at me, but it looks more like a wince.

"What's on your mind?" I ask.

"Don't be mad."

I feel a little nervous. "I won't."

"I was just thinking how it's too bad you won't see all the fish up close. You'd have to get in the water for that."

I don't say anything.

But while Rowan collects our backpacks, I kneel at the edge of the dock. I can hear two sets of waves: the tiny ones lapping at the shore and, out at sea, bigger ones surging against the reef—the second-largest barrier reef in the world.

The breeze shudders in the palms. And for the first time, I finally feel the distance between me and Toby, me and my parents, me and the life I've left behind: hundreds, thousands of miles, even millions.

I feel like I can do anything.

Rowan's standing beside me, one backpack in each arm. We're the only ones left on the dock. "Sure you're prepared for this?" he asks.

"Prepared for what?"

"The madness." He smiles that strange smile again, the wincey one I can't decipher.

The engine of the water taxi starts, and I glance over. A new crowd is sardined inside it, their vacation at an end. Like mine will be in just ten days. Half my trip's already passed. It makes me feel like crying. I wish there were a way to make time slow down.

"I guess," I say.

But I don't get up. I spread my hands on the dock. It's baked warm, even though the sun is almost gone. Then I lean back until I'm lying down, both my hands flat against the gray wood. I try to take up as much surface as possible, absorbing the lingering sunlight, the anticipation of tomorrow.

I hear Rowan kneel beside me. I glance over at him, and he smiles at me; it's a real one this time. "I guess there's no hurry," he says.

I pat the dock, and he obliges, lying on his stomach with his cheek on his arms and closing his eyes. I watch him for a while, feeling sort of possessive. Whatever Rowan's been through in the years that separate us, now he's just trying to be good. It's ironic, almost, that I'm trying to be the opposite.

"Thank you," I say.

His eyelids flicker open. "For what?"

"For this." I reach toward the horizon, grasping at it with my fingers. "All of it. I wouldn't be here without you. And I haven't thanked you yet."

"It's nothing. My pleasure."

I tip my head to the side so I'm facing the sea. But I'm still aware of him, lying beside me.

All of a sudden, the dock starts to vibrate, then pound. I shriek and sit up as a spray of water hits me in the face. A dripping-wet, massively tall guy has thrown himself on top of Rowan's back.

Rowan curses, reaching around to swat him. "Get off me, you ogre. Bria . . . meet Jack."

Jack kisses Rowan on top of his head, then rolls off. With a start, I recognize him: the third backpacker from the airport. Minus the stocking cap, his head's shaved down to a layer of sheer blond fuzz. His apish arms dwarf Rowan's. When he extends a hand to shake, mine disappears. "You've got to be the dive partner," I say.

"Divemaster," Rowan interjects, sitting up. "He leads the classes. I just assist."

"In other words, he gets paid even worse than I do," Jack says. He has an accent—probably Scandinavian, although I can't deduce which country. "He just can't stick in one place long enough to finish his training."

"That's because he's afflicted with . . . ," I begin, but stop myself just in time.

"How's Marius?" Rowan asks.

"Sick as a dog. He's staying with his parents in San Ignacio. You've saved us, my friend. All the dive shops are booked. The island's already packed, even though Lobsterfest isn't for days. People want to get their dives in before they're too bombed to see the fishies. We can help with that, too—"

"I'm not helping with anything. How many students do we have?"

Jack laughs and tugs Rowan's ponytail. "We'll talk about it later. But yeah, we've got four students. Or five, maybe—is she diving?"

They're both looking at me. Rowan shakes his head. "She won't dive."

In the wake of their weird exchange, his comment bristles me more than ever. I don't want this new guy thinking I'm afraid of the water. Even if I sort of am.

"How do you know, if you've never asked?"

Rowan looks at me like I've sprouted moose antlers. "Fine, Bria. Do you want to dive?"

"Probably not."

He exhales noisily. Jack grins at me, then Rowan, displaying a pair of cavernous dimples. "She's a challenge, isn't she? This is great. You've found yourself a brand-new Starling!"

Rowan and I avoid each other's eyes.

"Oh, come on," Jack says, grabbing my arm and hauling me to my feet. My head reaches only his chest. "Our friends are waiting at the shop. With boatloads of rum punch—my special recipe." He lifts both our backpacks and, with one on each shoulder, heads for shore.

"Show-off," Rowan mutters.

17

Day 11
Island Life

"Rowan's got Hyperactive Diver Disorder," Jack tells me at breakfast.

I glance at Rowan. He's sitting at the other end of the table, nursing a mug of coffee. He hasn't touched his fry jack: warty-looking parcels of deep-fried dough. We're sitting around a picnic table outside the dive shop, the color of a ruby red grapefruit. A stack of yellow kayaks sits beside it. It's built over the water, which I can hear sloshing beneath my feet. Though it's just before nine, the dive instructors from last night's festivities are there—even the most prolific drinkers.

"That sounds a little dangerous," I reply.

"He doesn't have it when he's teaching, luckily. No, then

he's responsible. He only comes down with it when left to his own devices."

"What does he do?"

Jack stabs a wedge of pineapple and brandishes his fork. "Sometimes he zooms around like Superman, all drunk off his senses, rushing to take in as much as possible. And then other times he'll find something *pretty* and hover in front of it for like fifty percent of his bottom time while his dive buddy— usually that's me—has to wait around."

"Sounds like our Rowan," says Devon.

Devon's one of the dive shop owners. She's thirty or so, with strawberry blond hair and skin the exact color and texture of a baseball glove. The sight of it last night frightened me into applying extra sunscreen this morning.

"I'll drink to that," adds Clement, the other owner and Devon's boyfriend. He's Belizean, with muscles that resemble ropes of onions.

They're right. It *does* sound like Rowan. I still can't get over how long these people have known him. And despite the shadowlands of his past, everybody seems to adore him.

The dive shop served as the headquarters for last night's celebration. Islanders and instructors from other companies swarmed on the dock and inside the bedroom-sized space, swigging rum punch from plastic cups. I don't know if Jack's recipe is representative of Belizean rum punch in general, but after last night, I'd rather drink rainwater collected in a spare tire.

Jack's Rum Punch Recipe
Orange juice
Pineapple juice

201

Cashew wine
The dregs of every booze bottle from the
back of the cupboard

Pour everything into big yellow keg
stenciled with McDonald's logo and stir
with chunk of driftwood until beverage
tastes of rotting seaweed.
Serve!

At twenty-one, Jack's both old enough and gigantic
enough to make me feel like a spooked mouse. Apparently,
he's the one who taught Rowan to dive two years ago. Since
then, they've worked at various dive schools, most notably in
Honduras, where they got into "the best sort of mischief."
Before Jack could elaborate, Rowan materialized and steered
the conversation away.

Jack wasn't the only one thrilled to see Rowan. All the
divers adored him. He was their muse, their idol, their little
brother. At his side, I became an instant celebrity. When I
explained he and I weren't together—not, you know, like
that—they almost fell over.

Every single one of them. Like diver dominoes.

Rowan wasn't exaggerating—their version of him is entirely different from mine. Which version deserves the "Good
Parts" status is arguable, though.

But as the night progressed, I began to realize that no one
knew Rowan *well*. The dive instructors tripped over Starling's
name: Sterling, someone called her, while others shortened it
to Star. Their recollections clashed as well. Depending on
who I talked to, Rowan had been in Vietnam or Ecuador last

March. He'd befriended a wounded monkey, or a coatimundi in a Latin American cloud forest, and sobbed when he had to set it free. In December or November, he drank too much rum punch, or smoked too much ganja—what everyone here calls marijuana—and swam across the island's channel to sleep in the mangrove forest. Or he'd done the same thing totally sober, but naked. Unsurprisingly, he was always playing pranks on unsuspecting tourists. Convincing them Icy Hot worked as insect repellent. Directing them to far-flung hotels and idyllic beaches that didn't exist.

Several times I caught him watching me, looking sheepish.

Which means there have to be *some* truths. All night, I gathered the stories like puzzle pieces of Rowan's history, trying to match them together. And what fit formed a much different illustration than the one I sketched in my head.

Maybe Rowan was a bad boy.

But he was a *fun* one.

I glance at him now as he sips his coffee and try to imagine him crashing through the mangroves, high as a satellite, a CENSORED brick hovering over his lower parts. I admit: it's tough. Especially when I realize I've never seen him take a single sip of alcohol. He was the only sober one at the party.

Throughout the night, I wondered whether I should confront him about what Jack said on the dock: *We can help with that, too!* Getting people bombed, it seemed. But in the aftermath of all Rowan's non-partying, I'm glad I didn't get the chance. Rowan wants me to trust him. I owe it to him to try. And anyway, people on this island seem to have no problem getting bombed on their own.

"No more," I tell Jack, covering my cup as he attempts to top off my mimosa.

He laughs boomingly. "It's the best way to clear my head before a dive, I've found. But you never heard me say that."

"Well, I did," Rowan says. He leans over the table and grabs Jack's drink, dumping it over his shoulder into the sea.

"Intercepted by the ethics police," I joke.

"The ethics police?" Jack laughs again. "Rowan? That's rich."

Ignoring him, Rowan checks his dive watch. "It's nine. The students should be arriving."

Jack glances at his own dive watch, which looks like an entire computer strapped to his wrist. "Professor Spoilsport's right. We should head on over to the classroom—we're not diving, anyway. Day one's for bookwork. Bria?"

I have to tip my head back to look at him. "Yeah?"

"Don't get into any trouble." He reaches out and musses up my hair.

The instructors disperse, dropping cups and paper plates into a rusty trash barrel. Clement heads into the dive shop, Devon for the dive boat parked at the end of the dock. Rowan pauses beside me. "Sorry to abandon you like this."

"Why would you be sorry? It's your job. It's why we're here."

He shrugs. "If you need something to read, there's a book exchange in the Internet café, next to the ice cream shop on Front Street. You'll probably be drawing the whole time, anyway."

I smile. "Who knows?"

"Show me sometime?" He averts his eyes almost guiltily, all too aware he's violated our list. Unfortunately for me, it's pretty damned cute.

"We'll see," I reply.

"You can use any of the bikes behind the dive shop, by the way. The island's nothing but a squat, curved strip—kind of shaped like a bird's wing. It'll take you like half an hour to see the whole thing. Just make sure you lock up your bike wherever you go. And look out for potholes. . . ."

"You're protecting me again," I tease. "Don't worry, I'll be fine."

"I know you will."

"Just don't run off with any of your students." Oh God, I'm turning magenta. "Otherwise, Starling will feed me to the sharks." Nice save.

"Now who's protecting whom?" Rowan turns to go, then stops. "I almost forgot," he says, reaching into his daypack. "I grabbed this for you. If you can carve out some time for it between your picture-makings, I think you'll find it electrifying."

He holds up a book. Not just any book, but a worn-out old dive manual, mildewed, the photo on the cover flaking off.

I frown at it. "Rowan, you know I don't want that."

"It might grow on you."

"What, like a rash?" I open the book to its first page. "'Chapter One,'" I read. "'Let's Explore the Deep!' You've got to be kidding."

"Look," Rowan says. "The truth is . . . I thought it would be nice if you knew a little about what I do. Then I'd have someone to talk about it with. Other than the Swedish Lumberjack."

"Oh, you poor, poor thing. I can smell a guilt trip from a mile away." But because I know he's being sincere, I stuff the book into my daypack. Rowan beams.

Our hostel is a massive, rambling beach house painted neon yellow, with sprawling balconies, a common kitchen, and three levels of dorms. It's like a backpacker fun house. I get lost twice trying to find my room.

Pros & cons of staying in supersize backpacker hostels

Pros:
Low prices
Free bananas
Free make-your-own pancakes, aka
    panqueques
Fifteen minutes of free Internet daily
"Camaraderie"

Cons:
Bunk beds
Guys who start washing their socks in the
    sink of the coed shared bathroom even
    though you're standing there with a
    mouthful of toothpaste
Loud voices in the hallway when you're
    trying to sleep, and people who look at
    you like you're the spawn of Satan
    when you ask them to please quiet
    down a bit
Saggy mattresses
Dirty panqueque pans
Nocturnal naked piggyback rides down the
    hallway*

*I was not involved.

Last night, I was the only one in a six-bed girls-only dorm—Rowan's staying with Jack and Clement downstairs—but it looks like my new roommates stopped by while I was at breakfast. Their backpacks must have exploded, judging by the clothes draped over the bedposts, the beds, and even the fans.

I'm pretty certain I see spangles.

Although my roommates are probably busy in the classroom, I change into my swimsuit as quickly as I can in case they come back. I've never been one of those naked girls. Unlike Olivia, who takes it off whenever, wherever, including in Mexican border towns that will remain nameless.

My first stop is a gift shop, where I select a blank book with a red cover. New Bria, new journal.

"Mayan ladies made it," says the woman at the counter. She has to be over fifty, but she's dressed like a devout backpacker, in a shapeless tie-dyed dress and loops of beaded jewelry. When she reaches for a plastic bag, I notice a patch of gray hair in her armpit. "Some of the profits go to sustaining an indigenous community near the border."

Starling would be proud.

I consider borrowing a bike but decide to explore on foot. At first, I feel random and awkward and aimless without a destination. I visit my dorm room two more times, for absolutely no reason at all. I spend way too long picking out a candy bar in a Taiwanese-owned liquor store.

But eventually, I get the hang of it: wandering.

The populated portion of the island is less than a mile long, and two-thirds of it is residential. Those are the parts I like best. I pass houses with open doors, children playing in the sandy yards. I follow a trail through a thicket of mango trees. I kick a soccer ball back to a huddle of shouting kids, missing them by yards. Apparently, my skills haven't improved.

On the main street, I sift through the jewelry piled on folding tables, even though I know I don't really have the money to buy anything. There are beaded necklaces, hemp bracelets in Rasta colors, heavy wooden bangles. I wonder what the locals think when travelers wear their jewelry. Is it flattering, or does it make them look like poseurs? And what about the Mayan skirts for sale in Guatemala? Obviously, I'll never pass for Mayan. Although I'm about the right size.

On the next table, I find a giant basket of coconut rings, exactly like Starling's. There must be hundreds of them.

By the early afternoon, it's as hot as Hades. The heat inspires me to do what I meant to do all along—head to the swimming channel on the north side of the island, strip down to my eggplant bikini, and at least *look* at the ocean.

At the channel, a crooked cement pier extends over the water. A few people are sunbathing on top of it. They don't pay me any attention as I step over them, heading for an empty spot. I toss down my daypack, spread my towel, and for the first time, stick both my feet in the Caribbean. It's warm. Crabs skitter sideways over the sand, and spear-shaped predator fish hover over clouds of minnows. Green ribbons of sea grass sway in the current. Farther out, it looks like someone's swirled a turquoise-tipped finger across a canvas of deep blue.

Happiness begins at my toes and swells into my chest, until I'm beaming like a lunatic. A Belizean guy with cornrows in twin buns catches my eye and whistles. I know it looks like I'm grinning at him, but my face has frozen this way.

"Bria!"

I grin in the other direction.

Rowan's heading toward me, flanked by two half-clothed girls. It turns out my face isn't frozen, because I can feel my smile wilting. I look down quickly and catch an eyeful of my own nakedness. It's too late to cover up. *Act busy.* I tug my new sketchbook from my bag and begin to scribble, hating my sudden shyness. I don't know where it came from—this is *Rowan.* I've given him a mud unibrow, for crying out loud.

"Fancy finding you here." He crouches beside me and lifts his sunglasses.

I shrug. "It's the place to be."

"Actually, we saw you from the boat." He nods at the two girls standing behind him. "These are two of my students—your roommates, Emily and Ariel. They're from Florida. Eighteen, just like you."

We eye each other in that suspicious way that's such a betrayal of our gender. Ariel has long blond braids and wears a T-shirt over black bikini bottoms. Emily has cropped black hair and a double nose piercing. She wears tiny shorts and a yellow bikini top. They both hold bottles of Belikin beer. Their sunglasses are enormous. Spring Breakpackers, I presume.

"Are you an artist?" Emily asks, pointing to my sketchbook. "I am too. Can I see?"

I shove it into my daypack and zip it up.

"Yikes," she says.

I feel like a jerk. "Sorry. . . . It's just kind of personal."

"Just wait until you have a juried exhibition. *Then* it gets personal."

"There wasn't a jury!" Ariel objects. "Just teachers. And it wasn't an exhibition—it was a show in the school cafeteria."

"That still counts."

As they bicker, Rowan sits beside me. I pull my daypack onto my lap in an effort to cover a fraction of my nakedness. Why am I acting so strange? I am baffling myself. I have to remember these girls know Rowan even less than I do, and they have no problem with their respective lack of shorts and shirt.

"So how's your day been?" he asks, unaware.

"Hot. Yours?"

"Refreshing. The water felt great."

"You went in the water? I thought today was for, like, bookwork in the classroom."

"We took the boat out to the reef for a bit. Brought some snorkels, splashed around."

No wonder he seems so relaxed. I picture Ariel and Emily, entirely shirtless and shortsless, splashing around beside him. I clear my throat. "So what did you see underwater? Anything vicious?"

"One stingray."

"There aren't really stingrays. Really?"

"He was just a small one."

"It looked pretty big to me." Emily squats between us. "Bria, are you certified?"

Ugh. "No, I'm not."

"So why aren't you learning to dive with us?"

I sigh, because it's getting old. Last night I suffered through the interrogation of various drunk divers. Apparently, when you're a die-hard scuba aficionado, the nether regions of the sea equal nirvana.

It strikes me as strange Rowan hasn't spoken about diving much. Then I recall the way he guiltily slipped me the dive book. He probably doesn't want me to think he's pressuring me by talking about his greatest love. It makes me feel like an evil person.

"I'm sure it's amazing and all," I say diplomatically, "but it's just not my thing."

"Mine neither," Ariel says. "But I'm still doing it."

Emily smirks. "She's right. She was utterly chickenshit, but I convinced her."

"It didn't help that my parents wanted me to, and they paid for this trip."

"For *your* trip. I had to pay for mine."

"With money your parents gave you!"

"My parents don't even know I'm here," I say.

All three of them stare at me. Too late, I realize how it sounds—like I'm trying to make Emily and Ariel look bad. It's not like my money didn't come from my parents, technically, though I earned it doing paperwork and data entry for my father.

"What are you—like, a runaway?" Ariel asks.

Quickly, I shake my head. "What I mean is . . . my parents know I'm in Central America. But they don't know I'm on this island. They think I'm with a tour group. Rowan and his sister helped me escape." I grin, like it's just so incredibly funny.

"So you're *kind of* a runaway."

"That's pretty intense," Emily says, looking at me with obvious respect.

"Your parents still think you're with that tour group?" Rowan asks. He leans back on his hands so he can see me better.

"It doesn't matter. They wouldn't care."

"But have you talked to them at all?"

I don't like the tone of his voice. It makes me feel anxious, even though I'm not exactly sure what I've done wrong. "Rowan, you know I haven't. You've been around me the whole time. What's the big deal, anyway? I'm eighteen."

"Eighteen is only a few months away from seventeen."

"And nineteen's only a few months from eighteen," I argue, even though I know he's almost twenty, so that isn't exactly true. But he ran off a couple of weeks after he turned

212

eighteen. He told me at the lake; I'll never forget it. So why's he acting all self-righteous?

"How do you know that Marcy lady didn't call them?" he says. "According to what you said, she seemed pretty irate. I can picture it now: 'We last saw your daughter with some hippie druggie girl, and we're terrified she's gone and joined one of those jungle cults you hear about down here, one of those Jim Jones things—'"

"Rowan, would you stop? It's my business whether I call my parents or not."

"I suppose." With one finger, he taps his sunglasses so they fall over his eyes. "But I still think it's immature."

I feel like I've been punched. "Well, do *your* parents know where you are?"

"My parents are off-limits," he says, unfazed. "Remember our list?"

My jaw drops. I can't believe Rowan brought up our list in front of these strangers. Even though it's been only a few days since we wrote it, the thought of it humiliates me. Especially after our conversation yesterday in Belize City. I thought we'd moved past that.

"What list?" asks Ariel.

"Never mind." I stand up. "Look, I'll catch you all later. This heat is making me sleepy." I dig through my daypack until I locate my shirt. I feel three pairs of eyes watching as I tug it over my head, get stuck for a disconcerting second, and then yank it into place.

I don't notice Rowan following me until my first foot hits the sand. "*What?*" I demand.

He holds up his hands. "Wow—you're prickly today."

213

"I refuse to validate that with an answer."

"It wasn't a question."

I try to stalk away, but Rowan catches my daypack and swings me back around. It might be cute if I didn't feel like slapping him with a stingray.

"Look," he says. "I really do think it's important you give your parents a call. Or an email, or whatever. Just so we don't have to think about it for the rest of the trip. I don't want to see your face on CNN . . ." He trails off. "Okay, sorry. No more jokes. But—you'll talk to them. Right?"

I wonder why it bothers him so much. I hate to back down, but I don't want to fight. On this island, he's all I've got. "Sure, Rowan," I say with a sigh. "Of course I will."

I just don't say when.

18

Day 11
Friends or Siblings or Whatever

"But Rowan's so hot," Ariel says, too close to my ear. "You *sure* you're not sleeping together?"

"I'm pretty sure," I reply.

We're sitting on rope swings at an outdoor bar called Coco Plum. There's no floor, only sand. As soon as we arrived, Emily ditched Ariel to go flirt with the other two dive students: a pair of dreadlocked guys who'd look like twins if they didn't have different-colored skin. Ariel, however, seems to have one particular guy in mind. A guy who was supposed to show up an hour ago.

"If I was traveling alone with Rowan for a week, you'd better believe I'd have jumped him by now," she tells me. "Have you seen his back?"

"His back?"

"He's so cut. Emily says he's like some kind of rock star, all drug-damaged and wild under this balladsy surface. After you left the channel, Jack came and told us all these stories about him. Rowan got kind of agitated. It was cute."

I find myself wishing I had been there to defend him, or at least to deflect Jack's attention. Although I admit I'm curious about the stories.

"Like did you know he used to twirl fire batons?" Ariel asks.

"He *what?*"

"You'd think he'd have caught fire, with all the stuff he was on. He swears he isn't like that anymore, but you *know* the crazy is just waiting to come out again. . . ." She winds one of her long blond braids around her arm. "So you sure you're not sleeping together? Because if not, I've got to get him before Emily does. Don't you think he's hot?"

"If you like the unwashed bohemian type," I say, feeling mean.

"His eyes are the color of dark blue jeans, did you notice?"

I try not to scowl, despising the way I feel. I know I don't have any right to Rowan. But even though I suspect Ariel isn't his type any more than I am, her comments make my skin itch. And since it appears he isn't going to show up anytime soon, I decide I've had enough.

"I've had enough . . . to drink. I think I'm going to bed."

Ariel perks up. "Do you think Rowan's back at the hostel? Want me to walk you?"

"It's okay. Really. He's in bed, I'm sure. He goes to bed early. Or sometimes he reads, but he doesn't like to be disturbed. . . ." I shut myself up.

"See you tomorrow, then."

I nod. "Tomorrow."

I leave my drink on the bar and shuffle through the sand toward the exit, where I almost bump into Jack. "Bria! You're not leaving already?" He stands so close I have to crane my neck to meet his crinkling eyes. "Or are you off to see Rowan?"

I shake my head so adamantly he grins, dimples slashing his cheeks. "I'm just tired. You people wear me out."

"Just you wait. Lobsterfest blows this all away. It's like your favorite dream and your worst nightmare drowned together in an ocean of rum punch."

"Can't wait."

I take a step toward the exit, but Jack doesn't move. He smells like fabric softener. It reminds me I need to do my laundry. I could ask Jack where he does his, but I don't really want to draw out the conversation—even though he's attractive in a big, goofy, Scandinavian way. "So I guess I'll see you tomorrow morning," I say pointedly, wondering if I'll have to shove.

"Probably not. We'll be in the water by seven-thirty. Then back in the classroom. Then back in the water again. You won't see us until four, four-thirty for the next few days. Our classes are intense—it's really too bad you're not taking them. They pay shit, though, so it's good we've got a few things in the works on the side."

The beach has turned to quicksand. "Who's *we?*"

"Don't worry. I won't get your travel brother into trouble, I promise."

Jack reaches out and musses up my hair, like he did this morning. When I slap his hand away, he catches mine and twirls me around before freeing me to go.

217

I find Rowan on the rooftop verandah of our hostel, relaxing in a hammock with his eyes closed. As usual, a book rests on his lap: *Lolita*. He's wearing clothes I haven't seen before—a baby blue linen shirt and frayed white shorts. It's unfair. He keeps coming up with clothes I haven't seen, while I'm already rewearing everything. His backpack's like a perpetually expanding magic trick.

Should I tell him what Jack said? Or should I give him an opening to tell me? The problem with our mutual touchiness is all the uncertainty: I don't know what will seem like distrust. I'm about to bring it up anyway when I notice the plastic cup balanced on a ledge beside him.

"Are you drunk?" I ask in disbelief.

Rowan opens his eyes. "Hey, you." He stretches, sending the book tumbling to the ground. "I was wondering when you'd show up. The drink's yours."

"Is it rum punch? Because—"

"Actually, it's an apology."

"The drink's an apology?" I ask warily. "Why are you apologizing?"

"I never gave you a seaweed."

"A *what*?"

"A seaweed! That classic Belizean beverage I told you about in Punta Gorda."

"Oh, right." I peer into the cup. "Smells like nutmeg."

"Taste it."

I try one swallow and shudder. It's not vile or anything—mostly it tastes like milk and spices—but it *slimes* down my throat. "Why is it so slippery?"

218

"That's the seaweed."

"Actual *seaweed*? I thought that was just a nickname! Thanks, but . . ." I pour the rest of the drink over the edge of the balcony. Then I spit for good measure.

Rowan laughs. "I'm glad you feel comfortable enough around me to spit."

"So where were you tonight?" I ask, wiping my mouth.

"I just needed a break."

"You wimp. It's only our first night here!"

"Don't remind me." Rowan crosses his arms, the eye of his dragon peeking through his fingers. "Anyway, I have another apology—but you have to get in first."

"The hammock?"

"That's right."

I reach out and test the sturdiness of one of the posts. "Seems wobbly."

"Who's the wimp now?"

He's got me. I climb in beside him, playfully pushing his feet from my face. I remember how shy I felt the last time we did this, back at the Rainforest Retreat. I can hardly believe only five days have passed since then. Or ten days, according to Olivia's sister's dorm-time scale. It feels like weeks and weeks.

"So what else are you sorry for? Besides tricking me with liquefied seaweed."

"For not trusting you."

That's not what I expected. "To do what?"

"To do what's best for yourself. When it comes to telling your parents."

I try not to squirm. "Don't worry about it."

"Especially after I'd asked you to trust *me*."

I'm still not sure if I do. "Well, I told you I'm untrustworthy when it comes to doing what's best for myself. And by that, I mean what's *really* best. Not other people's ideas of what's best."

"Like your parents'?"

I nod. "They were okay with the tour group. Well, they said, 'Guatemala? Why would you want to go there?' But they put a lot of faith in structure. Plus, they're dealing with a lot of personal stuff. They fight all the time—and I mean *all* the time—but just can't bring themselves to actually get a divorce."

"I'm sorry. That's rough."

"Honestly? I wish they *would* split." I try to shrug, but my shoulders are wedged in too tight. "Some people just aren't meant to be married."

Rowan nudges the wooden post with his foot so the hammock starts to sway. "It's too bad, what you said about the structure, though. That's exactly why I hate tour groups like your Global Whatevers—they stick to the well-trod trails. They avoid anything new or different. They're like hummingbirds scanning a landscape for red flowers: hover, swoop, then dart away."

Put like that, it sounds a little like Hyperactive Diver Disorder.

"I just think it's a shame, is all," Rowan continues. "To miss the beauty in all the details. The side streets and smaller islands. The overlooked places. Like the way we saw Livingston—you enjoyed that, right?" He looks so hopeful it's endearing.

"Of course I did!" It's true. Even during my brief few days off the beaten path, I'm amazed, even *stunned,* at what I've seen. Not just in Livingston, but along the banks of the Río Dulce. Through the windows of the chicken buses to Guatemala City and across Belize. And today, on the back roads of Laughingbird Caye. Color and frenzy and beauty and poverty that make me want to simultaneously stare and cover my eyes. Backpacking really does push aside the curtain.

Maybe everyone should be required to sign up for a dose.

But then . . . I think about my father. His lonely train trip across Canada, the one he traced for me on his maps. And that family trip to Spain he always talked about—it'll never happen. Of course he wouldn't understand fearless travelers like Rowan and Starling. Neither would Glenna

Heron, professional beadworker. Global Vagabonds is the trip of her life. And I just can't bring myself to look down on that.

"The thing is," I begin, "not everyone can travel like you do, Rowan."

"Sure they can—as long as they have the money. They just need to open their minds."

"But most people aren't raised to think this kind of travel's an option. Like me—I just fell into it accidentally."

"Best bag you ever lost."

I smile.

"But I'm being honest," he continues. "I don't see how anyone moderately educated and raised in Western civilization can't be enchanted when they hear about places like these. Like Livingston, or Antigua Guatemala. Or the lake. Do you know what Aldous Huxley called it?"

"'The most beautiful lake in the world.' As a matter of fact, I read about it in my Global Vagabonds itinerary."

"Really?" Rowan cringes as his entire belief system comes crashing down around him. "But still. What I say stands. Groups like that visit Tikal—on day trips. They visit Panajachel, which is great, but never make it to the other villages: Santa Cruz, San Marcos, Santa Lucía. They hear about the offbeat places. Why don't they go?"

"Because they hear about the dangers, too."

Rowan tries to sit up straight, almost flipping us out of the hammock.

"Sure, traveling can be dangerous. People get robbed, and stabbed, and raped. More likely, they get the runs. They get bitten by mosquitoes, and stray dogs, and exotic arachnids, and sometimes their parts swell to enormous sizes. They itch, and they sting, and they burn in the sun. They tumble off highways in chicken buses, and crash in tourist-class minivans. They even get their purses stolen in Mayan marketplaces."

I wrinkle my nose.

"But all that's hugely unlikely—with the exception of mosquito bites and sunburn. And yet even experienced travelers are still afraid.

"What everyone forgets—even me—is the people who actually *live* here. In places like Central America, I mean. Southeast Asia. India. Africa. Millions, even billions, of people, who live out their whole lives in these places—the places so many people like *us* fear. Think about it: they ride chicken buses to work every day. Their clothes are *always* damp. Their whole lives, they never escape the dust and the heat. But they deal with all these discomforts. They *have* to.

"So why can't travelers? If we've got the means to get here, we owe it to the country we're visiting not to treat it like an amusement park, sanitized for our comfort. It's insulting to the people who live here. People just trying to have the best lives they can, with the hands they've been dealt."

I open my mouth to reply, but I can't untangle my brain from his words.

All stuff I know, of course. I *know* people live in Central America all their lives. And I know people are people, be they professional beadworkers or Garifuna, Spring Breakpackers or Mayans. But on this trip, I've never let my brain dwell on those thoughts. I've never bothered to imagine myself in someone else's place. Like the kids selling key chains in the streets of Antigua. Or the mother with the screaming

223

toddler in the Guatemala City bus station. Because then I'd have to admit that in the grand scheme of things, I'm pretty well-off.

I mean . . . art school. *That's* what I'm agonizing over? The missed opportunity to pay bunches of money to paint and draw?

I know how shallow it sounds. And yet . . . it's not like I can instantaneously extricate all my emotions from it. My problems might be superficial on a global scale, but they're real to me. Just like my parents' marital problems are real to them. And Rowan's hang-ups are real to him.

"You're right," I tell him. "But you're wrong, too. Because you just can't speak for everybody. Not even every traveler. You can't begin to know what *anybody's* going through. It's almost like . . . you only have empathy for those less fortunate than you are."

"Come on!" Rowan cries, indignant.

"You do come off as feeling awfully superior."

"I don't think I'm superior."

"No offense, because I think you're the most insightful person I've ever met . . . but you seem to have a lot of pent-up disappointment in travelers who aren't you or Starling." I know I'm really stomping on his feelings at this point, but I make myself hold his eyes.

Finally, he cracks a grin. "Thanks," he says.

"Are you being sarcastic?"

"No. I'm really not. I'm thanking you—for the first thing you said. About being insightful. That's just . . . Wow. I'm honored. It almost eclipses what you said next, which was pretty mean. But point taken."

I poke my fingers through the netting of the hammock.

"Anyway, who am I to talk? I'm probably more judgmental than you are. I judged Dan as soon as I saw his comb-over."

"Who's Dan?"

"Marcy's husband. I judged Marcy based on her velociraptor fingernails."

"I judged you when I saw your Windbreaker."

"Asshole! That's a low blow and you know it. At least I'm not a boy wearing a stack of multicolored bracelets on his leg."

Rowan sticks his foot in my face. I grab it and trap it under my arm.

"You're right, though," he says. "It's about time to take these damn things off, isn't it?"

"Tonight?"

"Soon. It'll be, like, a rite of passage. We'll have a ceremony. And until then . . . I'll try to be more accommodating of Spring Breakpackers."

"I will too. Also, Global Whatevers."

"And even Global Whatevers."

For a moment, we're just smiling at each other, and it's kind of weird but also really nice. Rowan clears his throat like he has something important to add, but all he says is "Look up."

Mystified, I tip my head back.

I don't know how, but I forgot about the stars. They coat the sky like smeared wet sugar, so many the whole night seems to glow. When was the last time I looked up?

"Bet you don't have stars like that back home," Rowan says.

"No way! In Los Angeles? Too much light pollution, even in the suburbs. If I'm lucky, I see about ten or twelve of them."

"Just wait until I take you to the Corn Islands in Nicaragua. Especially Little Corn. Or Isla del Coco. It's in Costa Rica, miles and miles offshore. But if I took you all the way out there, you'd have to dive."

"Naturally," I say, playing along.

"Or maybe I'll take you to this tiny Garifuna island off the coast of Honduras. Chachauate Key, they call it. At low tide, you can hike from the main village across a sandbar and put up a hammock on a deserted isle. Between two coconut trees. Like out of a movie. And the stars—you wouldn't believe.

"Or we could go to the Tikal ruins, just over the border in Guatemala. You can stay at a budget hotel in the park, then wake up before dawn and climb to the top of the highest temple to watch the sun rise over the jungle. You'll swear you can see the whole wide world."

None of it will ever happen. We both know I'm not going anywhere after Laughingbird except home. But the images are so gorgeous, his words so beguiling, that a sentence slips out without my permission: "Hold my hand."

Rowan stares at me.

I would stare at me too if I could.

"It's just—what you said was so perfect. I'm not, like, coming on to you."

After a moment, he reaches out. Because of the way we're lying, we can only hook our fingers together clumsily. It's more awkward than anything.

"Anyway, I know you wouldn't," he says.

"Wouldn't what?"

"Come on to me."

"Of course not," I say quickly.

"So . . . we're friends? Or siblings, or whatever it was Starling said? Brother and sister?"

"Of course. Hooking up would be immoral. Like, travel incest."

Rowan grins at me, then closes his eyes. We sit there awhile longer, listening to the waves, the grackles trilling in the trees, the soft thump of reggae music from the bars down the street. I want to let go of his hand. But I don't want him to think anything's wrong.

19

Days 12–15
Transformed

I have mastered the island.

Okay, so it's not that much of an accomplishment, considering it's so narrow in some places I can see the ocean on both sides. But when you're from the Los Angeles area, you can't master much outside your own neighborhood. You know where you're going, but it's almost impossible to know all the corners. You know the good parts and bad parts, but not all the parts in between.

Every morning, I borrow the same purple bike from the dive shop and set out to reexplore all the places I've already been. And hour by hour, trail by trail, I'm changed.

Externally, it's obvious. My sunburn turns to tan. My wind-thrashed hair is almost untamable, even by Rowan's rolled-up bandanas. Bug bites materialize on my legs, though I never catch a single mosquito sucking at me. When I show Rowan, he tells me about other Central American beasts that bite. "Sea lice. Sand flies and fleas. Sea serpents."

"I call bullshit on your serpents."

"There really are sea snakes, though."

As if I needed another reason to stay out of the ocean.

Biking barefoot with my sandals in the basket, I fly down Front Street. I dodge potholes on Middle Street. Clutching an iced papaya drink in one hand, I sail down Back Street. I wave at everyone I pass—locals, backpackers, guys and girls and children—but I'm speeding way too fast for conversation.

I stop only to draw.

Wanderlove
an illustrated tale of travel magic!
by Bria Sandoval

(no beasties were smushed in the making of this book.)

Until now, I've been pecking at my sketchbooks, erasing, sketching with painstaking care, perfecting every line. Like every single page I drew was designed to impress my invisible critics. Well, one critic in particular. But on this island,

I don't care what he thinks. I have really, truly left him behind.

I draw pelicans, frigate birds, grackles, gulls, herons.
I draw iguanas, weathered old dinosaurs basking in the sun.
I draw island dogs.
I draw island kids.

I sit on a tombstone, which I hope isn't disrespectful, and draw the island's tiny graveyard. I draw the briar patches of the mangroves, trees that grow right out of the sea. I draw the ice cream shack when I'm craving a second scoop but am too embarrassed to go get one. I draw until I fill my sketchbook and have to buy a third.

I'm so happy I can barely stand it.

But my happiness comes with one major stumbling block: it makes me even more aware of how little time I have left.

My plane leaves from Guatemala City four days after Lobsterfest. College is supposed to start a month after that. I've been so busy I haven't thought about it in days.

Once I remember, time starts rushing by even faster, so fast I can see the minutes zipping around me like one of those cartoon time warps. I feel unhinged, propelled forward, as if the wind's bashing me in the face even when I'm off my bike, and time's flying, I'm flying, and real life and the college I don't want are speeding toward me like the front bumper of a semi truck.

The only thing that anchors me is Rowan.

Every afternoon, I wait at the dock for the dive boats to come in.

First there's Devon and Clement's boat, for certified divers exploring the deeper, farther places, like the legendary Blue Hole, which I picture as a bottomless pit filled with thousand-tentacled creatures baring fangs bigger than Belize City light-houses. Jack climbs off the second boat first, with a stack of weight belts slung around his neck and a dive tank in each hand. He always has something smart-assed to say to me. Like "Hungover, as usual. Didn't I warn you to stop at number nine?" Or "It's because you're bite-sized, isn't it? Good thing—those hammerheads looked hungry today." I've been avoiding him as much as possible, because the sight of him makes me wonder about things I don't want to wonder about.

Next come the dreadlock twins. Emily and Ariel follow, bickering loudly.

Rowan always emerges last, looking like some sort of ponytailed mer-creature in his unzipped wet suit. He grins boyishly and says, "Don't listen to Jack. Next time, you should come along."

And I shake my head and grab an armful of flippers before following him to shore.

In the evenings, Emily and Ariel act like puppies, jostling for Rowan's attention. He's civil—at least, he doesn't play any of his notorious pranks—but it's obvious he prefers my company.

Just not in *that* way.

It's a relief, really, that we established our relationship once and for all, that night we shared the hammock. The murkiness has been clarified, the tension dispersed. At last, there's an easy peace between us.

We find the time to talk before dinner, or after we excuse ourselves from the group at night. Before long, everyone knows those hours are ours, even Rowan's fan club.

Rowan's sixth travel rule:
Downtime is the best time.

Rowan admits that one day, he'd like to write books. There's no shame, he claims, in being a Flashpacker: a backpacker with a laptop and other techno-toys. I describe my histories with Reese and Olivia, the way I drifted from one to the other, then away from both. And I talk about how I used to love to swim at one particular beach, my beach, a long time ago but not anymore, even though I don't tell him why.

Rowan tells me about the dad he shares with Starling: a failed architect turned landscaper, terminally unhappy, always on the move to escape a boss, a woman, or another imaginary enemy. He doesn't talk about his mother, and I don't ask.

I tell him about the art school girl, and even my art school dreams. But I don't tell him my reasons for discarding them, and he doesn't ask.

Little sacrifices to keep us content. To convince us we're making progress.

And maybe we are. It's like carving a sculpture from a hunk of marble. Exposing the artwork hiding inside, chip by chip. But the process is slow. Too slow, when our trip is already winding down. Which I don't want to think about.

One time, Rowan asks if I'll ever draw him. We're sitting

on the beach, atop an overturned rowboat. I shake my head. "It's just too . . . intimate."

"Really? But don't you draw, like, models? Strangers?"

"It's different then. When I'm drawing a stranger, it's easy to break them down into lines, shapes, edges. Forgetting the person isn't a problem, because you don't *know* the person. That's how I can draw an old man's . . . you know, and not be embarrassed. And also, models rarely ever see the drawing—there's no pressure to achieve a likeness they're happy with. But friends are different."

"I wouldn't care if your drawing didn't look like me."

"You *say* that." I roll my eyes. "Drawings are interpretations, right? By definition. But when I draw a friend, I can't just interpret *clinically*: I see them through a veil of what I know, what I feel. That's what I mean about the intimacy. About how it's personal, for both of us. So the process is already different. But the product is what really stops me."

I think of the time I drew Olivia. She claimed she really liked it . . . *except.*

"When people are faced with their flaws—and my artistic limitations—they're never as happy as I need them to be. I know it's dumb that I need validation. If I ever want to be a professional, I'll have to swallow all that to earn a paycheck. But for now, I can't help it. It's too important to me."

When Rowan doesn't say anything, I glance at him. "What?"

"Nothing. I just love to hear you talk about art." He pauses as a pelican dives into the water right in front of us. A piece of my chest seems to plunge with it. "Do you think you'll ever show me your drawings?"

The pelican surfaces, a fish flopping in its enormous beak.

"Soon," I promise. "Will you ever tell me about your sordid past?"

Rowan laughs and shakes his head. "Soon."

Although we're both all too aware our time is running out.

When you spend days aboard a rickety beach bike and there are potholes all over the place, it's basic probability: you're destined to take a spill. Lucky for me, my wipeout occurs on the south side of the island, and my audience is mostly birds and lizards.

Mostly. Because when I finish cursing and totter to my feet, I discover I've fallen in someone's yard. A woman stands nearby with a spatula in her hand, like she's about to smack me. She's even shorter than I am, with an enormous bosom that tapers to skinny legs and tiny feet. She wears a wrinkled Sesame Street T-shirt, with Elmo and Grover beaming freakishly across her chest.

"What you looking at, girl?"

"Oh, n-nothing," I stammer. "I—"

"Well, what you waiting for? These *plátanos* is getting cold."

I gape at her, trying to figure out what the heck a *plátano* is.

The woman mutters something in Kriol. "Quit yawning at me. Are you a baby bird or a girl? You can call me Sonia."

"I'm Bria." Finally, I leave my bike on its side and perch tentatively on a picnic bench. I'm not really sure what's going on, but she seems friendly. Like a wolf wagging its tail. Despite her tiny feet, she moves quickly, zipping between the grill and the table, loading two plates with a Belizean breakfast of refried beans, tortillas, scrambled eggs, and fried plantains, which are probably what she meant by *plátanos*. She sits across from me and shoves a plate my way. "Really? You don't mind?" I say.

"Mind what? You joining me this breakfast? I should thank you." She rolls a tortilla into a shovel shape and scoops a heap of beans. "Morning's boring as shit. My husband, he fishes dawn till dusk."

"What does he fish for?"

"Fish. Conchs." She pronounces it *conks*. "But now is lobster season, so he fishes for lobsters. You going to the lobster party?"

"Sure—how could I not?" It's all anybody talks about, with the exception of Rowan.

"So you're a backpacker?"

I shrug. "I have a backpack, at least."

"I was a backpacker too," Sonia says. "Girl, don't look so surprised! We got travelers *from* here as well as *come* here." She spoons a giant pile of sugar into her coffee and stirs. "So you like my island?"

"I love your island."

She chuckles. "If you love it now, you should see it before. Back before there's more hotels and bars than shells. Back when only real backpackers come and visit. You're too skinny," she adds. "Eat more eggs."

I take a bite. "What do you mean?"

"Eggs give you big tits."

"No! About the real backpackers."

"Oh. Well, it's thirty years ago or more. You know La Mariposa? By the main dock?"

"Sure," I say. The hotel with the butterfly paintings. By

236

now, I know where everything is. I could draw an entire map out of my head. Maybe I should.

"La Mariposa is my sister's hotel. But she's a *bruja* and we don't talk no more. Anyways, the whole southern part of the island, from the channel to the main dock, is mangrove forests thirty years ago. Now there's a thousand people live on this island. Then, there's just three or four hundred.

"In those days, only the *real* backpackers visit. Those carrying real backpacks—not these giant monster bags, look like a turtle house. There's no water taxis, no airstrip. To get to my island, you have to pay a fisherman in Belize City to take you on his boat. Maybe if you're lucky, he put you up in his house. Or you find two coconut trees and put up a *hamaca*, and hope no coconuts falls on your head in the night."

"What did people eat?" I ask, imagining *Survivor*-type hippies scavenging for shrimp and mangos.

"They eat what everybody eats," Sonia says. "You pay a family in the morning, and in the evening, you have what they have—stew chicken, fried fish, *pollo a la plancha.*"

I wonder if Rowan's ever traveled like that. It's easy to picture him hailing a fisherman, stringing up a hammock. I remember the island he told me about—the one with all the stars. And suddenly, I want to see it so badly my stomach aches. I want to string up a hammock under the stars and eat *pollo a la plancha*. I don't ever want to go home. "It sounds amazing."

Sonia nods. "But now, the word is out. And to this day, we can never go back."

We can never go back.

I see what she's saying. To a seasoned traveler like Rowan, with his piles of passport stamps, this island isn't much edgier

the swimming
channel

① art gallery #1
② ice cream!
③ art gallery #2
④ gift shop

lobsterfest!

BACK STREET

MIDDLE STREET

FRONT STREET

①

②

③

④

Coco
Plum
Bar

OUR HOSTEL

soccer
field

TAXI

MAIN
DOCK

the
Dive
Shop

Sonia's
house

graveyard

AIR STRIP

The Belize Barrier Reef

Mangrove forest

Map of
Laughingbird
Caye
(NOT TO
SCALE!)

than a Sandals resort. Not to mention Sonia, who's seen it swell from a heap of sand into a starred Lonely Planet destination.

But then again, to my friends back home, the entire Central America isthmus would still seem impossibly remote, a storybook realm of bandits and bananas. That's how it seemed to me as I stared at the Mayan temple photo in my Global Vagabonds pamphlet.

I guess it all depends on how you look at it.

Bria's first travel rule:
Travel is a matter of perspective.

"You think there's any place left in the world nobody's been before?" I wonder.

"I stopped traveling many years ago," Sonia says. "So I don't know the answer."

Then she leans forward, wedging her coffee mug in her cleavage. "But what I do know is this: you got to find your own places. The places you *get*, girl, the ones that stick in your heart. And if you're lucky, you find people to share them with." She pauses. "Just don't marry a goddamned fisherman."

She takes our empty plates and puts them on the ground for the dogs. When I reach into my daypack, she snaps, "And don't try to pay me. I be very insulted."

20

Day 15, Night
Skeletons

That evening, the Florida girls want to play skeleton in the closet.

Five of us sit on the floor of the dive shop: Rowan and me, Jack, Emily, and Ariel. The dreadlock twins are back at the bar, while Clement and Devon headed home. Apparently they've outgrown that kind of nonsense. I wish I could say the same. I'm facing the open door, wearing a pair of Rowan's sunglasses, even though it's almost dark out. Jack passes around a joint and a flask of something called Garifuna giffity, which tastes like scorched gasoline. As usual, Rowan doesn't drink or smoke. I spend so much time deciding between staying sober and carpe diem, they finish the joint without me.

The game is Emily's idea. I expect Rowan to make up an

excuse to leave, but instead, he turns to me and says, "I'm in if you are."

I shouldn't be shocked. By now, our evasiveness has become a joke. Like the other afternoon before dinner, when we visited one of the island's art galleries. Rowan was browsing on the other side of a row of glass shelves, his face doubled and split, when he called to me. "Look what I found." In the crook of one arm, he cradled a gnarled hunk of wood, made glossy, with a tiny knob the size of a popcorn kernel in the center. I pinched it open. A drawer.

"For secret-keeping," I said.

Rowan set it back on the shelf. "We don't need any help with that!"

Hilarious. So even though I don't want to play, I convince myself that I'm okay with this. That I don't have anything to hide. And really, I don't. My relationship with Toby isn't exactly tabloid fodder. Rowan, on the other hand . . . I just can't figure out why he's okay with this when he can't bring himself to confide even in me.

But then he whispers in my ear, and it all makes sense: "Feel free to lie," he says.

"So how do you play?" I ask Emily.

"It's like truth or dare, without the dare. We go around the circle, and one by one we ask a question—any question. Everyone but the person asking has to answer."

"And what if we won't answer?"

"You take a penalty shot of giffity."

"That stuff's foul." And even though he's never said so explicitly, I add, "Plus, Rowan doesn't drink."

"I'm more worried about you, Bria," Jack says. "You sure you can handle it?"

"Of course. Can you?"

He chuckles. "Sure. I love this stuff. But you, you're such a little thing. How tall are you—one hundred fifty?"

"Huh?"

"He means centimeters," Rowan explains.

Emily leans over and seizes a dusty conch shell from the bookshelf. "I'll start," she says, "because I've got the conch."

Rowan crosses his arms. "I'm glad this game's democratic."

"I don't get it," Emily says.

"*Lord of the Flies*. You know, Piggy? 'I've got the conch'? When they . . . Never mind."

"How do we know who goes next?" Ariel asks, flicking her thumbnail against her teeth. She's too tidy of a girl to actually bite.

"We can spin the conch."

"Like spin the bottle? I'd rather play that."

"Let's not," Rowan and I say at the same time.

Emily kneels with both hands on the seashell. "Okay," she says. "My question is . . . Have you ever cheated on someone?"

Ariel and Jack answer yes, while Rowan and I say no. I'm impressed until Rowan winks at me and I realize I don't know whether he's lying.

Great. This is going to be a mindfuck.

Emily spins the shell, and the pointy end stops at Jack. He leans against the wall, extending his infinite legs in front of him. "Have you ever carried drugs across an international border?"

There's a pause as we all weigh the weirdness of his question. Especially me. I can't help thinking of the pounds of bananas that weren't bananas. It fits too well. I glance at

Rowan, who just happens to be avoiding my eyes, and then I speak.

"I have—I bought a box of Alka-Seltzer in Tijuana once."

True story. I was trying unsuccessfully to ward off a hangover after my fifty billion kamikazes. Everyone laughs except Emily. "That's not what he meant," she complains.

"So what?" Rowan says. "Then he should have worded it differently. I've carried all kinds of drugs across borders: Tylenol, aspirin, malaria pills."

Jack grins. "Foiled."

The game goes on. Heavy-lidded from the joint, Ariel asks about sex in public places. I ask about shoplifting. "*Boring*," says Emily, even after Rowan relays some elaborate story about hiding a container of pistachio ice cream in his pants. She asks about threesomes, and I decide not to mention me, Toby, and Toby's sketchbook. Then it's Jack's turn again.

"Have you ever been jailed in a third-world country?"

Emily and Ariel both shout, "No!" I consider making up a story, but I'm not fast enough. I shake my head. Only Rowan is left. And for some reason, he's not answering.

"Rowan's taking too long," crows Ariel. "Drink! Drink!"

Jack grins and holds out the bottle. To my surprise, Rowan accepts it. He swallows, making a terrible face. "This shit's wretched."

"If you'd stop being so damn cagey, you wouldn't have to drink it," Jack says. "Come on, man. What's it going to take to get you to talk to me?"

"Not bringing up shit like that."

"This isn't the same sort of situation, I told you. Not even close."

I'm starting to feel dizzy. It could be from the smokebox

we're sitting in, but more likely it's the secrets whirling through the air. It's almost like Jack's trying to blackmail Rowan with his past. Who does that? But I don't know what else to think, especially when Rowan's still avoiding my eyes.

"Why has everything got to be so serious with you nowadays? How about this?" Jack reaches for the shell and points it at Rowan. "Your turn. Give me your best shot."

Rowan scowls. It makes him look like a little boy. "Oh, I've got questions for you," he says. "How about, *Have you ever left a friend to take the fall for you? Or, Have you ever had an ulterior motive when you told your pal about a job lead? Or how about, Have you ever slept with your best friend's sister, then lied about it?*"

Oh. My. God.

"That's not fair," Emily says with a scowl. "The question has to apply to everyone."

"Quiet," Ariel says, looking intrigued. "Did you, Jack? Really? His *sister?*"

My dizziness has turned to nausea, and the smoke and giffity are only making it worse. I want my denial back. I want to run outside and stick my head in the sand and pretend that I haven't heard anything, that Rowan's the brilliant, perceptive, utterly decent guy I've come to care about more than I'll let myself admit, nothing more, nothing less. But as tempting as a getaway sounds, I can't leave the others to talk shit about Starling. Not while she's busy martyring herself for the greater good in some impoverished village.

"That's what you're so bent out of shape about, Rowan?" Jack is saying. "Really? Because she's the one who—"

"I slept with Rowan's sister!" I shout.

Everyone stares at me in disbelief.

244

"Well, I did. In Río Dulce. Starling and I slept together. Literally. In the same hotel room. Not in the same bed, though. Sorry."

"Stop misinterpreting the questions!" Emily exclaims. "And take those sunglasses off. It's night."

I shove the sunglasses to the top of my head as Rowan stands.

"Don't leave." Ariel tries to get up, giggling, but she's too stoned.

"Rowan, no hard feelings," Jack says. "Seriously, I was just kidding around. We had great times back then, didn't we? Anything I did to hurt you, then or now, I'm really sorry. Look. . . ." He holds up the flask, tips his head back, and swigs. When he lowers it, Rowan grabs it from his hand.

"Rowan, you don't have to . . . ," I begin.

For an instant, his angry eyes flash my way. I've never seen him look like that. I've seen him frustrated, annoyed, exhausted. But never angry. He unscrews the flask and swallows. And swallows. And swallows. He recaps it, tosses it in Jack's lap, then stalks off into the night.

I give him a head start before running after him.

Outside, people from the beach bars spill onto the sand. I dodge them, hopping over the seaweed that drapes the shore like stinking rags. Near the main dock, I finally catch up with Rowan, walking with his hands in his pockets.

"Jack knew the answers to those questions," he says.

"Yeah . . . I got that."

He kicks a piece of driftwood. "Jack's no angel, just so you know. I meant what I said, about taking the fall for him back in Honduras. If he'd gotten caught, the dive shop owners would have had him deported, or worse—it wasn't his first transgression. I was lucky I didn't get in more trouble. But I lost a job I loved, on an island I adored. And now there's no way I can go back, not even for a visit."

"But . . . what did you take the fall for?"

Rowan waves his hand, like I should know.

"Drugs? Is that what you're telling me? Jack blamed his drugs on you?"

"They weren't just his," Rowan says.

I pause. "Oh."

We're walking down the main dock now, where the water taxis come in. I can hear the waves crashing against the barrier reef. The sound track seems to make the whole world stall, as if we're suspended here in this landmark moment, bound by Rowan's words.

"I was young, and new to the travel scene. Selling drugs to tourists seemed like easy money—and it was, at first. Also, Jack can be awfully charismatic—even after the first couple times we almost got caught, and I swore to myself I wouldn't fall for his fast talk ever again. God, it was all so idiotic. We could have been jailed for years. Hell, we could have been killed, considering some of the sketchy characters we got involved with." He shakes his head. "*Now* you see why I didn't want to tell you."

I stumble on an uneven plank, and Rowan grabs my arm to steady me. He pulls back quickly, like he's suddenly too shy to touch me. It makes me want to hug him, but we've never done anything like that, and now's probably not the best time to go there.

"Why did you agree to play Emily's game in the first place," I say, "if you knew Jack had all that ammo against you?"

"Jack and I might have had our issues, but it's been a long time. He was great when we caught up in Guatemala City. And . . . well, you have to know Jack. He doesn't mean things to come out as harshly as they do. Sometimes he's just so enamored with the potential *humor* of a situation, he doesn't realize he's making everyone around him uncomfortable. And I suppose in this case, he's still a little hurt."

We've reached the end of the dock. I stay a couple of feet back, while Rowan steps right to the edge.

"Why is Jack hurt, exactly?"

Rowan sighs. "Just . . . he and Starling had a thing, I guess. Late last year. I suspected it, even though I didn't know for sure. She didn't know about my problems with Jack until later."

"But what's he blaming *you* for?"

He shrugs. "I guess you could say Starling left him for me."

Everything's beginning to come clear now, sun through the clouds. "How do you figure?"

"I'd just arrived at Lake Atitlán, and I . . . sort of had what you'd call a breakdown. Hit bottom. Starling came down to take care of me. It was awful, but it was what I needed to give me a kick in the ass. Everything's been so much better since then. Until now. I should have known this job was just an excuse as soon as Jack called."

And suddenly, the sun's obscured by black thunderheads. "An excuse? An excuse for what?"

Rowan runs his palm over his eyes, looking weary. "It's nothing. Just a connection Jack has. A way to make extra money, when all the crowds are here for Lobsterfest."

"He wants you to, like . . ." I can't bring myself to say the word again. "To sell . . ."

"It's not a big deal or anything."

"But it *is* a big deal. After everything you just told me?"

"It really isn't. Compared to the kind of situations I used to get into, it's nothing. I've already said too much. Don't worry about it."

"You're not going to do it, are you?"

"I said don't worry about me, Bria! I can take care of myself."

I can't let it go. "But—"

"Hey, look!"

I turn and look. In a silver pool of light from a dock lamp, sinuous black shadows move through the water. Rowan steps closer to me.

"Baby nurse sharks. They come out at night. Aren't they graceful?"

Any other time, I'd be captivated. Or joke about another hazard keeping me from the water. But this time, my stomach reels with frustration. It's not the first time Rowan's tried to change the subject right when we're getting somewhere. I'd hoped we were past that stage, but apparently we're not.

And this time, we're talking drugs across borders. Jail in third-world countries. Drug deals that might not be entirely dealt with. I know I should have expected this, after what Starling said, what Liat said. And I did expect some of it. Drugs, maybe. Girls. Scores of girls. But not all this. I mean . . . my God. *Rowan.* No wonder he didn't want to tell me about his past.

Especially since it's looking likely that it's not in the past at all.

My emotions are twisting together, so dense and dizzying I can hardly speak. My head aches, and Rowan's not helping by striding way too fast down the road to our hostel. He drops me off at my room with barely a nod for a goodnight.

I stand with my ear against the door until I hear his shut.

I count to sixty.

Then I hurry back downstairs to the hostel lobby, where the night clerk's still manning the desk. With his help, I call the number Starling gave me back in Río Dulce, the emergency number I'm supposed to call if anybody needs saving.

"I think Rowan's in trouble," I tell her.

21

Day 16
Letting Go

Lobsterfest is tomorrow.

It sticks up from the landscape of my journey like a volcanic peak. The inevitable climax of my days in Central America. Exciting, intimidating. Unavoidable.

And now Starling will be there. She's flying in from Flores tomorrow morning.

"But do you really have to come all this way?" I said on the phone last night. "Can't you call Rowan and, I don't know, talk some sense into him?"

"That wouldn't work," she explained. "First, because it would make him angry, and less likely to listen to me. Second, because he'd know you called me. By showing up for the party, I can pretend it was a surprise—my intention all along."

He'd know you called me. I never thought of that. I tried to imagine Rowan's reaction if he learned I told on him, and it made me want to down an entire keg of Jack's toxic punch.

"You're sure about this, Bria? Because if you're wrong . . ."

I told her I was certain.

And I thought I was. But this morning at breakfast, I can barely look at Rowan. It's for the best, I tell myself. I'm doing this because I care. And *he's* the one betraying my trust. Though every time I think of last night's furtive phone call, it feels like it's the other way around. I just wish I'd given Rowan another chance to explain. Or demanded an explanation.

But now it's too late.

I need to keep busy, I tell myself. It's the only way to keep my mind from stumbling backward into last night's minefield.

After breakfast, I hurry back to the hostel. When the coast is clear, I wash a few tank tops, a couple of pairs of shorts, and all my underwear in the sink of the shared bathroom. I drape them over the balcony outside our room to dry.

I hang out at the edge of Sonia's backyard until she comes outside and calls me a creep. While we listen to a bootleg CD of her favorite soca music, she tells me a story about a white man her husband took lobster fishing, mocking him in a deep, dopey voice. "So he says, 'I nailed this one guy so big you wouldn't believe. The guide said it musta been fifteen years old. Did he ever fight! A furious sonofabitch. I had to rip off both his antennae and a leg or two to get him on the boat.'" She spits. When I ask why, she explains, "He got no respect. He should have left that ancient old creature alone. That lobster probably was ten times smarter than he is, the filthy potlicker."

After lunch, I consider getting out my sketchbook, but I don't really feel like drawing.

Instead, I ride my bike to the airstrip and watch a plane land. It looks like an aerial chicken bus. I weave a handful of bougainvillea into a bracelet, which breaks when I try to slip it on.

For the trillionth time, I visit the island's two art galleries. There's folk art, watercolor portraits of locals, island scenes constructed from torn tissue paper and shells. I wonder if they sell art by visitors, or just the islanders. I wonder how many drawings you'd have to sell to make a living, at these prices, in this place. Maybe if you supplemented your income with another kind of job, like working the desk at a hotel, or administration at one of the dive shops. Rent has to be cheap here. It wouldn't be that hard.

When I hop off my bike to watch uniformed school-children cavorting in a playground, a little girl runs at me and hugs me around my knees. For no reason.

I buy a bag of roasted peanuts and a plastic bag of green mango slices coated in chili and lime. I sit at the channel and eat, scanning the horizon for Rowan's boat, my feet in the water, the dive book in my lap.

I wonder if he and Jack have had the chance to talk.

I wonder how Rowan's feeling. If he's feeling regret.

Because I know I am. Regret that I let myself trust a guy, yet again, when the first time failed so miserably. Trust that he was "reformed." That he'd do the right thing around me, like Starling said. That he'd eventually explain everything to me, like he promised under the lighthouse in Belize City, and again when we sat on the overturned boats a few days ago, and other times too. He only told me under duress, and that's not the same.

How could I trust him when all I had was what he'd given me?

If Rowan hadn't remained so closed off, I wouldn't have had to run to Starling. But he's made it almost impossible for me to confront him. Now he's about to wreck everything we've built traveling together. And there's no time to recover.

Because there's barely any time left.

In the late afternoon, when the palm shadows are turning purple and the dive boats are almost due to arrive, I park my bike beside a wide stretch of sand. With my arms crossed, I watch a group of laborers unfurl a chain-link fence.

The divers call tonight Lobsterfest Eve, like Christmas Eve. Apparently, it's tradition to abstain from drinking, to save up for the next day's epic liver-pickling session. But the dive students want to celebrate their spanking new Open Water certifications. So Jack concocts several pitchers of mocktails, which taste like watermelon smoothie mixed with cough syrup and agony.

We sit at the picnic table while Jack, Clement, and Devon enthusiastically exchange stories of Lobsterfests past. As usual, I have nothing to contribute to their talk of vomiting up lobster-flavored ice cream in the vacant lot behind Gilligan's Grill. Emily and Ariel keep trying to change the subject to the exploits of the past few days: equalizing, regulators, wet suits with saggy asses, surprise barracudas.

"Do you remember what happened to Ariel?" Emily shouts across the table. "When she lost her mask at sixty feet?"

"During a skill set," Ariel explains to me. "You have to take your mask all the way off for an entire minute. I dropped it when Ethan kicked me with his flipper by accident."

Ethan, I gather, is one of the dreadlock twins.

"Thank God Rowan found it," Emily says.

"It was hooked on a piece of coral at *eighty feet*."

"Jack and I had to hold her in place so she wouldn't freak out and swim to the surface."

"Bria, you would have been so scared. I thought I was going to drown!"

While Ariel continues her story, Emily turns to Rowan. She's dominated his attention all through dinner—not too hard, since he obviously doesn't want to talk about Lobsterfest. I'm bothered. Shouldn't be, but I am. Because here's the thing: if I think about it, I have to admit that Emily's more Rowan's type than Ariel is. She's edgier, opinionated. Definitely the boss man. And she *loves* to dive.

A bee lands in my mocktail. I try to use my straw to rescue it, but it's not working. Finally, I pour the drink into a bush.

"Hey!" Jack says. "I saw that. I put lots of love into these beverages."

"And a whole lot of rotten fruit," I mutter.

All evening, Jack's hand has been knocking into mine under the table. By the fourth time, I suspect it's not an accident. Part of me is compelled to get up and leave. Ambush flirtation is sort of shady. Plus, Jack had that thing with Starling. Doesn't that make his attention inappropriate?

Sounds like *I'm* the ethics police.

Not really, though. Even though any attraction to Jack

would make me a hypocrite, if I'm completely honest with myself, another part of me feels flattered. Because if Jack is interested in me, and he had a "thing" with Starling—she of the coconut rings and indigent villages and Mayan head scarves and phone book–sized travel journals—then it almost makes us equals. Which might be silly, but it feels really good. Like I've reached my *potential* after all.

Jack clutches a fist to his chest, as if my insulting his mocktail savaged his heart. "Just wait until tomorrow. Add a bit of booze, and you won't even notice the taste."

Just wait until tomorrow.

My eyes drift back to Emily and Rowan. He and I haven't spoken since last night, other than mumbled *good mornings* at breakfast and *how are you, I'm fines*. I wonder if he's suspicious of me. I wonder if he knows about Jack's overeager hands.

I realize I don't see Rowan's hands. Or Emily's.

"You know what? I think it's time for bed." I untangle my legs from the picnic bench. Then, on impulse, I add, "I hope the geckos don't keep me up tonight."

Rowan squints at me. I stare back.

"Geckos?" Ariel looks around. "Where?"

Finally, lightbulbs appear in Rowan's eyes. "I guess—"

Before he can finish, Jack claps a mammoth hand on my shoulder. "Do you want me to walk you to your hostel?"

Shit. I shrug at Rowan, who shrugs back. "No, I'm fine. Don't worry about it."

I'm only a few steps away when Emily calls, "Hey! You forgot your sketchbook."

I whirl around. "Thanks, I—"

And then I stop. Because she's flipping through it.

"You're pretty good," she says.

I can't move. My feet are adhered to the dock.

"Hey," says Rowan. "Seriously, that's not cool."

He reaches for my sketchbook, but Emily holds it away. "Holy shit, Ariel, she drew us! Aw, come on. My legs aren't that fat."

Ariel bounces out of her seat and leans over Emily's shoulder. "I think they look about right." She turns a page, and then another. "I like the dog. He's cute. He looks like Yoda."

"How come you never drew Rowan? Oh, wait—there's his foot. With all the bracelets."

"You drew Rowan's *foot?*" Jack asks.

"Who's this backpacker girl you keep drawing?"

My tongue has turned to wadded cotton. They've jammed a periscope inside my brain. Rowan reaches for the book a second time, but again, Emily dodges him, skipping a few feet down the dock. Ariel scampers after her.

"Dude! You've got to see these lists. They're hilarious. Rowan, you've got travel rules?"

"What the hell's *Wanderlove?*"

And with that, I turn and run.

I admit it. I cry.

Okay, fine. I do more than cry. I dead-bolt the door of our dorm and squeeze onto our tiny balcony, fold myself into a weather-stained rattan chair, and bawl.

The tears come for the obvious reason: that these girls I barely know took something good and made it something to mock. But that alone wouldn't be enough to make me cry this hard. I'm sobbing because it hits all too close to home. The places I swore I wouldn't bring to this island, which is turning out to be the exact opposite of the idyllic paradise I thought it was. And I cry harder, because my overreaction embarrasses me. I cry because I'm crying. Which means I will probably cry forever, in a Möbius strip of endless tears.

Someone's knocking on the door.

"Go away," I shout. Emily and Ariel can sleep on the beach tonight for all I care.

"Please, Bria. Let me in."

It's Rowan. I freeze mid-sob. Before I can chicken out, I pull up my tank top and use it to wipe my face, then march inside and throw open the door.

He's holding my sketchbook.

My traitorous arms rise to hug him, but I restrain them just in time. I grab my sketchbook and fling it onto my bed before heading back to the balcony. Only then do I remember all my underwear lying out to dry. "Shit," I say, scooping it into my arms. A pair of pink bikinis flutters to the ground right as Rowan steps outside.

"Need help with those?"

I glare at him with the intensity of a thousand hellfires. Then I squeeze past him into the room and dump the pile into my backpack. They're not completely dry, but that's the least of my concerns. I return to the balcony, my rattan chair, and my scowl.

"I want you to know," Rowan says, "I didn't look."

"What, at my underwear?"

"At your sketchbook. It was really screwed up of Emily to grab it like that, and I told her. Repeatedly. So did Jack and the others. I want you to know."

"It doesn't matter." I shrug. "So what? I'm the neurotic

257

one. They're a bunch of stupid drawings. Why should I care if people look at my art? Isn't that the point of it?"

"I don't think there has to be a point."

I shrug again. "It's my fault. I'm the one who made it into a big deal. I'm the one who gave up art in the first place. I didn't have to. No one made me."

"But you draw all the time."

"Not in the same way. I used to be serious about it. It was my whole life. I mean it—I've never cared about *anything* as much as I cared about art. And then . . ." I wave my hands through the air like a melodramatic orchestra conductor. "I stopped. I let it go."

Rowan's still leaning against the door, and it's making me feel self-conscious. I pound the seat of the adjacent chair. He sits, careful not to touch me.

"Can't you just . . . take it seriously again?"

"You don't get it, Rowan. With art, it's different. You have to work your ass off nonstop to get good. The competition out there's staggering. And I'm not even going to art school. I'm not . . ."

Oh, for fuck's sake. I'm crying again.

"Don't," I say, even though he hasn't said anything. "It's stupid. It's my fault. I believed Toby when he said we'd go to art school together, no matter what."

"Toby . . . your boyfriend."

"Yep. Surprise! He was real—just past tense, not present." I wipe my eyes. "He was an artist too. And he was really good. Like prodigy good. You'll have to take my word for it. His father was a professional artist, and it made him obsessively disciplined. Before I met him, all I did was doodle."

That's what Toby called it, at least. Wistfully, I recall my fairies, my woodland creatures, my cherubs looped with ivy. My sea monsters.

"I hate to admit it, but Toby made me good. Made me serious. He's the reason I started to study art. And maybe I never cracked the whip like he did, but I saw my drawings get better. Until I could hardly believe what came out of my pencil."

"So what happened?"

"He was jealous, I know that now. I got into Southern California Art Academy's fast-track program, and he didn't. The plan was *who cares who makes the program: we'll both go to SCAA anyway.* I was naïve enough to believe him. But after months of doing this stupid secretive dance, where we both kept avoiding the subject, he informed me he was going to the Art Institute of Chicago. He'd known for ages, but didn't tell me until it was too late."

"Too late for what?"

"For me to apply to other art schools."

"But what about the art academy? Can't you still go?"

"Nope! I never sent in my acceptance." I shake my head, laughing through my tears. Rowan probably thinks I've gone mental. "I told my parents that they were right, it was too expensive, and that I wanted the flexibility of one of my state school fallbacks. And they barely even questioned it! I swear, they didn't even notice when I stopped drawing. Like they thought it was a passing phase the whole time. I didn't want to think about art until I decided to take this trip. At the time . . . well, it sounds really, really screwed up, but it was easier to let it go."

"I get it," Rowan says after a pause.

"What do you get?"

"How it's possible to give up something you love."

I can't speak, so I tear off a strip of rattan and crumple it in my palm.

"Because I know what it's like," he says. "To throw away all the good things you've got going for you. *Nothing* makes you hate yourself more than that." He reaches over and takes the crumpled strip of rattan from my hands. "I've come to realize that sometimes, what you love the most is what you have to fight the hardest to keep."

"Isn't it the opposite? If you love something, set it free, or whatever."

"I don't think it's the opposite, necessarily. If you really, truly love it, it'll find you again, no matter what." He shakes his head. "I mean, look at you! I've never seen anyone draw so much. Isn't that your second sketchbook, the one Emily stole?"

"It's my third," I admit. Then, inexplicably, I find myself laughing again. "You know what's crazy? My dad bought me the anatomy coloring book in the first place—"

"Stop right there," Rowan says. "Did you say 'anatomy coloring book'?"

"I did," I say.

"For coloring? Like, with crayons? When you were a kid?"

"A little more recently than that."

"Why in the world?"

"Well, it was really a medical reference, for med students . . . not as exciting as it sounds. I went on this field trip to visit art schools sophomore year, and it's what I saw lots of students using. For memorizing anatomy. For art. Like kind of a hands-on approach . . ." Aware I am only embarrassing myself further, I shut my mouth.

"I think it's the best thing I've ever heard."

"You would."

"So do you know your anatomy?"

I pull off my bandana and run my hands through my wild hair. My face feels tight with dried tears. "I'm not sure if I like where this is going."

"Innocent speculation, I swear. I almost took an anatomy class this summer. Online, of course. It's always fascinated me."

"I know it okay. Not as well as a doctor, or one of those Marvel Comics artists, but I'm decent. For someone my age. For a girl artist."

"A girl artist?"

"Well, guy artists who are into, like, superheroes tend to know it better. I just memorized enough to get by. It helps me draw from my head. Or finish a drawing when my reference is gone, so they don't look like Muppets."

"What's this called?" He points to some indiscriminate place on his arm.

"That's between the bicep and the tricep. You probably know those. But then there's the deltoid. . . ." I reach out and touch his shoulder. "One of my favorite muscles. You've got to study not just the shape of it, but also the way it moves. It pulls up and out. Try it."

He lifts his arm. I feel his muscle flex beneath my hand.

"The deltoid runs up against the trapezius. Stand up and I'll show you." When he stands, I slide my hand to the top of his back, behind his shoulder. "The trapezius runs down your spine, where your latissimus dorsi comes around. . . ."

"Latissi . . ." He stumbles over the word.

I laugh. "Latissimus dorsi. That one's a mouthful."

"Here?" He touches my upper back.

"Lower." I arch my back as his hand slides to my waist, the heat of his touch making me suck air through my teeth. We stay that way for a moment, our hands on each other's backs. If there was music, we'd be dancing. But instead, we're just standing here awkwardly, in an anatomical half hug.

"Did I mention I love it when you talk about art?"

"You might have." I pull away, clearing my throat. "Well . . . big day tomorrow. And I'd like to be at least feigning sleep by the time Emily gets here, so I don't punch her in the face."

I follow Rowan to the door. He opens it, then hesitates.

"Bria . . . Damn it. I'm so sorry."

"Sorry about what?"

"That I've been so stupidly secretive with you. I didn't know what you went through with that ex of yours, but that's no excuse."

"Come on. That was way different."

"Close enough. And being embarrassed is no excuse either. I told you to trust me, but why would you? How could you, if you didn't know the whole story?"

"Rowan, I—"

"But I need you to know that I'm not getting into anything with Jack. No drug deals. No deals of any sort, and not any kind of real friendship, either. I never planned to. I realize it might have come off like I was considering it, but I wasn't. I swear to you. I wouldn't do that to you, or to myself."

Shit. *Shit.*

"And I'm pretty sure I talked him out of it too. From now on, you can ask me anything you want, and I'll answer. Truthfully. In the name of overcoming the past. Sound good, Bria?"

I smile weakly.

"If you're lucky," he adds, "I'll even tell you my whale shark story."

Now I grin. Because despite the plummeting sensation in my stomach, Rowan is irresistible when he's like this. "I would *love* to hear your whale shark story."

"Tomorrow." He salutes me.

As soon as I close the door, I press my forehead against it, counting to one hundred just to be safe. Then I hurry back outside and back downstairs to the lobby, desperately hoping it's not too late to call off my whole misguided espionage attempt before it blows up in my face.

22

Day 17, Morning
Suspended

Early the next morning, a vigorous knock wakes me from a stressful sleep. All night, I kept reliving my call to Starling. I thought she'd be relieved, but instead, she was annoyed. She'd already booked a plane ticket and could get only a partial refund. It was all I could do to get off the phone.

I glance at the other girls. Emily's sleeping backward, with her feet on her pillow. Ariel's still wearing her shoes. Since the two of them aren't about to resurrect themselves anytime soon, I shuffle out of bed.

"Who is it?"

"Your knight in shining armor."

"You've got to be kidding." I open the door. "Rowan, what . . ."

When I see him, I cover my face with my hands. He's wearing a wet suit, half peeled, like a black banana. I try to shut the door before my loopy brain starts cataloguing his stomach muscles, but he catches the knob.

"This is your last chance. Devon offered to take us out on the boat, but we have to go now. Lobsterfest kicks off just after noon, and we'll probably want to be back in time to shower."

"You know I don't swim."

"Won't swim. You used to swim at your beach all the time—you told me. And I think it's exactly what you need. It'll be a rite of passage."

"Like your bracelets? Which you still haven't removed."

"Give me one good reason why you won't dive."

I scowl at him. The problem is I don't have a good reason, and both of us know it.

"It doesn't have anything to do with that guy, does it?" Rowan touches my hand. "Come on, Bria—do you really want to give him that kind of power over you?"

My mouth hangs open so wide a frigate bird could fly inside it. I back into the room and sit on my bed. Ariel mumbles something incomprehensible.

"Wait." Rowan sits beside me. The cheap mattress almost touches the floor. "Look. I know that's hitting below the belt. But isn't he the reason you're holding back? I hate that fucker having any influence on you, especially when it comes to something I think you'll love. You see so much, Bria. . . . It's like traveling with a little kid."

"What?" I screech.

Rowan laughs. "I just mean . . . everything seems new through you. I don't know if it's your being an artist, but you see things in a way I haven't for a long time. If ever."

My anesthetized heart twitches feebly.

"So will you come?"

I shake my head. "It's not just Toby. I'm scared."

"You said you used to love to swim!"

I suppose I did. "It's not that I'm scared of swimming, exactly. Anymore. But . . . I'm scared of scuba diving—of being underwater. What if something happens?"

"That's my job," Rowan says. "Literally. It's my job. I'll be with you the whole time, right beside you, and I'll talk you through it all before we go under."

"But you can't prevent everything. What about, I don't know, nitrogen narcosis? Or what if I get the bends?"

"You read the dive book!"

"I did," I confess. I read it cover to cover.

"We won't go deep enough for you to worry about all that. Twenty, thirty feet, tops. You could rocket to the surface at that depth and nothing would happen."

"I might *rocket to the surface?*"

Rowan sighs. I sigh. We sigh together.

"Damn you," I say. "*Fine.* I'll dive!"

He leans over and hugs me.

Rowan has never hugged me before. And I've never hugged him. But instead of hugging back, I just sit there like a Bria-shaped rag doll, cursing that stupid silly thrill in my chest.

"You should draw me in my wet suit," Rowan shouts over the roar of the engine. We're sitting on the dive boat, on our way to the Hol Chan Marine Reserve. I can tell he's trying to calm me by changing the subject. But he's not picking the right one.

"That would be beyond lame," I tell him.

"Really? You don't think this is a good look for me?"

I can't help laughing. "I don't think wet suits are a good look for anyone. And anyway, I know you remember what I said. I don't draw friends."

"You drew Emily and Ariel."

"Not friends! And anyway, they weren't supposed to see."

"What about Starling?"

"Same."

"We're getting close," Devon shouts back at us. She's wearing a skimpy black bikini, the better for showing off her baseball glove skin.

"Well, what if you drew—"

"Shut up and talk about diving."

"But we've already gone over everything! And you've read the book."

"I want you to tell me what you love about it."

He grins. "Well . . . I love moving in extra dimensions. Not just backwards and forwards, but up and down and around. And fins. I love swimming with fins—human feet are practically useless underwater. I love all the unique things you see on each dive. Millions of little aquatic soap operas playing out between all the creatures. And the silence. Well, it's not really silent down there, but the roar of bubbles blocks any other sound. . . ."

It's beautiful, what he's saying. I've never seen him as excited as he is right this minute, with the ocean shimmering in his eyes. But the more he talks, the more nervous I feel. I'm glad I still have his spare pair of sunglasses to hide my anxiousness.

"We're here!" Devon announces.

I look around. "Really?" I'm not sure what I expected: a sign poking out of the water, maybe, or a fleet of other dive boats. But there's only one other boat, anchored to a pumpkin-orange buoy. Devon directs our boat alongside it and cuts the motor.

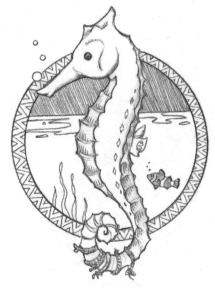

"That's the park ranger," Rowan says. "I'll pay our entrance fee. Why don't you put on your wet suit?"

Now that we're floating in one place, I can really feel the boat rocking. Bracing myself against a bench, I wrestle with the wet suit until I'm more or less inside it. It's like prying on another person's skin. Rubbery, disturbingly warm skin.

"You could pass for a pro." Rowan hands me a weight belt.

I grab it the same instant the boat tilts, and I end up sitting on the cooler. "Ow. I feel so uncoordinated."

"Just wait until you put on the rest of your equipment," Devon says, rolling a Belikin beer can up and down her leathery thigh. I can tell she's antsy to get to shore. On our way to the boat, we passed scores of islanders setting up grills and blenders behind the chain-link fence.

"This is nothing like swimming, you know." I lean forward and clip the weight belt around my waist. "There's too much *gear.*"

Rowan shrugs. "It's all weightless underwater. Now, spit," he orders, holding out my mask. "It prevents your mask from fogging up."

"Don't forget to tell her our mantra," Devon adds. "The greener the cleaner."

I wince. "So I'll be gazing at fish through how many generations of other people's snot?"

Devon laughs. "Hundreds."

Once I am encased in the rest of my scuba paraphernalia, Rowan has me totter backward in my fins to the edge of the boat. I peer at Rowan through my mask. "How do I get in?"

"Backwards. You know that—it was in the book."

"Everything's backwards."

"Including you."

I glance over my shoulder. The water pitches and sloshes. It might be clear near shore, but here I can't see anything but impenetrable blue. I hope that doesn't signify a bottomless pit.

"I'll stay right beside you the whole time you're underwater, I promise," Rowan says. "I won't leave your side for a second. The water here isn't more than ten or twelve feet deep, by the way. It's like a swimming pool. Now, put your regulator in your mouth."

I wedge the regulator—the contraption you breathe through—in my mouth. Recalling my chewed-up straw in Río Dulce, I try not to gnaw on the rubber.

"Now, hold it with one hand, and hold your mask with the other."

I try to say something, but it comes out a burble.

"What?"

I remove my regulator. "I said, push me in."

Rowan shakes his head. "Are you kidding? You're doing this yourself."

I try to make myself relax, but panic keeps corrupting my throat. It doesn't help that the air from my tank tastes like laundry room. I spit out my regulator again. "I'm still scared."

"Do you want me to go first?"

"I guess."

He lumbers over beside me. "Devon, can you help her in?"

Devon pauses in her beer can rolling to give Rowan a lazy thumbs-up.

I pull off my mask and watch Rowan tumble in. He surfaces a second later, pressing a button and inflating his dive vest—his BCD, said my dive book—with a hiss. He removes his regulator. "See? No big deal, right?"

"I think I'm going to be sick."

"Come on, it's not that bad."

"I'm serious."

"Shit!" Devon exclaims. "Not in the boat!" She rushes over to help me out of my tank. I stagger to the other side and lean over just in time. I hope the fish enjoy my breakfast.

I unzip my wet suit and battle it from my body. In my bikini, I flop back-first onto the bench, pull up my knees, and close my eyes, listening to the clunks and splashes as Rowan climbs aboard. At least the topsy-turviness in my stomach supersedes my bashfulness at displaying so much skin.

After a moment, something wet falls over my eyes. I touch my face. Rowan's bandana, soaked in fresh water. He sits beside my head as Devon starts the engine.

"I'm sorry," he says.

"You need to stop apologizing to me! I'm the one who got seasick."

"You know what I mean." I feel his hand braced against the seat, his wrist touching my shoulder. Suddenly, I'm thankful for my blindfold. "I'm probably the worst person in the world to be giving advice on moving forward."

"Right now I don't feel like moving at all."

"Fifteen minutes after you step ashore, you'll feel good as new. That's the great thing about seasickness. But if you don't feel better . . ."

"Don't worry," I say quickly. "I'll make it to Lobsterfest."

"I was going to say, if you want to sit it out, I could stay with you. It wouldn't kill me to miss it."

I try to laugh. "Yeah, right."

"I'm serious."

"You have to go, Rowan. You'll break too many hearts if you don't."

"Whose heart?"

"You know," I say vaguely.

He pushes the bandana to my forehead. The sudden sunlight makes me squint. "No, I don't."

"Don't make me say it."

He prods my side. I double up and sputter, "Quit it, ass-face! I'm sick."

"So who?"

271

I shove the bandana over my eyes so I don't have to look at him. "Emily. And Ariel. And probably every single backpacker chick on the entire island. You are one popular dive instructor."

"Assistant instructor."

"Whatever." I throw my arm over the bandana, double-shielding my eyes. Like if I can't see Rowan, he can't see me.

"Anyway," he says, "it's not important."

"Lobsterfest?"

"All of it." I feel his leg slide against the top of my head as he gets up.

I don't know why he's acting so offended. It's impossible he didn't know how adored he is, unless he's denser than a conch shell. Which is possible.

Because he's also wrong about tonight. It *is* important— the most important night of our whole trip. And tonight, I decide, will be the night I'm all in. No more holding back. Especially after my humiliating non-dive. Now, more than ever, I need to prove that I can participate. That I'm not going to let anything or anybody hold me back again. To Rowan, and to all the others, but especially to myself.

23

Day 17
Lobsterfest

After I shower (the water as arctic as ever), I dig through my backpack until I find my flowy white skirt, crushed into a ball at the very bottom.

I shake it out, touch the silver piping at the hem. It's the one I wore back at La Casa Azul. There's a smudge of dirt at the hem. Lake dirt, from Santa Lucía. I remember sitting on the bank while the backpackers skinny-dipped, feeling like I'd never be brave enough to join them. Maybe a white skirt's not the ideal thing to wear on a chicken bus, but it's perfect for a beach party. And pretentiousness be damned: I'll wear my silver necklace, too.

I paw at my clothes, searching for a shirt. I shudder as

I recall Olivia's spangly contraption that Starling flung into a wastebasket. Which makes me remember the sweatshirt I stuffed on top of it. Finally, I choose a pale gray halter I've only worn once, in Antigua.

I don't have long curvy legs like Emily, or acres of blond hair like Ariel. But maybe I can be that La Ruta Maya girl I imagined once upon a time. Gracious and profound, but also a little bit wild. Since real butterflies aren't about to flutter down anytime soon, I pull out a pen and redraw the butterfly on the back of my hand.

On my way to Rowan's room, I reach over the railing to pick a flower from a gardenia bush. I check for insects, then stick it behind my ear.

"We match," I say when Rowan opens his door. "Sort of."

He wears a short-sleeved white shirt over gray shorts, tattered at the bottom, like everything he owns. His Mayan necklace rests in the center of the tanned triangle of his chest. I smile at him, feeling almost floaty in my gladness that Rowan isn't getting into anything shady after all, that calling off Starling worked (apart from her irritation), and now, minus this morning, we have nothing between us other than tonight.

"So you're ready?" I ask him.

"Or not." He pauses. "Here we come."

We're halfway down the stairs when I notice his ankle. "Your bracelets—they're gone!"

He grins almost guiltily. "Yeah, I know. They were getting itchy after so much time in the ocean. I didn't want my foot to fall off."

His band of untanned leg is at least six inches wide. It looks brand-new, like baby skin. A rite of passage, he called it. I hoped he would invite me to take part, even if it was kind of repulsive. But he didn't. I guess it seemed like a bigger deal to me.

We stand in a long queue of islanders and visitors, waiting to enter the celebration. On the other side of the chain-link fence, the sand swarms with tropical anarchy.

Blackboards painted with rainbow chalk advertise drinks, desserts, and—you guessed it—lobster. More lobster than I've ever seen. It's practically grotesque. Grills are heaped with multitudes of the ill-fated shellfish, served whole or in any other form conceivable: rolled in burritos, mashed and smeared on corn tortillas, pureed in bisque, speared on kabobs, breaded and deep-fried in greasy, crunchy fritters. Smoke rises from the barbecues in salty billows. It soaks into our clothes until we smell like lobster, until we can't smell anything else. And that's before we get inside the gate.

As soon as we pay our five dollars, I am bonked on the head with an inflatable lobster. It's Clement. I swipe the lobster and bonk him back.

"Finally!" he exclaims, clearly plastered. "We're all over there."

I hook my index finger with Rowan's as we weave through the crowd. Dancers appear and disappear in the smoke. Music pounds from speakers as large as doghouses—not the reggae I imagined, but rock. I see local girls dancing barefoot with wreaths of flowers on their heads and emerald glitter around their eyes. Children chase each other—turns out Lobsterfest is family-friendly. Sonia waves at me from a pack of women in beach chairs. A pair of hunchbacked old men sway together as a young boy thrashes a steel drum.

275

Next to a yellow circus tent, we spy Emily and Ariel dancing atop a picnic table. I see Jack, Devon, the dreadlock twins, and about a dozen other people with them. Some I recognize; others I don't.

"Rowan!" Emily calls.

Then she sees me standing behind him. So far, we've managed to avoid each other in our waking states. To my surprise, she hops down from the tabletop and rushes straight to me. My finger falls from Rowan's as she pulls me aside.

"I wanted to apologize, Bria. It was really bitchy grabbing your sketchbook like that."

I'm sort of taken aback, but I manage to say, "You're right. It was."

"Seriously, I'm sorry." She tugs at her tiny shorts. "You know, you look great tonight."

"Um, thanks."

"Watch. Hey, everyone! Doesn't Bria look hot?"

Before I can even register my humiliation, the entire group looks over. Jack whistles. So does Clement, even though he's already seen me. I am blushing from forehead to toenails. I feel like I've downed an entire flask of Garifuna giffity, and cannot look at Rowan for the life of me.

Ariel calls to me. "Come dance!"

I take a deep breath.

Forget diving, and not diving. Forget manipulative ex-boyfriends and platonic travel brothers with shady pasts. Forget the clock spiraling toward the end of my trip, seconds rushing through an overturned hourglass so fast I can almost hear them. Forget *everything*.

This is going to be the night of my life.

I feel the same way I did when I squashed Reese's raspberry apology. But better. Because what I've squashed this time is much larger, and much more satisfying. Tonight, I am the bohemian beach fairy of my fantasies. Tonight, I am the art school girl.

I shove past Jack and Rowan. Then I climb up on the picnic table and reach for Ariel's drink.

The darker it gets, the rowdier the crowd grows. Fights break out twice, creating a current in the masses, idiots shoving each other to see. The third time the crowd surges, it's because a group of judges has crowned a local girl Miss Lobsterfest. Her waist is so narrow she resembles a twisted balloon. A pair of guys leap onstage and lift her. She holds her crown with one hand, squealing.

By then, our picnic table is a wasteland of paper plates and cups, kabob sticks and lobster carcasses. I shuffle through the mess as I drink and dance, and eat and dance, and throw back my head and dance.

Ariel keeps laughing in my ear. "I can't believe it! What's gotten into you? You're so much fun!"

Emily has scampered off to find Rowan again. All afternoon, Emily and Ariel have alternated in their pursuit. So far, neither seems to have been successful. *Don't give up the fight*, I think at him.

Which makes me realize I haven't seen him in a long time.

The thought tugs at my middle. I should go find him before I drink too much. But the problem is the drinks keep coming.

Before I left for Central America, Reese emailed me

articles about date-rape drugs in foreign countries. (And guerrilla warfare. And unanticipated volcano eruptions. And botfly larvae, which you really shouldn't look up. Really.) As a result, I won't drink anything I don't order myself. But that doesn't stop guys from sticking bills in front of my face to pay.

I dance with Ariel the most. But the guys are everywhere. They creep up from behind and accost me, sneak dance attack. They hold out burnt offerings of lobster, chicken, shrimp in exchange for just one song. When I let the Belizean guy with the double cornrow buns buy me a drink in exchange for a dance, I sort of feel like a hooker.

And then there's Jack. As scarce as Rowan seems to be, every time I turn around, the Swedish Lumberjack is pulling me into a dance. After everything Rowan's told me, I don't know why I'm even giving this guy a second of my time. He was the instigator, the force behind Rowan's fall, and yet there's something appealing about his attention, made so obvious, especially after traveling so long with someone who's made it *perfectly clear* I'm not his type.

Or maybe it was Starling who said that.

Suddenly, it's hard to remember who said what, and why. I'm starting to regret my last drink. When Jack grabs my hand for the thousandth time, I turn my face, trying to find an opening in the crowd where I can breathe. Past the chainlink fence and the palms and buildings, the sky smolders mandarin orange. It's magical. But I can't deny it—I'm starting to feel sick. And throwing up twice in one day, for different reasons, is a travel badge I'm not exactly seeking.

"Do you know where I can get a bottle of water?" I ask Jack. My mouth tastes like coconut, sickeningly strong.

He shakes his head. "How about another beer?"

I duck under his arms and head for a clearing, holding on to a palm until the ground stops mimicking Devon's dive boat. The final scraps of island fantasy drift away. And it's like I've woken up inside a painting of the underworld by Hieronymus Bosch. In the sunset, everyone's faces are colored red. The lobster smoke reeks like Hades. My feet hurt. My throat feels raw.

Ariel crashes into me. She's reapplied lip gloss, and even that seems ominous, her mouth a glistening pink gash. "I've got shots of Malibu!" she shrieks.

I push past her. I don't know where I'm going, if I'm planning on leaving, and if I leave, whether I'll come back, but I halt in my tracks when I see Rowan.

He's standing against the chain-link fence looking desperately uncomfortable, like a chaperone at a high school dance, someone's beatnik big brother, with one hand in the pocket of his ragged shorts, the other holding a nearly full beer against his knees.

"Rowan," I call.

He lifts his beer in greeting but doesn't budge from his spot. He just stands there, watching me. And then, slowly but deliberately, he shakes his head.

What the hell's that supposed to mean?

He can't be serious. I feel his eyes on my skin and I want to cover up. How long has he been watching me? Has he been counting my cocktails? Have I been laughing too loud? I've always felt like Rowan was judging me, but never in this way. I wonder if he's embarrassed for me, behaving like such a silly girl, so obviously overcompensating for the things I told him last night.

And then I begin to feel resentful.

Just because Rowan's wild years are over doesn't mean he has to tread all over my night like a ponytailed Godzilla. I'm almost two years younger than him. For all those months I wasted with Toby, I deserve this. How dare he judge me? I've never judged him. Not really. Okay, maybe sort of, but still.

When Jack's arm snakes around my middle yet again, I feel both sick and glad. "I come bearing meat," he says, holding out a lobster kabob.

Aware of Rowan's gaze, I tear off a hunk of the smoky shellfish and eat it with my fingers. I try to turn that feeble gladness into something more gratifying. But when Jack's sticky hand reaches for mine, the gladness seeps away and I just feel sicker than before.

Who am I trying to fool?

I shove Jack's hand away. "Sorry," I tell him. "But I'm just not interested."

Like a pinball, I ricochet through the crowd until I'm standing in front of Rowan. I give him a push in the center of his chest. "So whatever happened to joining in?"

He just looks at me.

"Rowan, come *on*. Liven up!" I put my hands on his hips, trying to make him dance. When I feel him respond, I put my arms over his shoulders and press up against him. I'm startled by how good it feels. He cups the back of my head in his hand, leans in.

"Don't do this," he says in my ear.

I pull back, forcing a laugh. It sounds like I'm hacking. "Do what?"

"You know what I'm talking about."

"Oh, give me a break. I've had, like, three drinks!"

Rowan stares at me, unblinkingly, until I want to cover his eyes.

"You need to stop parenting me, Rowan. Just *let me go*."

He doesn't argue; he just leans back into the fence. The party continues all around us, more jovial and boisterous than ever. But the night has officially lost its thrill, thanks to him.

"I think I need a walk," I announce.

Rowan just stands there, his beer against his knees.

24

Day 17, Evening
Jump In

I stride along the seaweed-clotted shoreline until the sounds of the party fade. Once I'm sure I'm alone, I grab my skirt and run.

When I stumble over a Coke bottle trapped in a tangle of sea grass, I kick off my sandals. I leave them where they land and keep running, dodging palm trees, slopping through milky puddles. I run until I've almost reached the tangle of mangrove forest, and then I let myself fall, first onto my knees, then onto my back.

I lie there until the ground stops swaying.

Then I sit up. Beyond my bare toes, the water flickers with lights. Spirit orbs. The horizon's so dark it blends in with the sky. Above, night clouds obscure the stars in patches silvered by the moon. All I hear is the lapping of tiny waves. The entire island has shifted to the other end.

And here I am, alone.

I feel so sorry for myself I want to cry. I *want* to. I find myself searching for that familiar knot, that parcel of emotion tucked inside my chest the moment art began to break my heart. But for the first time, I *catch* myself trying. And as soon as I uncover it, remove it like a manhole cover and roll it away, the real emotion's exposed.

Anger.

Not just anger, but outrage. The kind that glows orange at the edges and steams and stinks like when you flatiron your hair too long. Outrage. Outrageous outrage. I am so damned outraged I could scream. I do scream.

The waves lap-lap back.

I mash my fingers into my eyes until all I see are Kandinsky splotches. Then I reach into the sand and scoop massive fistfuls, squeezing it, letting it bleed between my fingers as I savor my anger.

There's anger for Toby, of course. And my parents—for being too preoccupied to question me when I gave up art school and art. There's some for Starling, because what the hell was she thinking, asking me to look out for Rowan? She knew I was vulnerable. She's got no right to be irritated after I made an honest mistake. And there's even some anger left for Reese and Olivia, for backing out on our trip. In hindsight, I'm glad they did, because otherwise I wouldn't be here. And maybe I wasn't the best friend to them when I was with Toby. But our friendship should have been stronger than that.

Most of all, I'm angry at myself.

Because I'm the one who gave it up. Of course I'm talking about my art, but not just my art. That's not all I lost. I gave up who I was when I was an artist—a version of myself so happy it scared me. Not the invented party girl I tried to become tonight. I didn't like her at all, actually. I like Bria who drew. Bria who was happy.

I've spent so much time blaming everybody around me for what happened in the last few months. But in the end, I was the one who let myself go.

And it pisses me off.

A rim of gold glows along the reef. I walk a long time before I have any idea where I am. I must have run half a mile. I wonder where I left my sandals.

I stub my bare toe on something, and I glance down. A stick of driftwood. I almost kick it away, but then I pick it up, turning it over in my hands.

Once upon a time, whatever troubled me could be scratched away by my pencil, smudged out with the side of my palm. But then Toby came along, and art seemed to become what *created* my problems. Letting it go meant I had no outlet. Maybe that's one reason I stockpiled my anger until it colored my world black and red.

I twirl the driftwood stick between my fingers.

Then I crouch in the moon-bright sand. And I begin to draw.

First I draw a nautilus shell. Nothing momentous. But my relief is instant as I mimic its cavities and whorls, endlessly swirling, my broken chunk of stick waltzing across the sand. I draw a leaping dolphin and then scratch it out and draw a killer whale in its place. On impulse, I add fangs.

I kneel and draw a goggle-eyed lobster, its antennae trailing like seaweed. A conch shell. A whale shark with leopard spots and an open mouth, swallowing a scuba diver, because damn it, I *told* him I didn't want to dive. I toss the stick aside in favor of my fingers, carving out clumps of wet sand. I start to draw a mermaid, then scratch her out and draw a sea serpent in her place. A Pegasus with butterfly wings. I'm like a crazy person. It's as if all these fantastic creatures have been caged in my brain since the day Toby first flipped through my sketchbook, and now they're all stampeding out.

I'm finishing the talons on a dragon when Rowan comes up beside me. "Caught you."

I jerk in surprise. My knee skids across the poor dragon's face. Stricken, Rowan yanks me back by my waist.

"I've ruined it!" he exclaims.

"It's not—"

"I thought if I didn't surprise you, you'd stop drawing. And now I've gone and wrecked it."

"Are you kidding? The wind's going to wreck them all anyway. But it doesn't matter. . . ." I lean down and pick up my stick. With a few strokes, I fix the dragon.

Rowan just shakes his head.

I watch him examine each of my drawings, carefully stepping between the creatures. He smiles at the lobster, the vampirish killer whale. When he sees the sea serpent, he grins.

"I drew sea lice, too," I tell him, "but they're too small to see."

"Bria, you never stop amazing me." With exaggerated

285

caution, he hops over the nautilus shell and comes to stand beside me. "And you're a mess."

I look down at my skirt. It's practically tie-dyed with tar and smears of seaweed. My arms are coated up to the elbows in pale, sugary sand. I make claws at Rowan. He catches one of my arms and brushes the sand from it, sending a million tiny shivers through my skin.

"Are you angry?" he asks softly, still holding my arm.

"You didn't do anything wrong." I pause. "Are *you* angry?"

"Not at you."

"Who, then?"

He takes my other arm. "I hated seeing Jack touch you," Rowan says. "*Hated* it."

I try to reply, but I can't breathe deeply enough. My heart's getting in the way of my lungs.

"And I know it was my fault," he goes on. "I mean, it kind of sucked, because you know about our history, but it's not like I asked you to stay away from him. Not that I can tell you what to do. It's just . . . I should have . . ." He sounds as nervous as I feel. "I've given you so much grief about hanging back, about not jumping in, when I've been just as afraid myself—"

I pull away. Because if I let him hold me for one second longer, I am going to spontaneously combust, and although it would be impressive, that's not how I want this night to end.

"Then let's go."

Rowan looks mystified. "Where?"

"If you're not ready, I'll have to go alone."

"Go where?" he shouts after me as I jog away.

When I reach the shoreline, I hurl my stick into the sea. It skips once. Not bad for a stick. Rowan catches up with me at the end of the dock.

"So . . ." My toes curl over the edge. "Do you think I'm ready?"

"I think you might be drunk."

"I think," I say, and then I step into the water.

There's no shock of cold, like I expect. Only a sudden, soothing warmth. The tickle of sea grass, the gentle suck of sand. I push off the bottom and try to shoot forward, but the current nudges me in another direction. It's almost like the waves are playing with me. *Bria! You're back!*

Each summer until this one, I swam at my favorite beach almost every day. I went with Reese or my parents at first, but once I got my license, I preferred to go alone. It wasn't the biggest beach, or the closest, or even the most scenic. Definitely not the best place to scope out guys. Olivia always wanted to drive to Santa Monica, or to giggle at the crazies in Venice. But when I was by myself, the isolation was what I loved. Knowing that I could sit and not be hassled when I pulled out my sketchbook. And that my sketchbook would still be there when I came back from a long, slow swim in the water, which was always freezing. Nothing like *this*.

Belizean water feels like a hug.

Something shimmies by my ankle. I squeal, but I feel no fear. Even if I'm chewed to pieces . . . In the ocean? What a way to go.

Okay, maybe I'm a little drunk, but it's far better than death by Guatemala City sinkhole sludge.

There's a splash, and Rowan surfaces beside me. He's shed his shirt. I feel my breath catch, and this time, I let it. Let

287

myself notice the way the moon highlights his skin like white charcoal. The shape of his collarbone, with his Mayan necklace right in the center. His chest. His shoulders.

"Trapezius," I tell him.

He flexes his arm.

"Wrong muscle."

"I *knew* I'd get you in the water one of these days."

"Or nights," I say with a grin.

"Race you?"

Without warning, I lunge for the horizon. He grabs my calf and yanks me back. "Cheater!" I scream as he charges ahead.

I catch his foot just in time, and I pounce and push him under. I try to swim away, but my legs tangle in my godforsaken skirt. He wraps his arms around my hips and lifts me in the air. I manage only one short scream before he tosses me over his shoulder and I'm underwater.

When I burst up, laughing and spitting, he grabs me around the waist. I bite him in the trapezius. He tries to escape, but neither of us can swim, we're both laughing so hard.

And suddenly, we stop. And we're just looking at each other, panting.

We come together in a series of motions. He catches my hands. I wind my fingers through his. He brings my arms behind his waist.

The water shifts endlessly, knocking us together, pulling us apart.

Then my back hits something. When I turn to look, Rowan grips me under my arms and lifts me out of the water, until I'm sitting on the dock. He climbs out after me, trapping the sopping layers of my skirt with his knees. I fall back and pull him with me, my hands running over his chest and back, his skin wet and smooth, all the vital muscles just waiting to be named.

He reaches for my hands, pulls them over my head, and holds them. And then my heart turns over, because his mouth has found mine.

25

Day 17, Night
How It Ends

Here's what's *supposed* to happen.

Everything's supposed to culminate that night on the dock. Okay, maybe not *on* the dock, because that would be splintery. But the arc that began with a glance in the Guatemala City airport brought to its inevitable conclusion in a hostel bed, with the music from the beach party filtering through the window, the wind gone wild right outside.

But in reality, we don't even make it to the hostel.

And unfortunately, I don't mean it like *that*.

Here's how it really ends.

I'm lying on the dock, and Rowan's on top of me, and

we've been kissing for so long my whole face feels numb—but the good kind of numb, which I swear exists. The world could screech to a halt on its axis and the dock could be swept out to sea in an apocalyptic current, and we wouldn't notice. Our universes have condensed into each other.

At long last, Rowan rolls to the side and tugs me up. We stumble down the dock, then through the sand, playfully, him half carrying me, but we don't get very far, because we keep stopping to kiss. At one point, I trip over the root of a coconut palm and fall, and it's funny, but it also kind of hurts.

Rowan's kneeling next to me, holding me, kissing me. And I want to go on, I want to continue, but something inside me has started to pull back.

It's the most intense moment of my life, and suddenly, that scares me. I know this was the whole point of my trip. I'm finally living out my promise to Olivia. To find somebody to make me forget. But this isn't just somebody.

It's Rowan.

"What's wrong?" he asks.

I shake my head. He takes that to mean everything's okay, and he weaves both his hands through my hair and kisses me again. Mentally, I fight to keep myself here, on this island, on this beach, in this moment, but it's too late. *I can't, I can't, I can't.*

"Bria?"

"I can't."

Rowan looks confused for a second. Then he pulls his hands from my face.

"I'm sorry," I say. "It's just . . . I promised myself. It just hasn't been long enough since . . . I mean, I promised myself

I wouldn't, unless . . ." It sounds so idiotic coming out, but it's too late to stop. "Unless it can be meaningless."

"Meaningless?"

It's not a harsh word, but the way he says it, each consonant feels like a finger-jab in my chest. "I know it's too late for that," I say hurriedly. "I know. I shouldn't have . . . It's my fault. I just never thought this would happen. We're like brother and sister."

"Bria, give me a break. You know that's bullshit."

"But it's what you said—"

"I thought it was what you wanted."

I shook my head. "No, it's what *you* wanted."

"No, it's— I'm not going to argue about this. You were the one who said you had a boyfriend."

"Because I was scared!" I pound my fist in the sand. "Of *this*!"

Rowan lifts his hand, and then it falls back on his knees, a dead bird.

"I've got to think of myself, Rowan. And for a while longer, that means thinking *only* of myself. I just can't give any more of myself away. I'm sorry."

"This is your life, Bria."

"I know that—"

"I'm not finished," he says. "This is your life. But it's mine, too. And I'm sick, I'm tired, I'm so damned *exhausted* of wasting it on *meaningless* things. If you want to go down the same path I did, I can't stop you. But I won't help you either."

"I'm not asking you to help me!" My voice breaks. "Just that . . . Rowan, please. I can't stand it if both of you are mad at me."

"Both? Me and who else?"

"You and Starling."

"Wait, what do you mean, Starling? Why's Starling mad at you?"

Oh God. Now I've done it.

I squeeze my arms around my middle to restrain the sick in my stomach. I want to lie, but I can't. Not after everything that's happened. And he'll find out from Starling anyway—something I should have realized this whole time. "I talked to her last night," I admit. "And a few days ago. She wanted me to call her if I suspected anything. Any trouble."

"Bria . . . are you saying you called my sister to tell on me?"

I hug myself more tightly. "I thought I was doing the right thing. We were worried about you. . . ."

"I don't believe this!" Rowan kicks at the sand. "Why didn't you talk to me first? After I was completely honest with you? About everything?"

"I'm *sorry*. She was going to come here, but I called her off. It's fine. She's pissed at me, not at you, okay?" I grab at Rowan's hands, trying to pull him toward me, but he shakes me off.

"Way too late for that, Bria."

"That's not what I meant. I just—I don't get why it has to be all or nothing! Can't we just go back to the way things were? What about all those places you wanted to take me?"

Rowan shakes his head scornfully.

"What about Wanderlove?" I ask, but he's already turned away.

As I climb the stairs to my room, full-body shell-shocked, the wind rattling my brain in my skull, my arms and legs doped with the worst kind of numbness, I have to keep telling myself that as bad as it hurts, it would hurt so much more if I'd let what almost happened happen.

If I'd let myself fall for him.

But the next morning, when I push open the door to Rowan's room and find his bed empty, his backpack missing, I know that's the biggest bullshit of all. Because it's too late—I've fallen.

PART
4

The Ruins

I've been absolutely terrified every moment of my life—and I've never let it keep me from doing a single thing I wanted to do.

~*Georgia O'Keeffe*

There are always flowers for those who want to see them.   ~*Henri Matisse*

26

Day 18
Afterward

I walk through the remnants of Lobsterfest. It looks like a battleground, with lobster claws and confetti for weapons. An invisible haze of smoke seems to hang in the air, scorching my already aching throat. Last night's winds hauled in a tumble of clouds. The sea looks more gray than turquoise.

I stop by the dive shop. Devon's there, puffy-eyed, organizing the rack of wet suits. They remind me of the hog corpses in the Mayan butcher stalls.

"I thought you left," she says. "Rowan came and got his check late last night. He said he had to catch the first water taxi this morning. He didn't say anything about the two of you parting ways, though, so I thought . . . Is something wrong?"

They don't do goodbyes.

"Everything's fine." I'm amazed by how cheerful I sound. All those months of faking happiness have really paid off.

"So now you're on your own?"

"Well, I . . ." It hasn't hit me until she says it.

I am on my own.

"If you want to meet up for dinner tonight," she says, "I think a few of us are going to Gilligan's for drinks. Almost everyone will be gone by then, though. After the party's over, the island empties pretty quickly."

I tell her I'll think about it, even though I know I won't go.

In the afternoon, I put on my bathing suit and head to the channel. I walk to the very end of the cement pier, shedding my shorts and shirt as I go. When my face hits the water, I don't remember diving in.

I climb out and dive in again, over and over, until I'm exhausted. Then I crawl out and lie on my back. I watch goose bumps rise on my stomach, my thighs. I've grown so tan over the last few days I hardly recognize my skin as my own. I try to breathe deeply like I did last night, lying on the sand. But my chest feels shallow, my throat parched. I think the numbness has spread.

Desperate to feel something, I attempt to coax out the anger that poisoned me for so many months. But when I picture Toby lying with his hand on my stomach, I think of Rowan lying beside me on the dock the day we arrived. When I picture my parents failing to notice when I put away my pencils, I think of Rowan consoling me after Emily whored out my sketchbook.

I think of him bringing me his old backpack in Panajachel, the lake like a crinkled sheet of foil behind him. I think of him in Livingston, storytelling the legend of his dragon tattoo.

I'm glad I learned it so young. To depend on myself, and no one else.

But didn't Rowan depend on me by the end? I think about how much he opened up to me over the course of our trip, and how much I opened up to him. I spent so much time gaining his trust. His respect. And I lost it all, in one stupid night.

I know what it's like. To throw away all the good things you've got going for you.

Even if I want to track him down, I don't have his email address or his cell phone number—if he had a phone, the damned hermit. I don't have any way to contact him, other than calling Starling again, and I can't do that, not after how our last call went. Now that I've wasted an entire day on the island, he could be anywhere. And my plane leaves Guate-mala City the day after tomorrow. I can't afford to postpone my flight. In every possible way, I have royally fucked this up.

Nothing makes you hate yourself more than that.

In the evening, I sit at the end of the dock. Our dock. The sun is just starting to set. I open my sketchbook to a blank sheet and stare at it. If I were in a movie, I might tear out the pages one by one and fling them into the water. But I don't want to litter.

It's too dark to draw, really, but I know I need to. Because I'm already forgetting.

I can remember the moments. Smearing mud all over him.

299

Sharing too-small hammocks. Sitting on an overturned rowboat and talking about my art. Listening to him talk about diving, about his tattoo, about his regrets. But his face is dim, like a faded photo. A travel ghost.

I start flipping through the pages of my sketchbook. I've had no problem drawing Starling. And no matter what Emily said about her own sketch, I totally nailed her likeness, legs and all. I can draw pelicans from memory. The dive shop. The dock. I can name every single one of Rowan's muscles. I just can't draw him. I should have when I had the chance. But instead, as usual, I let fear get in the way.

I hung on to my relationship with Toby so long, I thought the best antidote was doing the opposite. To run without looking back. But that's just another way of compromising. Another way of letting Toby have power over me. I was so afraid of anything getting in the way of my independence, I couldn't see that Rowan had helped me find it in the first place. That's probably why I let myself think the worst when it came to Rowan and Jack.

As long as I had a reason not to trust Rowan, I couldn't fall for him.

Or so I thought.

And now I'm leaving Central America. I've learned hardly any Spanish. I won't see Laughingbird Caye again. Or Santa Lucía, or Livingston. I haven't visited a single Mayan ruin, which was what inspired me to pick Central America in the first place.

I imagine myself showing up at my friends' houses the night I get back, suntanned and sage-like, imparting all my travel wisdom. Reese would probably be disappointed by my lack of serious peril, other than my stolen purse. "You mean, you didn't see even *one* botfly?" she'd say. Olivia's reaction would be markedly different. "Tell me more about the make-out session on the beach," she'd demand. Or "You mean you didn't get laid at all? You prude!"

They wouldn't want to hear about the baby iguanas skimming across the river. Sonia's soca music. My Technicolor rainbow glasses. The jungle. The island. And the lake—how it looked coming through the mountains. Like a shock of blue light.

Or they'd listen, but they wouldn't care. No one would. Hearing about vacations is like hearing about dreams— no one cares except the person who's experienced them. Without tastes and scents and context, they're meaningless.

Meaningless. I hate that word. Even more than *potential*.

I turn another page and find a drawing of the art school girl, paint-brush in hand, running barefoot down the hall. The girl I'd thought I would become, before I met Toby and altered my future in an attempt to synchronize it with his. I wanted her happiness more than anything in the world. But why was I so

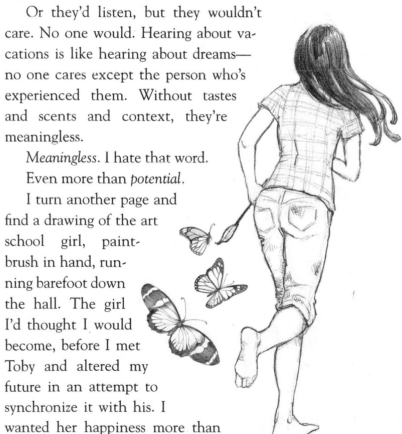

certain she was happy? I never even saw her face. Maybe she was running because she was crying.

Maybe she'd just made the biggest mistake of her life.

I'm on my feet before I know it, halfway down the pier before I've crammed my sketchbook all the way into my day-pack. I've got one last chance, one last hyenashit-insane scheme, and it's not going to be easy. It's going to be brutal. But I know I've got to try.

Sometimes, what you love the most is what you have to fight the hardest to keep.

27

Day 19
Flowers

Starling sits atop a desk, cross-legged, an ivy-colored skirt gathered between her knees. She wears Birkenstock sandals and a white headband instead of a Mayan scarf. Her hair is coiled in two Princess Leia buns at the base of her neck. She's peering at a thick book over the top of her glasses, the red-framed ones from the lake. I rap my knuckles on the doorjamb.

She looks up. "Holy fuck."

"You read my mind. You're an English teacher? I thought you were, like, teaching business basics to impoverished families."

"What are you doing here?"

"Looking for you, obviously."

"Why didn't you call first?"

"So you could yell at me again? You wouldn't even let me explain."

She closes her book and sets it on the table. "I'm sorry about that. . . . I was upset. But why in the world are you looking for me?"

I can't tell whether she's playing dumb, or she really has no clue why I'm here. Maybe I'm acting brave, but my relief at finding Starling is so earthquaking I'm amazed my knees don't give out. The trip from Laughingbird Caye to Flores, Guatemala—*alone!*—was the toughest journey I've ever taken, in more ways than one. Since I don't have the energy for hinting or guessing, I opt for full disclosure.

"Because Rowan left me on the island, and it's my fault, and I want to make amends. And if anyone knows where he is, it's you."

"Unfortunately," Starling says, "I don't."

My expression probably resembles a deflated pig face. "He hasn't talked to you?"

"Nope. Not yet."

"So he could be anywhere."

"Could be," she agrees. She checks her phone. "Is it after five already? You're lucky I'm still here—usually I'm long gone by now. How about we grab something to eat?"

She probably hears my stomach snarling. I haven't eaten since a sweet corn tamale in Belmopan, the Belizean capital, six or seven hours ago. And to be honest, I'm not sure I entirely believe her, and it might be more difficult for her to lie sitting across from me over a meal. "As long as I can leave this damned thing here," I say, shrugging out of my backpack

and tossing my daypack on top of it. Some travel companion—
it's killing me.

Flores is located on a tiny island in a lake called Petén
Itzá. Like Antigua, it's Spanish colonial, with pastel-
colored buildings and cobblestone streets. At the top of
the hill, a white double-domed church seems to glow in the
dark. The prices at the café Starling chooses are so cheap I
order a feast: hot chocolate, steamed vegetables with tofu,
french fries, and *pollo a la plancha*, which turns out to be grilled
chicken.

"So how in the world did you find me?" Starling asks.

"You told me you were in Flores—it was never a secret."

"Yeah, but I never said *where* in Flores. And I never told
you how to get here."

"It wasn't hard. Flores is a popular destination." I'd used
my fifteen minutes of free hostel Internet wisely. Rowan was
right: all the travel information I needed was a straightforward
Google away.

"But how did you travel here, exactly? Did you fly?"

"Are you kidding? I'm broke."

Starling exhales noisily. "Can you just explain yourself
already? Fine, I admit I underestimated you. You made it
back to Guatemala alone. I just want to know how it went
down!"

I squeeze a glob of neon-green ketchup onto my plate. I
eat three more french fries, which are so squishy they're more
like mashed potato spears, and tell Starling the story I docu-
mented in my sketchbook on the bus to Flores.

My Epic Journey

Phase One: The Boat

I left a note with my email address on top of Ariel's head. I left another note in the dive shop mailbox addressed to Devon and Clement, and a second for them to give to Sonia. Then I waited at the main dock for the day's first water taxi. In the early morning, the Caribbean looks pink.

Phase Two: The Taxi

To my surprise, I had the same Belize City cab driver as last time—the one with the jalapeño-flavored Pringles. I swear he still smelled like them.

Phase Three: The First Bus

I pictured all of Belize as spindly beach forest, but the back side of Belize is real forest, almost as dense as the jungle in Livingston. On our way there, we passed the sign for the turnoff to the Community Baboon Sanctuary, and I admit it: my heart did a pirouette. A lonely one.

Phase Four: The Border

Ugh. Ninety-degree heat with a billion percent humidity, and a line as long as a football field. When I finally made it to the immigration office, I was inexplicably terrified they'd deny me access to Guatemala. Like maybe my mom and dad had called and told them to deport me back home to the United States. Luckily, I got across all right. I had to leave my English at the border: Your language is no good here. But as it turned out, *once I needed it, I remembered more high school Spanish than I thought I did. Who knew?*

Phase Five: The Second Bus

Someone must have buried a fleet of bowling balls under the road from the border to Flores. Thank God the scenery distracted me from my tailbone. A basketball court filled with goats. Churches with names like Iglesia Evangelical de la Luz y Vida Eterna. Men beating weedy lots with machetes. Shacks folding in on themselves. Cattle pouring over the road like a river of brown butter.

~ July 30, somewhere in Guatemala

It was dark by the time the bus crossed the bridge to Flores, which looked like a fantasy kingdom to me in my strung-out state. Until I climbed off the bus and realized I had no idea where to go.

"So you've done it," Starling says, applauding. "You've mastered Central American transportation."

"It's not hard when you know your destination."

"But how the hell did you find my school?"

"First, I found a kid."

"A kid?"

"Actually, she found me." I was standing on the busy side-walk, a boulder splitting a brook, when a local girl took pity on my helplessness. Miracle of all miracles, her sister was in Starling's class. Well, Flores is a tiny village, but still. For the first time since I met Rowan and Starling, it felt like the fates had flicked a little happy dust my way. "She happened to know who you were. The rest is history."

307

Starling points at my food with her fork. "You know, tofu's made of soybeans. Same as tempeh."

"I know that, Starling."

"You said you were allergic to tempeh."

It takes me a second to remember what I said in Panajachel. "I did say that. But you said you didn't know where Rowan was. So we're both liars."

It's a gamble. But a good one. Gradually, Starling starts to smile.

"So where is he?" I ask. "Is he in Central America, at least?"

"Think about it. It's been, what—three days? Two? He barely makes any money diving. Just enough to get by. And he refuses to take money from me, unless it's a real emergency."

I poke at my *pollo a la plancha*, my appetite fading as my mind stacks the Central American destinations Rowan told me about. Utila. Little Corn Island. Chachauate Key. Costa Rica. So many places. Damn Rowan and his Wanderlove. And didn't he say something about heading south when we first met? But does that mean farther south in Guatemala? Or Brazil? He could have wrangled up a subzero parka and headed to Antarctica, for all I know. I wouldn't put it past him.

Starling steals a fry from my plate. "Anyway, how do you know he wants to be found?"

"I don't. But like I said, I want to make amends. I don't know what he's told you. . . ." I think of our dock, and my face heats up. "But he found out I called you, Starling. That's not all, but it's what's important." Or at least, what I'm willing to tell. "He's angry, and really hurt."

"In which case, I'd hope you'd respect his decision to disappear."

When she reaches for another fry, I slide my plate away.

"Look who's talking, Starling! You're the one who keeps enlisting strangers to 'protect' him. He's almost twenty years old! Talk about a lack of respect."

"You don't know what I know."

"I know more than you think—but it doesn't make a difference. If you hadn't underestimated your brother so much and planted all those stupid suspicions in my head, I wouldn't be in this mess, would I? If you're not going to tell me anything, I might as well go."

I stand up, then sit back down.

"I left my money in my daypack," I admit.

Starling hands the server a couple of bills. "Where the hell are you planning to go, exactly? It's getting dark. Do you have a place to stay?"

It's times like these I really, really wish I wasn't broke and clueless.

"Are you inviting me over?"

"No. I'm letting you sleep out in the street. Of course I'm inviting you over. You'll give me a headache all night, but I'm not as much of a bitch as you think I am. Believe it or not."

An armed security guard cranks open the gate to Starling's building, which has white iron cages on all the windows. On our way to the stairs, she stops by her car. That's right—Starling has a car. A Toyota Camry, parked in a tiny carport inside the gate.

"A rental," she confesses, seeing my expression.

"I don't get it. Can't you walk to work?"

"Obviously. But it's way more convenient to have a car. They just put in a supermarket outside Santa Elena."

I guess I can relate. My high school was less than one mile from my house, but I drove there anyway. I'd have thought Starling would be different, though.

She unlocks the door to her third-floor studio apartment. It's small, with a red tile floor and a window overlooking the Flores rooftops. A massive table serves as a desk, cluttered with papers, travel journals, and computer paraphernalia. The kitchenette in the corner is equally messy, the sink heaping with dishes. An orange apron hangs from a hook on the wall. Next to her bed, there's a framed photo of Starling and Rowan standing atop a Mayan ruin. Rowan looks younger, his hair shorter and hanging in his eyes. I wonder if he's been here since he left the island. Wondering makes my stomach hurt.

"I don't get it," I say for the second time. "You just got here. How come you have so much stuff?"

"This is where I lived before. I kept everything here when I went to stay with Rowan." She kicks off her shoes. They strike the opposite wall: bang, bang.

"In Santa Lucía?"

"Sure. The owners kept it for me. I paid, of course."

I watch Starling fill two coffee mugs from a jug of purified water and stick them in the microwave. "Where do you get all this money?"

"My stepdad. He's loaded. He and my mother use money as a substitute for affection, and I've decided to be okay with that."

My thoughts start to sputter. I always assumed people who lugged around backpacks and stayed in places like the Rain-

forest Retreat did it because they couldn't afford anything better. Coming from money is the last thing I would have expected from Starling West, the backpacker ideal. She drops tea bags in the mugs and brings them to the table. I glance at the label: Tazo Wild Sweet Orange. Isn't that the Starbucks brand? I feel like I've tumbled down the rabbit hole. "If money's no problem, why in the world do you backpack?"

Starling sits across from me. "You think only broke people can backpack?"

"No, but . . ."

I guess I never really thought about it. On first reflection, simulating poverty seems deceitful, like panhandling for fun. Isn't it offensive to the truly impoverished? But then again, anyone who can afford a plane ticket is doing better than most of the world. I guess that's something you carry with you as a person who travels with his or her eyes all the way open.

"But what?" Starling prompts.

"Well, Rowan and I discussed this kind of thing a lot," I say slowly. "How a person sees more by traveling cheap. More of the real world, at least. And then, once you've traveled this way . . . it probably wouldn't feel right to travel in luxury, even if you could afford it." I pause. "Though maybe I'll feel differently when I'm sixty with a bad back. But it's why you volunteer all the time, isn't it? That guilt?"

"I guess it's part of the reason," Starling agrees. "First-world guilt. You know what, Bria? You're a walking contradiction. You come off one way, but you're really someone else entirely."

"Thanks. I guess."

"It's funny to think back, isn't it? I was so surprised to see you in Santa Lucía. I thought maybe I'd misjudged you on the plane—but then, you seemed so uncomfortable around the other backpackers. Also, you were kind of bossy. So I thought there was a good chance you'd keep Rowan from the island. Or at least from Lobsterfest. Before you yell at me again, I'm not saying Rowan can't take care of himself, okay? But there's no need to revisit the scene of old crimes."

"I wanted to go to Lobsterfest more than he did."

"You did?"

"It's true. Rowan tried to get out of it, but I pressured him to go. And he hated it. But I didn't notice—I was just so into my own little party."

"I suspected you had your own shit to deal with. Considering you invented a boyfriend and all."

"I didn't *invent* him! I just lied about our breakup."

"Why'd you lie?"

"I don't know. It's not like I thought it through. I guess I

312

wasn't ready to be completely accountable for myself. If that makes sense."

"It does." Starling gets up and crosses the room to her dresser. In front of me, she changes into a pair of gym shorts and a T-shirt. I am not surprised Starling is one of those naked people. When she rejoins me at the table, I see her shirt reads *Banana Republic*. Talk about walking contradictions.

"You're staring." She swivels around. "Look at the back."

"'Honduras,'" I read.

"The real banana republic."

"Got it." I bounce my tea bag in my mug, even though the water has reached the point of supersaturation. I know I need to bring up Rowan again, but my mouth won't form the words. "So . . . has this ever happened before? With other girls?"

"What, the stalking?"

"Starling! Come on, I'm not . . ." Wait, am I?

"I'm just teasing. No, I'm pretty sure none of his girls lasted longer than a week or two. But as you know, Rowan was a lot different back then. He had the same good heart. Three sizes too big, if you ask me. But it's only recently that he's turned some of that love on himself."

"So he loved them?"

"Love?" Starling scoffs. "Are you being funny?"

"I thought . . . I don't know. Wanderlove, and all that."

"Don't you remember what I said? It has nothing to do with love."

"Maybe."

"Maybe? I'm the one who came up with it."

"But it's not your philosophy. It's Rowan's."

"Whatever." Starling wedges her knees against the table.

313

"I'm realizing I have no idea what he's told you over the past couple weeks. Did he tell you how we met?"

"Met?" I blink at her. "How you met? But you're brother and sister. You've always known each other."

"Nope. We met when I was your age."

My age? I'm speechless. *But what about your secret language?* I almost ask, and then I remember: I made it up. I invented their childhoods together.

"I didn't even know Rowan existed," Starling explains. "All I knew was what my mother told me—that my dad was a loser and a drunk and probably dead, and they hadn't been in touch since before she had me. I was clueless until my freshman year of college, when this sixteen-year-old guy showed up on my doorstep in Berkeley. He'd tracked me down. Rode a Greyhound all the way from Oregon. I couldn't believe it."

I can't believe it either. "You're saying your mother didn't know about him?"

"That's what she said, but I didn't believe her, and I still don't. Rowan always knew about me—his dad's not the type to protect anyone from anything. Our dad, I mean. Apparently, he'd tried to get in touch himself. Probably for the wrong reasons—he must have known my mom married rich. But I was an adult! I deserved to know I had a brother."

"At least you have him now."

"As much as anyone can *have* Rowan."

I can't help thinking about my own parents. Maybe they could be more outspokenly supportive of my art talent, more perceptive, more harmonious, all the qualities I find them lacking. But they've always been truthful. They've always been open in their love for me. And the other stuff—well, they're people. Flawed people, just like me. I need to stop blaming them for not asking the right questions when I could have volunteered the answers at any time.

I should probably start by telling them where the hell I am.

My eyes migrate to the photo beside Starling's bed. "That's at Puerto Sol, in Nicaragua," she says. "Almost two years ago."

"When Rowan came to meet you in Central America."

"Yep. When he caught the travel bug. Met Jack. Began to dive."

"And never looked back."

"And began making a real mess of things." Starling tugs off her headband. "He was always a party animal. When I left him to head home and finish college, I should have known things would escalate. I graduated early last winter, and we did some traveling before I came to work up here. That's when the shit really hit the fan."

She unwinds her Princess Leia buns until her hair dangles in two pigtails.

"When I came down to Lake Atitlán that time, he was the lowest I'd ever seen him. Someone in a boat from San Pedro la Laguna caught him trying to swim across the lake. In the middle of the night. Do you know how far that is? He was so depressed. Practically out of his head. Hal Cavendish—you know, the guy from La Casa Azul—Hal called me and told me what was going on. I gave the school a day to find a replacement teacher. And then I went."

I think about the bus breakdown, when Rowan wouldn't share his scary story. "Was Jack with him? At the lake?"

Starling wrinkles her nose. "He was with me, actually.

Here in Flores. Visiting from Laughingbird, where he'd just started working. It wasn't serious or anything. After I found out how he'd left Rowan in Honduras, I was completely over it. And so I left. Fast."

"But you were with Jack at the airport."

Starling nods. "Despite Rowan's better judgment, they got back in touch. Jack stayed at the lake a couple days, before you got there—that's when he invited Rowan to Laughingbird Caye. That jackass has got a sixth sense for vulnerability. Back in Honduras, I'm pretty sure—"

"Don't tell me."

Starling squints at me. "Really? I thought you'd be dying to know what happened."

"Rowan told me a lot. But what I don't know . . ." I wrap the string of my tea bag around my finger. "It's Rowan's story. You know? He should be the one to tell it—if he wants. It's all that talking and wondering and speculating that got me in trouble in the first place. And even if I never see him again, at least I'll know I haven't done anything else to compromise his trust."

Starling keeps staring at me, her head tipped slightly. In the silence, I can hear tuctucs beeping in the streets below. Someone's playing Latin accordion music in the next apartment over.

"You're right," she says at last. "I guess I've been underestimating everyone lately."

For the first time, I see the resemblance between her and Rowan. Something in the shape of their eyes and mouths. It makes me miss him more than ever, and I have to look away.

"You really think a lot of him, don't you?" she asks.

"How can I not?" I touch the butterfly in the crook of my

hand. It's fading; I'll have to retrace it. Maybe I should tattoo it there. But then it'd ruin all the fun in drawing it. "Can you tell him I'm sorry?"

"Why don't you tell him yourself?"

I look wildly around, heart pounding. Is Rowan here? Has he been hiding in a closet, listening?

"He's not here! If that's what you're thinking. Not right here, anyway. But he is nearby."

"Where is he?"

"You're going to have to get up really, really early," she says, reaching for her phone.

After Starling finishes talking with the shuttle company, I ask if I can call my parents. I could use my phone, but racking up roaming charges isn't the best way to atone for my lack of status updates. Starling brings a book and a flashlight to the balcony to give me privacy.

"I'm all right," I say as soon as my mom answers.

What follows is a whole lot of yelling, and a whole lot of tug-of-war as my dad battles for the phone, before they finally put me on speaker and give me the chance to explain.

"But what were you doing in *Belize?*" my mom demands. "We were so afraid you'd end up all alone in Nicaragua or El Salvador, somewhere dangerous."

I swallow the groan rising in my throat. As it turns out, Marcy called my parents the day after I left the Vagabonds. All they knew was that I'd gone off with some backpacker girl. Like Rowan said, they probably thought I joined a jungle cult. "It's fine, Mom," I insist. "There are travelers everywhere. And I've been with friends."

"With friends?" The relief in her voice is obvious. "You made friends. So you haven't been alone."

"Of course not!"

"I *told* you," my dad says. "Didn't I tell you she'd be fine?"

"She disappeared in a third-world country. What was I supposed to think? Bria, I don't understand why you didn't contact us two weeks ago."

"I was upset."

There's a silence, so long I think we've been disconnected. Then my mom chuckles nervously. "Upset? About what?"

I trace my finger over the wood grain of Starling's table. I should have called my parents days ago, when I was still feeling angry. Now I just feel distracted by tomorrow's journey—shorter than today's, but much more intimidating. "Why didn't you say anything when I stopped drawing?"

"Drawing? What has drawing got to do with Central America?"

"Everything." I pull the phone from my ear to glance at the time. "Look—I'm exhausted, and I have to get up in just a few hours. I'm going to try to explain. Will you listen? For once, without interrupting to tell me what *you* think is best for me?"

I brace myself for an argument. But all my mom says is "Of course, Bria. We're listening."

So I tell them. The crib notes version. About Toby, and art school, and how I stopped drawing as soon as it became a struggle, and how maybe some part of me was afraid of my success, relieved by my fall, and this trip has helped me kick that side of myself in the ass. "And I still haven't sent in my housing forms for state. Which means I've probably lost my spot. And I'm fine with that, really I am. I figure I'll start out at community college, and in a couple years I can transfer. Or I'll study art later, in some graduate program. It's not the end of the world. . . ."

My mom interrupts me. "Bria. Have you read *any* of the emails we sent you?"

I pause, feeling ashamed. "Not really, no."

"Your father found your forms after we dropped you off at the airport. We made some calls. It's not too late—you can still go."

Suddenly, my heart swells in my chest. "To art school?" I squeak.

"Not to art school. But to state."

My heart deflates with a pinched-balloon squeal. "Oh."

"They *do* have an art program, though. I checked."

"You did?" I say incredulously. I mean, I already knew they had an art program, but that my mom checked? Wow.

"Is that so hard to believe? Anyway, I know it's not the same . . ."

"But your mother and I hope you'll consider it, Bria," my father finishes, in that low, strain-to-hear tone he saves for truths he feels with his whole heart. "Take it from me. Even when life turns out different than what you planned, it's always better to try and fail than to wonder what could have been."

I'm still processing this when a sound makes me jump. Starling's knocking her flashlight on the sliding door. "Can I come in yet?" she shouts. "It's freezing!"

28

Day 20, Morning
Tikal

Happy Forever

• *My dad gave me my very first sketchbook when I was*
three years old, after he caught me drawing on the walls of
his office. Who could blame me? Walls are so big and
white and boring. It's no wonder people paint them bright
colors, hang paintings and tapestries, and feel suffocated in
hospitals.

    Now I realize the sketchbook had to be one of his old
ones, maybe with the used pages torn out. He told me I
could draw on the floor anytime I wanted—just not on the
actual floor, or the walls, or the ceiling, either.

    That sketchbook was like a wardrobe to a magic
kingdom. When you're three, you don't draw what you

see—you draw upon your imagination. Nobody tells you to stop putting wings on people, unless you have a most unfortunate preschool teacher. You are intoxicated by your own magic. Everyone draws as a little kid, but most people lose it as they grow up. For any number of reasons: lack of skill, lack of motivation, lack of encouragement.

Miraculously, somehow I hoarded that power longer than most people—the power to draw out the brilliant parts of the real world on paper, until art became an entire world of its own. I think I could be happy forever, straddling both worlds, one foot in each. Most people don't get that opportunity. Even if—

The shuttle bus beeps outside Starling's window. I date my journal entry and put down my pen. It's still dark out. I'm dressed in a tank top, my sneakers, and a pair of Starling's drawstring pants. "Cherish them," she said. "They've back-packed around the world. Now I'm passing the torch." In the morning chill, my Windbreaker has made a comeback, but thank goodness it's not so crispy anymore. I've crammed a bottle of water, my third sketchbook, and my favorite pencils into my daypack. My overstuffed backpack leans against the door.

I go over and shove Starling's shoulder. She groans.

"I'm leaving," I tell her. "If this doesn't work out, I might never see you again."

"That's crap," she mumbles. "You have my number. And you always pop up somewhere."

I pat her head. Whatever happens with Rowan—if I find him—it's nice to know Starling and I have passed the peace pipe. The peace pants.

On the shuttle, I sit on a bench seat in back. A pair of

teenage girls sit on either side of me, because they got here first and both want window seats. So for the forty-five-minute ride, I'm stuck between them, cringing beneath their squeals, ducking to avoid their excitable elbows. Nervousness is already salsa dancing in my stomach, so I distract myself by attempting to look out the windows.

The Petén jungle barricades both sides of the road. We pass a sign warning of falling rocks, which I decide not to think about. What are you supposed to do? Drive faster? Swerve? Once we pass through a checkpoint—military fatigues, machine guns—and enter the park, I see other signs looming in the dark: JAGUAR CROSSING, COATI CROSSING, DEER CROSSING, even TURKEY CROSSING.

At last, we pull into a big gravel parking lot, beside dozens of *turismo* buses and minivans. I guess we're not the only ones here to greet the sunrise. Our tour guide slides open the door to the sound of a whole chorus of cicadas, along with the sharp scent of wet soil. I see a few hotels—basic, budget places. I squeeze the straps of my daypack. Any one of them could be his.

As I climb the wooden staircase to Temple IV, which is so steep it seems more like a ladder than a staircase, the sun is already rising. Layers of gold and peach streak the stormy sky. The entire forest seems to vibrate, whispering up and down my bare arms, making the hair stand on end. When I finally emerge atop the crown of the Two-Headed Serpent—with a boundless jungle vista spread out before me, so vast I can almost make out the curvature of the earth—the satisfaction that sweeps over me seems so tangible, it practically sparkles.

322

It's the perfect moment to find Rowan. To run at each other (well, to walk briskly, since we're more than two hundred feet in the air) and to fall (but not really) into each other's arms.

I walk all the way around the top of the temple twice before I'm sure of it.

He's not here.

My stomach plummets all the way to the ground.

When Starling said Rowan might be here, on top of this particular temple, it made perfect sense. It's one of his special places. Like Sonia talked about—the places you *get,* the places that stick in your heart. One of the places Rowan said he'd take me, when we lay together in the hammock.

You'll swear you can see the whole wide world.

I step to the edge and stare out at the faintly shifting carpet of trees, the far-off haze of mountains, trying not to cry. The angular heads of other temples jut out from the canopy, glowing in the light of the sunrise. It's all as epic as Rowan said. And it wrecks me that he's not here beside me.

I'm facing east. So are the mountains I see the Maya Mountains? If I could somehow sharpen my eyesight, crank it up to telescopic Superman vision, would I be able to zoom right through the mountains to Belize City? Cross the water and revisit Laughingbird Caye? Our dock?

I back away from the edge and sit on a stone bench. I'm supposed to fly back tomorrow morning. As long as I take the night bus, I'll make it to the airport in time.

And my trip will be over.

This whole vacation, I've been throwing myself headlong into some situations, holding back from others, without any framework or road map—anything to extricate myself from

Toby and my past. And maybe that's what Rowan did, I realize, during those "meaningless" years before we met. If he kept moving from place to place, person to person, experience to experience, maybe somehow he'd stumble upon the best way to heal.

But there has to be a destination at some point, doesn't there? Otherwise, we're just wandering around aimlessly, endlessly.

At least I made it to the ruins. I run my hand over the stone beside me. This might be the exact place where a princess ran away with a warrior. Or a Spanish conquistador drove a sword through the heart of a high priest before flinging him headfirst down the steps. Did that kind of thing really happen? All I know about the Mayans comes from my muddy memories of tenth-grade world history. It's funny—I've been so upset with myself for not reading about destinations as they are. It never occurred to me I should also read about how they *were*. People really lived here: thousands and thousands of them. And now they're gone. From beginning to end, they completed their lives inside this ancient city. But had they been *complete*?

I hold out my arms, trying to feel the remnants of body heat, a scrap of enduring emotion. Something touches my arm. I draw it back against my body and see the raindrop, halfway up my forearm—like a glistening dragon eye.

If it's going to rain, I'd better get going.

So maybe I've messed up this Rowan thing. And it's going to hurt for a long while. But this time, I'm not going to let that pain hold me back. Instead, I'm going to let it propel me forward in the best way. I'm going to draw and paint like never before. I'm going to tell off Reese and Olivia, and then apologize, and I'm going to make other friends too. I won't let good things pass me by, ever again. And I'll always, *always* hold on to what I love.

I turn around right as Rowan appears at the top of the stairs.

I can't move. I'm a Mayan statue. I'm afraid the wind will knock me over, my stone legs locked together as I tumble onto the treetops. Because what if he doesn't want to see me? What if he doesn't want to be found?

He looks my way. His eyes take a second to focus, as if he's trying to figure out who I am.

Now or never. I take a deep breath and go to him, my hands in the pockets of Starling's drawstring pants. I wish I weren't wearing my Windbreaker, but it's doing its job.

"You didn't say goodbye," I say, willing my voice to hold still.

He stares at me.

"And maybe that's the way you and Starling do it," I continue, "but not me. So . . ."

I wait for him to reply. Something like, *What are you doing here?* Or, *Why aren't you on your way to Guatemala City?* Or maybe, *How did you find me?* There are a million questions he could ask. Or he could just say goodbye and climb back down the temple.

But instead, he keeps looking at me, and looking and looking. And then—unexpectedly, but somehow so fittingly—we both begin to laugh.

29

Day 20
Travel Ghosts

We walk along the trail toward the Grand Plaza, neither of us talking much. From time to time, our fingers touch, until Rowan puts his hands in his pockets. I try not to read too much into it, but it's hard. Especially after I've traveled so far.

Suddenly, I stop in my tracks. "This is it."

"Temple I? Yeah, it's probably the most famous one."

"It's the temple from my Global Vagabonds pamphlet." I glance at him. "Don't laugh. But it's what convinced me to come to Central America in the first place."

"Too bad we can't climb it." Rowan points at the Spanish signs propped at the bottom of each set of steps, which can only read DO NOT ENTER. TEMPLE OFF-LIMITS. NOT ALLOWED.

I take a few steps toward the temple, craning my neck to

look up at its hulking head and shoulders. I can picture the pamphlet photo exactly. The sunny-faced wannabe travelers, painstakingly racially diverse, probably Photoshopped in front of it. In real life, the temple appears even larger. There's a pale stripe across its face, broken by a black rectangular opening, like the eye of a Cyclops.

Then, something crashes into my legs. It's a kid with a stuffed spider monkey affixed to his neck. He throws me a terrified look before scampering away.

He's broken my trance. Now I'm aware of all the early-morning tourists milling through the courtyard like stirred-up ants. They take turns posing in front of Temple I, mimicking the beautiful people from my notorious pamphlet. Maybe it's because of the thunderheads gathering above, but everyone appears rushed. Power-walking between Kodak moments. Spending more time composing pictures than beholding the real-life panoramas in front of them.

It amazes me that I've traveled three weeks without a camera. It's definitely made me draw more. I wonder if it's also made my experience more intense. I don't need photos of the key destinations, anyway; I'll bet everything's available online. But then again, I don't have photos of particular moments. My most memorable vignettes. Or the people I've encountered. Glenna, Sandu, Sonia, and Jack. Ariel and Emily. Starling.

I don't have a single photo of Rowan.

We start walking again. Maybe we can't climb Temple I, but plenty of the ancient jungle gyms have been reinforced for foreign feet. At one point, an animal bursts out of the bushes below. I jump and Rowan grabs me, saving me from a three-foot plunge to certain death.

He lets go all too soon, laughing. "It's just a wild turkey."

"Yeah, thanks. I can see that now."

It's embarrassing, but it breaks the ice. Kind of. Okay, to be honest, there's still a great big white glacier between us, but at least now we're attempting to shout around it.

"So," Rowan says. "What's your plan?"

"Now?" I shrug, looking out at the treetops instead of at him. "I might stay a little while." In a few hours, my bank account should reflect the funds my parents transferred last night after I promised full-time paperwork duties for what's left of my summer break. Enough money to delay my plane ticket, if I need to. I have until the end of the day to decide.

"Just a little while, huh? That's what I used to say. 'A little while' has got a funny way of turning into longer than you think." We half smile at each other. "Where will you go, if you stay?"

I hate how there's a thousand ways I can read every single thing he says. I shrug. "I'm not sure."

"Don't stay for me."

I turn so he can't see my face, which feels slapped. "I'm not. I'm staying for me. Anyway, I really mean just a little while. A week. I've got college."

This whole trip, college has been another thing I've been running from. It's funny how you can run from the future and the past simultaneously. I spent a lot of time coming up with ways to avoid it. Teaching in a local school, like Starling. Selling my art in an island gallery. Maybe even traveling forever, like Rowan.

But it's like I said before. There needs to be a destination, even if it's way off in the haze of my unlived life. And in that life, I'd like to be an artist.

An artist who travels a lot.

"No kidding? I thought you were holding out for art school."

"Well, I'm going to major in art. And if I hate the art program, I'll transfer. I convinced myself I lost my chance, but that's not true at all. It just felt . . . safer to say so." I pause. "I've come to realize it really doesn't need to be all or nothing."

"True," Rowan says.

We round the corner and are faced with another sweeping view of the ruins. Nothing compares to the morning vista from Temple IV, but it's breathtaking all the same. "And what about you?"

"I guess it depends."

After that comes the silence. A silence that stretches longer and longer, thickening, amplifying into a current of jungle noise, a crescendo of insects and howler monkeys.

I turn to Rowan. "I want to draw you. All of you." Then I pause. "That came out wrong—you can keep your clothes on."

Slowly, he breaks into a grin. "You mean it?"

"I mean it."

"When? And where?"

"Anywhere. And right now."

Because if I put it off even an hour, I'll chicken out. Also, it looks like rain, and nothing ruins a good sketch more than a downpour.

"Just sit," I tell Rowan. "Like you'd sit if you were . . ."
"Sitting?"
"Right. Relax your back. And your hands."

He settles back on the ancient gray steps of Tikal's North Acropolis, holding a book in his lap. I spread out my Windbreaker on the wet grass and sit atop it, cross-legged. From here, his chin is lifted too high. "Look down," I say. "No, that's too much. You look like a sad puppy. No—now you look pissed off."

"Come show me."

"Fine." I go to him and put my fingers under his chin, tilting his face in just the right way. I can feel his breath on my palm. All I'd have to do is lean forward. I remember the way his skin felt after we jumped off the dock. The geography of his back.

"Okay." I back away. "That's good."

I sit down and open my sketchbook.

I try to pretend he's just a stranger, but I wasn't lying when I said it's almost impossible to forget. I have to erase more than usual; I want it to be right. In case we go our separate ways forever, this drawing is all I'll have of him. To gaze at or throw darts at, depending on how I feel when I get home.

Once I've built the framework of his pose, I start to render. Beginning with his ankles: right crossed in front of left. "Are you hiding your tan lines?"

He doesn't answer, but I can see him fighting a smile. Good model.

At his knees, I sketch the torn hem of his cutoffs. He hates when I call them that. Too many pockets—they're a bitch to draw. His daypack.

His hands.

His arms. I try my best not to make his dragon look like

330

the Loch Ness monster. His white shirt, unbuttoned three buttons. The angle of his clavicle. A place my mouth has been.

I release my breath slowly so he won't know I've been holding it. It's hard to believe he's not feeling anything, but if there's even a chance he isn't, I can't let him know I am.

Now his face.

It's the hardest part. Imperfections in the figure are forgivable, but achieving a likeness in the face is more important than anything else. I break it down into pieces—mouth, chin, ridiculous ponytail—convincing myself he's just another model, some stranger posing for fifteen bucks an hour. But every time I lift my eyes, I see his.

I've drawn people who made faces whenever I looked up. Don't do that, by the way, unless you'd like a pencil in the eyeball. But Rowan's not like that. He's taking this seriously. He just gazes at me, utterly relaxed, while *I'm* feeling so much my pencil's shaking.

The thing about drawings is you can work on them forever; they're never finished, not really. You can always find something to fix. I know I need to stop, but I'm afraid of what's going to happen afterward. I'm not so afraid of his opinion, although yes, my heart will shatter like a stomped-on piece of Mayan pottery if he doesn't like it.

But it's good, I think. It looks like Rowan.

So that's not what I'm afraid of. I'm scared that after I'm done, we'll stand up, and it'll be time for me to go back to my shuttle, and he'll go back to his hotel, or his shuttle or bus or wherever, and it'll be the end of my trip. Of our trip. Of us.

I waste a few more minutes on the background. Instead of

drawing the ruins behind him, I sketch the faintest outline of
volcanoes and the lake.

That's my Rowan.

Finally, I glance up at him. He's still as stone.

"Your tattoo looks like Nessie," I tell him. "But it's the

best I can do. You can move now. Maybe we can get lunch, and you can tell me your whale shark story—"

In one swift motion, Rowan hops from the steps and closes the space between us, reaching for me with both hands. It happens so quickly I'm still reeling as he sets my sketchbook on the grass and pulls me against him. When he kisses me, my entire body reacts, like I've taken that first step into a too-hot shower. I'm sure he can feel my heart pounding from my chest into his. I feel dazed, almost drunk from the reality of him— the heat of his mouth, the texture of his shirt in my fingers as I hold him tight.

I know that this time, the worst thing I can do is let go. And I won't be losing anything. Because it's the most selfish thing I could ever do—to allow myself to fall for someone worthwhile.

Not long after, the rain begins to fall. We hole up in the café of his guesthouse and order mugs of coffee. It only makes my heart more jittery, because Rowan's sitting right beside me, his fingers woven through mine. "I just need to make sure," he says with a slight smile. "This isn't meaningless?"

I use our linked hands to give him a push.

"It never was. You know that."

With his free hand, Rowan flips the lid of a container of condensed milk and splashes it into his coffee. "I really didn't think you'd come, you know."

"I didn't either."

"I figured you'd be hugging your airplane seat, you'd be so glad to get away. After all I went on about trust and over-coming embarrassment—I freaked out as soon as I discovered you hid one small thing from me. Now I get why you didn't tell me you spoke to Starling. But in the moment, on the beach . . . I imagined the two of you had this entire best friendship behind my back, and she'd told you every single humiliating incident from the past few years."

I shake my head. "I wouldn't let her."

"Let her do what?"

"Tell me about your past. Not any more than you've already told me. Because it's your story. Like you said when the bus broke down."

Rowan pauses, staring at me. And then he grabs my face and kisses me so hard I have to shove him away, laughing. "I can't believe you remember that!" he exclaims.

"Where'd you get it, anyway?"

"I actually got it from *The Horse and His Boy*. One of the Narnia books by C. S. Lewis. It was something Aslan said to Lucy, about your story belonging to you. . . . It just stuck." He brings our linked hands to his face. "I just thought—I thought that was the reason you ended things after Lobsterfest. Like if you could think I'd do something so stupid, that I'd regress like that, put you in any sort of danger . . . of course you wouldn't trust me."

"But I do. It just took me a while. As long as you don't leave in the middle of the night again."

"Technically, it was first thing in the morning." He takes a sip of his coffee. "So, Bria Sandoval. Where to next?"

"Well, I really only have a week."

"Only a week? You sure you can't stay longer? You could delay classes for a semester, and I could find you a job in a dive shop. Or there are other things we could do. Join one of Starling's volunteer programs, as long as it's on a coast so I can teach diving. Maybe even something that involves your art . . ."

I can't help grinning. "You sound like you've thought this out."

"Ever since Livingston, I've been trying to figure out ways to keep you here."

It takes me a moment to hear his words, to really hear them and comprehend. Then I drape my arms over his shoulders, and—who cares about everyone in the restaurant?—it's my turn to kiss him into laughter explosion. "I'm here now," I say, pulling away. "And the here and now is what's important. Isn't that what you said?"

Rowan's quiet for a moment.

"I could open a dive shop," he says slowly. "If I get my Divemaster certification. Bring the Belizean dive mentality to the United States. Too bad your water's so damned cold, though."

"My water?"

"In California. Right?"

I grin at him so hard my face hurts. "California—for now."

We stay in the café until the sun goes down. Then I use a pay phone to call my parents again and, after that, my airline. I can wait until tomorrow to call my college, where I'll probably be sleeping on a cot in the basement, but at this point, I don't care. When you fall for a guy like Rowan, nothing's certain. But I'm pretty sure we've found the antidote to Wanderlove: each other.

ACKNOWLEDGMENTS

I would like to thank:

Bryson Allen, my first and favorite backpacking partner, whom I knew I'd marry the moment I saw him scream with sheer joy at the sight of a baby iguana in Costa Rica.

Michelle Andelman, my brilliant agent, advocate, and literary soul mate, as well as the teams at both Lynn C. Franklin Associates and Regal Literary.

Everyone at Delacorte Press, especially my editors, Michelle Poploff and Rebecca Short. They know just how to deepen, mend, and enrich. I once heard someone say, "My editor helped me write the book I thought I'd already written," and that's exactly right.

My mother, Marcia, for serenading me throughout my childhood with tales of her solo trip across Europe, and for initiating all this Central America madness with a simple question: "How about Belize?" My father, Doug, for the crazy stories from his years wrangling grizzlies and crashing cars for the film industry, which inspired me to seek out a colorful life. My twin sister, Danielle, whom I will take backpacking one of these days. My wonderful in-laws, the Allens. My poor dog, Sky, for being such a trouper when I'm gone.

Michelle Haft, Rachel Arceo, Catherine Demdam, Jenny Hicks, Lisa McCune, Kristin Allen, Amanda Castro, and my other backpacking buddies and travel companions, including all the friends and family who joined me for my wedding on a certain Belizean island I couldn't get out of my head.

All my amazing writer pals, online and off, especially Michelle Schusterman, Kate Hart, Amanda Hannah, Kristin Miller, Kaitlin Ward, Emilia Plater, and the other girls of YA Highway—for support, critiques, and hilarity in the margins of my manuscripts. Someday, we will all travel together. It will be epic.

My art teachers at the Watts Atelier of the Arts, who encouraged my art despite my enrollment gaps and numerous travel absences; my singular high school art teacher, Jay Shelton; and again, my mother, the artist, who knows I'm not truly happy unless I'm drawing. Also, my patient figure models, Danielle, Kristin, and Bryson.

About.com, particularly the other travel guides and our editor, Brian Spencer. My years as the Guide to Central America Travel have kept me immersed in my favorite places—many of which are included, some thinly disguised, in *Wanderlove*.

Last but not least, all the extraordinary people I've met on my travels, including travel writers, hotel owners, and Central American ministers of tourism—but also the man who helped me save the baby mynah bird in Koh Chang, and that little Mayan girl who hugged my knees in Panajachel, and the literature professor with whom I shared a train car across Croatia, and the woman who painted my face in Nevada's Black Rock Desert. I'll never forget.

ABOUT THE AUTHOR

A travel writer and young adult author, Kirsten Hubbard has danced in a Serbian nightclub (self-consciously), been slapped in the face by a Thai monkey, discovered all manner of alarming creatures (including tarantulas) in hostel beds, and greeted the sunrise atop the highest temple at Guatemala's Tikal ruins. She prefers backpacks to suitcases, brings sketchbooks on every trip, and has served as the Guide to Central America Travel for About.com since 2006. When she's not off wandering, she lives in San Diego, California. She is the author of *Like Mandarin*, also available from Delacorte Press.